"Settle back and sav[...] has an intense brand of storytelling. He's a most welcome addition to the genre. The real deal, I look forward to reading more from him."

STEVE BERRY,
New York Times **bestselling author**

"Wow! Double wow! Starkly original, *Ghost Country* will make Asimov and Heinlein cheer with the angels. The techno-thriller meets sci-fi, and the result is mind-blowing."

STEPHEN COONTS,
New York Times **bestselling author**

The city was drifted with human bones.

Seven decades of wind had scurried them into piles against all obstructions. Cars, buildings, landscaping, walls, planter boxes. They were everywhere.

Travis let his eyes roam the nearest pile, seventy feet left of the exterior door. The bones had massed there against a different wing of the hotel. He could see them with enough clarity to discern adult skulls from those of children, and large ribs from small ones. The bones were scoured clean and white. Everyone who'd died outdoors had been quickly discovered by coyotes and foxes and desert cats, and whatever they'd left behind, the sun and wind had eventually taken care of.

"It's everyone, isn't it?" Bethany said. "They really did it. They all came here and just . . . died."

Travis looked at her. Saw her eyes suddenly haunted by a new thought.

"Maybe we were with them," she said. "Maybe our bones are out there somewhere."

By Patrick Lee

GHOST COUNTRY
THE BREACH

PATRICK LEE

Ghost Country

HARPER

An Imprint of HarperCollinsPublishers

HARPER

An Imprint of HarperCollins*Publishers*
10 East 53rd Street
New York, New York 10022–5299

Copyright © 2011 by Patrick Lee
ISBN 978-0-06-158444-2

First Harper mass market printing: January 2011
First Harper digest printing: January 2011

Acknowledgments

This part would fill half the book if I listed everyone. Thank you to:

Diana Gill and Gabe Robinson, for critical guidance throughout the story.

Christine Maddalena, Pamela Spengler-Jaffee, Michael Brennan, and more people than I can probably know, much less thank, at HarperCollins.

Janet Reid, my extremely cool agent, and everyone else at FinePrint, for a million reasons that would fill the other half of the book.

Ghost Country

EXECUTIVE ORDER 1978-AU3

Legal titles and definitions established in this document shall be binding on all signatories to the TANGENT SPECIAL AUTHORITY AGREEMENT (hereafter TSAA):

"BREACH" shall refer to the physical anomaly located at the former site of the Very Large Ion Collider at Wind Creek, Wyoming. The total systemic failure of the VLIC on 7 March 1978 created the BREACH by unknown means. The BREACH may be an Einstein-Rosen bridge, or wormhole (ref: VLIC Accident Investigation Report).

"ENTITY" shall refer to any object that emerges from the BREACH. To date, ENTITIES have been observed to emerge at the rate of 3 to 4 per day (ref: VLIC Accident Object Survey). ENTITIES are technological in nature and suggest design origins far beyond human capability.

In most cases their functions are not readily apparent to researchers on site at Wind Creek.

"BORDER TOWN" shall refer to the subsurface research complex being constructed at the VLIC accident site, to serve the housing and working needs of scientific and security personnel studying the BREACH. All signatories to TSAA hereby agree that BORDER TOWN, along with its surrounding territory (ref: Border Town Exclusion Zone Charter), is a sovereign state unto itself, solely governed by the organization TANGENT.

This document is legally binding and enforceable effective immediately, 3 August 1978.

EYES ONLY—DO NOT REPRODUCE

PART I

IRIS

CHAPTER ONE

Fifty seconds before the first shots hit the motorcade, Paige Campbell was thinking about the fall of Rome. The city, not the empire. The empire had gone in stages, with any number of dates that historians could argue over and call endpoints, but there was no disagreement as to when the city itself had been sacked. August 24, 410. Sixteen hundred and one years ago to the week. Paige didn't know the details beyond the date. Though she'd once planned to be an historian herself, before ending up in a very different line of work, she'd never studied that region or period in much depth. She only remembered the date from European history in high school. But she wondered. She wondered if the city's inhabitants had known, even a few months before the fact, that they would see it all come to its end. She thought about that and then turned in her seat and watched Washington, D.C., slide away behind her into the night. She could see the Washington Monument and the Capitol Dome lit up in the darkness. The winking lights of an airliner coming up out of Reagan National. The headlamps of cars behind her and on surrounding streets. Billboards and storefronts and arc lights, the glow of it all cast up onto the low cloud cover that lay over the city like a blanket. The infrastructure of the modern world. It looked like it would stand forever.

She turned forward again. The motorcade was heading east on Suitland Parkway, back toward Andrews Air Force Base, where she and the others had landed only a few hours earlier. It was seven minutes past midnight. The road was wet from the rain that had been falling steadily since their arrival. The pavement caught and scattered the glow of taillights ahead. Paige was in the rear vehicle of the procession. Martin Crawford was sitting next to her.

Behind them on the back bench seat, locked in its carrying case, was the object that'd prompted this visit to Washington. The Breach entity they'd just demonstrated for an audience of one.

"He was calmer than I thought he'd be," Paige said. "I thought he'd have a harder time believing it."

"He saw it with his own eyes," Crawford said. "Hard to dismiss that kind of evidence."

"Still, he's new on the job. He's never seen an entity before, much less one like this."

"He's the president. He's seen a lot of things."

Paige watched the traffic skimming by across the median, tires spinning up long ragged clouds of moisture from the roadbed.

"I thought he'd be scared," she said. "I thought, once we showed it to him, he'd be as scared as we are."

"Maybe he hides it well."

"Do you think he can help us figure this out?" Paige said. "How to stop whatever's coming?"

"We don't *know* what's coming yet."

"We know it's nothing good. And that we don't have a hell of a lot of time before it gets here."

Crawford nodded, staring forward. He was seventy-four and looked it, except in his eyes, which probably hadn't changed in decades. They looked troubled at the moment.

Paige glanced ahead and caught her own eyes in the rearview mirror up front. No lines around them yet—she was only thirty-one—but this job would put them there soon enough.

She turned and looked back at the entity's case, just visible in the rain-refracted city light. She thought of what she'd said to the president: that this entity could be considered an investigative tool. It offered a unique way of seeing the world—and a way of looking for things that could be found by no other means.

They were on their way to look for things now: the answers to the questions that had plagued them for not quite two days. Paige thought of Yuma, Arizona, the first stage of the search. The first place they would put the entity to use. Maybe the evidence they needed would be right there, obvious enough to trip over.

And maybe it wouldn't be. Maybe it wouldn't be there at all. Or anywhere else.

Paige tried not to think about that. She turned and stared forward through the beaded windshield. In the corner of her eye she saw Crawford turn toward her to speak, but then he stopped and cocked his head at a sound. Paige heard it too.

Somewhere ahead of them. Through the reinforced windows of the armored SUV it sounded like a playing card in bicycle spokes. Paige knew better. She felt her pulse quicken. She leaned to look past the driver's seat, and in the next second everything happened.

The SUV directly ahead braked and tried to swerve. Too late. It clipped the rear fender of the vehicle in front of it and spun hard, and an instant later its headlight beams were in Paige's eyes and the driver of her own vehicle was hauling left on the steering wheel. Also too late. The impact was like nothing she'd ever felt. Like someone had picked up a telephone pole and swung it as hard as a baseball bat into the front of the vehicle. Her seat belt slammed tight across her chest and the air surged out of her lungs and for a moment she couldn't get them full again. While she was trying, she felt the world shift beneath her. She looked up and saw the view through the windshield tilting impossibly. Forty-five degrees. Then steeper. The SUV rocked past the limit of its balance and came down on its roof. The struts collapsed and the windows, strong as they were, buckled and separated from their frames.

Just like that, the world of sound outside came in. The heavy rattle of the automatic weapon— maybe more than one—filled up the night. Some kind of monstrous caliber. Sure as hell not a light machine gun. Not even something firing 7.62mm. This sounded as big as a Browning M2. Fifty-caliber bullets, the size of human fingers, coming in at three times the speed of sound. Paige hung upside down in the seat belt, her chest still compressed and unable to expand. Over the gunfire she heard another sound, closer, like the patter of rain on sheet metal but amplified a hundredfold. It was the sound of the bullet impacts against the vehicles, and it was getting louder as she listened. She understood why. The shooters were methodically walking their fire back along the length of the immobilized convoy. Being thorough.

"Paige?"

She turned. Crawford was lying against the crumpled passenger door. His head was pressed at an angle against the roof below him. He looked determined not to be afraid. He knew what was coming.

Paige tried to see if the two men in the front seats were conscious. She couldn't tell. The vehicle had pancaked just enough that the headrests up front were touching the roof, and between the seats she could see only darkness.

The bullet impacts were very close now. Chewing apart the vehicle just ahead. Paige turned toward Crawford again. They shared a look. Almost certainly good-bye.

"It's already started," he said. "Whatever it is, it's started. And the president's part of it."

Paige nodded. Understanding settled over her. With it came anger. Enough to balance out her fear.

Then something in her chest let go and her lungs were free to expand again, and she sucked in a deep breath of air, and half a second later the bullets started hitting the vehicle.

She shut her eyes. The sound was louder than she'd expected. Metal screams that raked her eardrums. She couldn't tell them apart from human screams. Couldn't tell if she was screaming herself. Somewhere in the middle of it she felt liquid gushing over her. She wondered if it was her own blood, but didn't think so. Trauma survivors said their blood felt like warm water on their skin. Whatever this was, it was cold. She sucked in another breath, tasted gasoline vapor, and understood.

And then the shooting was over.

She was still there.

She opened her eyes in the silence. The gasoline was coming down from everywhere. Pooling in the concavities of the crumpled roof.

She looked at Crawford. Crawford was gone. Eyes wide open and staring at her, but gone. A shot had hit him in the chest. It looked like some giant animal had bitten away half of his rib cage, taking a lung and most of his heart with it. Past Crawford, through the open space where the window had been, she heard voices calling to one another. Then the flat crack of a pistol, maybe a .45. More voices. Coming closer. She couldn't actually see anything through the window. Because of her angle she could only see a few feet of the roadbed nearby.

She found her seat belt release and pressed it. Her body dropped hard against the underside of the roof. She was down level with the window now. She could see straight through it, all the way up the length of the crippled motorcade. Doors hung half open. An arm extended from one, blood streaming off the fingers in rivulets.

The shooters were advancing along the vehicles, carefully inspecting each one. She saw one man with a pistol and another with a PDA. The device's screen painted his face bright white in the darkness. The two of them moved from the first vehicle to the second. They stared in at someone on the passenger side. The man with the PDA pressed its buttons rapidly, and the light on his face flickered through a progression of shades. Paige guessed he was looking at a series of photographs.

"Keeper?" the man with the pistol said.

The other man looked at half a dozen more photos, then stopped and shook his head. "Just security."

The shooter leveled the gun through the vehicle's window and fired once. Then he and the other man continued checking the rest of its occupants.

Paige felt her breathing accelerate. In the fume-choked space, she thought she might pass out before long. The killers found another survivor in the second SUV, determined he was also no one important, and executed him.

Paige turned herself over and got up on her elbows. She looked around. The window facing away from the shooters, the one direction in which she might get out unseen and run for it, was compressed to four inches of space. No way through. Likewise for going forward or back. If she went between the front seats and out the windshield, they'd see her at once. And she couldn't reach the rear window: the back of the middle-row bench seat, where she'd been strapped in, was almost touching the roof now. There was maybe a one-inch gap below it.

The entity.

If she could get to it, she might get away. She'd

need room to actually use the thing—ten feet at least. That meant she'd still have to go out the windshield into open view. But after that she would only need a few seconds to switch the entity on, and then if she moved quickly, she'd be long gone.

She shoved her arm through the gap between the seatback and the roof. The padding gave a little, and so did the soft tissue of her arm, but she could still only reach about ten inches into the space beyond. She swept her arm left and right, fingertips extended as far as possible.

It wasn't there.

It might be only an inch out of reach, but that was enough. She made another sweep. Nothing. Her eyes were watering now. She wanted to think it was only because of the fuel vapor.

Another pistol shot. Closer. She looked. The killers were at the third vehicle. Maybe thirty seconds from finding her.

There was one other move to make. She didn't think she had time. She also didn't have a hell of a lot to lose in trying. She withdrew her hand from the gap below the seatback, rolled on her side and took her cell phone from her pocket. She switched it on and navigated to the macro list. You couldn't just speed-dial into Border Town. You had to call and then enter a code, then an extension and another code. A macro could do it all in about a second. She found the one she needed and selected it. She waited. It rang.

"Be there," she whispered.

She watched the shooters examine another victim in the third vehicle. They seemed to be debating whether the body was alive or dead. The one with the PDA looked through the photographs anyway.

The call rang again. And again.

The man with the PDA stopped on an image. Nodded at his partner. They reached inside the vehicle to drag the victim out.

The fourth ring was cut off by an answering click. Paige started talking before the other party could finish saying hello. The words came in a rush. She hoped to hell she was even understandable. There just wasn't time to say it all. It would've been tight even with a full minute, and she had nowhere close to that long. She found herself trying to prioritize even as she spoke. Trying not to leave out anything critical.

But she *was* leaving something out. She could feel the absence of it gnawing at her.

"*Shit, what else . . . ?*" she whispered.

She saw the killers turning toward her now, drawn by her voice, and a second later they were running, their footsteps slapping the wet pavement.

What the hell was she forgetting?

The other party began to speak, asking if she was okay.

She remembered.

She composed it into the simplest form she could think of and screamed it into the phone, and even as she finished she felt hands reaching through the window and grabbing her. Getting her by the calves, pulling her from the vehicle. She gripped the phone with both hands and snapped it in half. Heard the circuit boards inside break like stale crackers.

Then she was out on the pavement, turned over, pinned, the pistol aimed down at her. The PDA's glow on the killers' faces strobed through the photo sequence again. She looked past them and saw the body they'd pulled from the third SUV. She saw why they'd discarded it after all: one of its legs had been nearly severed by a bullet impact just above the knee. It hung on by only skin and a bit of muscle. The open femoral artery had already pumped a thick sheet of blood onto the pavement. Very little was still coming out. Very little was *left* to come out.

The killer with the PDA continued cycling through his pictures. Paige heard other men somewhere behind her, at the back of her own vehicle. Heard them kicking aside the crumbs of glass there, kneeling, cursing softly as they rummaged inside. Then came the clatter of the entity's plastic case, scraping over concrete as they pulled it free. She heard their footsteps as they sprinted away with the thing, back toward where the shooting had come from.

Above her, the PDA's flashing stopped. The man holding it looked down. His eyes went back and forth between the screen and her face.

"Keeper?"

"Oh yeah."

CHAPTER TWO

Travis Chase took his lunch break alone on Loading Dock Four. He sat with his feet hanging over the edge. Night fog drifted in across the parking lot, saturated with the smells of vehicle exhaust, wet pavement, fast food. Out past the edge of the lot, past the shallow embankment that bordered it, the sound of intermittent traffic on I–285 rose and fell like breaking waves. Beyond I–285 was Atlanta, broad and diffused in orange sodium light, the city humming at idle at two in the morning.

Behind Travis the warehouse was silent. The only sounds came from the break room at the far south end. Low voices, the microwave opening and closing, the occasional scrape of a chair. Travis only ever went in there to put his lunch in the refrigerator and to take it back out.

Something moved at the edge of the parking lot. Dark and low slung, almost flat to the ground. A cat, hunting. It slipped forward in starts and stops, then bolted for the foot of a dumpster. The kill reached Travis as no more than a squeal and a muffled struggle, a few thumps of soft limbs against steel. Then nothing but the swell and crest of the traffic again.

Travis finished his lunch, wadded the brown bag and arced it into the trash bin next to the box compactor.

He turned where he sat, brought his legs up and rested them sideways across the edge of the dock. He leaned back against the concrete-filled steel pole beside the doorway. He closed his eyes. Some nights he caught a few minutes' sleep like this, but most nights it was enough just to relax. To shut down for a while and try not to think. Try not to remember.

His shift ended at four thirty. The streets were empty in the last hour of the August night. He got his mail on the way into his apartment. Two credit-card offers, a gas bill, and a grocery flyer, all addressed to the name *Rob Pullman*. The sight of it no longer gave him any pause—the name was his as much as the address was his. He hadn't been called Travis Chase, aloud or in writing, in over two years.

He'd seen the name just once in that time. Not written. Carved. He'd driven fourteen hours up to Minneapolis on a Tuesday night, a year and a half ago, timing his arrival for the middle of the night, and stood on his own grave. The marker was more elaborate than he'd expected. A big marble pedestal on a base, the whole thing four feet tall. Below his name and the dates was an inscribed verse: Matthew 5:6. He wondered what the hell his brother had spent on all of it. He stared at it for five minutes and then he left, and an hour later he pulled off the freeway into a rest area and cried like a little kid. He'd hardly thought about it since.

He climbed the stairs to his apartment. He dropped the mail on the kitchen counter. He made a sandwich and got a Diet Coke from the refrigerator and stood at the sink eating. Ten minutes later he was in bed. He stared at the ceiling in the dark. His bedroom had windows on two walls. He had both of them open so the cross breeze would come through—it was hot air, but at least it was moving. The apartment had no air-conditioning. He closed his eyes and listened to the night sounds of the city filtering in with the humidity. He felt sleep begin to pull him down. He was almost out when he heard a car slow at the entrance to the front lot. Through his eyelids he saw headlights wash over his ceiling. The vehicle stopped in the lot but didn't kill its engine. It sat idling. He heard one of its doors open, and then light footsteps came running up the front walk.

His door buzzer sounded.

He opened his eyes.

He knew exactly who it was.

The guy in the apartment down the hall had an ex-girlfriend with a penchant for showing up drunk in the middle of the night, looking to discuss things. The last time, three weeks ago, the guy had tried to ignore her. She'd responded by hitting every button on the pad until someone else relented and buzzed her in, allowing her to come upstairs and pound on the guy's door directly. As a strategy it'd worked pretty well, so this time she'd skipped right to it. Nice of her.

The buzzer sounded again.

Travis closed his eyes and waited for it to stop.

When it sounded the third time he noticed something: he couldn't hear anyone else's buzzer going off before or after his own. He should have heard that easily. The tone was a heavy bass that transmitted well through walls. He'd heard it the last time this happened.

Someone was out there buzzing his apartment. His alone.

He pulled the sheet aside and stood. He went to the window and pressed his face against the screen to get an angle on the front door.

A girl was standing there. Not the neighbor's girlfriend. Not drunk, either. She was standing on the walk, a few feet away from the pad. She'd pressed the button and stepped back from it. She was staring up at the open window of Travis's bedroom—had been staring at it even before he appeared there—and now she flinched when she saw him. She looked nervous as hell. The vehicle idling thirty feet behind her was a taxicab.

The girl looked about twenty, but it was hard to say. She could've been younger than that. She had light brown hair to her shoulders. Big eyes behind a pair of glasses that covered about a quarter of her face—they were either five years behind the style or five years ahead of it.

Travis had never seen her before.

She'd seen him somewhere, though, if only in a picture. It was clear by her expression. She recognized him even by the glow of the lamppost in the parking lot.

She stepped off the concrete walkway into the grass. She took three steps toward the window.

Her eyes never left his. She stopped. For another second she just stood there looking up at him.

Then she said, "Travis."

In the time it took him to pull on a T-shirt and jeans, he ran through the possible implications. There weren't many. He thought of Paige, two summers ago, setting up the Rob Pullman identity. He'd watched her insert it into every database that mattered—federal, state, local. Retroactive for four decades. Then she'd erased every digital footprint she'd left in the process, and scrubbed the information from even her own computer in Border Town. No records. No printouts. It was no more possible to tie his new name to his old one than it was to reverse-engineer an ice sculpture from a tray of water.

No one but Paige could have sent this girl.

Travis stepped into the hallway and descended the stairs. The girl was standing at the glass front door waiting for him. She'd already sent the cab away.

Travis pushed the door open and stepped out into the night.

"What is it?" he said. "What's going on?"

Up close her nervousness was more apparent. She had a backpack slung over her shoulder and she was fidgeting with the strap. There must have been something in his expression that put her even more on edge. She looked like she wanted to back away from him, but she didn't.

"You drive," she said. "I'll talk."

"I–285. Hartsfield-Jackson Airport."

Travis took a right out of the complex.

The girl seemed about to speak again, and then her cell phone rang. She twisted in her seat and took it from her pocket. She pressed the talk button and rested the phone on her backpack, which was now in her lap.

"Hello?"

A man said, "Ms. Renee Turner?"

"Yes."

"Hi. This is Richard with Falcon Jet. I just wanted to let you know your aircraft is refueled and standing by, ready when you are. Flight time to Washington Dulles International will be an hour and fifteen. Does your guest have a preferred beverage?"

The girl glanced at Travis. He shrugged.

"We're fine with what's aboard," she said. "We'll be arriving shortly."

"Very good."

She ended the call and set the phone on the console. She still looked anxious. She hugged the backpack against herself. It flattened out. There wasn't much in it.

"Renee," Travis said. "Nice to meet you."

For a second she looked confused. "Oh, sorry, no. I'm Bethany. Bethany Stewart."

She stuck out a tiny hand. Travis shook it.

"Renee's a cover," she said. "She doesn't really exist."

"She sounds well off for someone who doesn't exist."

"I'll tell you all about her sometime."

"All right."

"I'm with Tangent. I guess you assumed that."

Travis nodded.

"I would have called ahead," she said. "I was just

afraid you'd hear the first five words and hang up, and you'd be long gone by the time I got here."

"Why didn't Paige call? She wouldn't expect me to hang up on her."

Bethany was quiet for a few seconds. "Paige is the reason I'm here. She didn't have time to call anyone but me. She barely had time for that."

Travis waited for her to say more, but instead she picked up her phone again. She switched on the display and brought up what looked like a file directory.

"This phone records every call by default," she said. She selected a file and clicked on it. An audio clip began to play.

Travis heard Bethany's voice first. She started to say hello and then Paige spoke over her, her own speech fast and panicked, struggling for clarity through hyperventilation: *"Bethany. Go to my residence. Override for the door is 48481. Open the hard storage in the back wall of the closet, star–7833. The thing inside is one of the entities I was testing, the same as the one I brought to D.C. Take it and get out of Border Town right now. Don't tell anyone anything. Get somewhere safe and then use the entity. You'll see what it does, and what you need to do. Whatever you learn from it, just make it public yourself, make it huge, do not go to authorities. Not the president. Not anybody. If you need help, find Travis Chase in Atlanta. Three seventeen Fenlow, apartment five, the name Rob Pullman. Shit, what else . . . ?"* Paige stopped to take a deep breath. Then another. In the background Travis heard a sound: running footsteps on pavement.

Bethany's voice came in on the recording: *"What's happening? Where are you?"*

Then Paige cut her off again, shouting. "*You can take it through and still come back! You can take it through!*"

On the last word something changed. Some expulsion of her breath, as though her body had suddenly moved. Or been moved. Then the recording ended as abruptly as if she'd turned off the phone, though Travis pictured something more severe than that.

The on-ramp to 285 came up on his right. He took the turn going too fast. His concentration wasn't on the driving.

He looked at Bethany. He waited for her to explain what the hell he'd just heard.

She went back to the directory on her phone and navigated to a new file. Its icon was a symbol of a filmstrip frame. A video clip.

"It was nine minutes after midnight, East Coast time, when Paige called me," she said. "And I captured this from CNN about an hour later, when I was already on my way here to find you."

She double-clicked the file, then handed Travis the phone. He propped it on the steering wheel as the video started to play.

News chopper footage. A row of vehicles crippled and burning in the street. Four SUVs jammed together like derailed train cars. The last of them was flipped over on its roof. The caption at the bottom of the screen read: MOTORCADE ATTACKED IN WASHINGTON, D.C.

The shot pushed in tight on one of the vehicles and Travis saw damage that couldn't be attributed to the flames alone. Massive holes in the metal panels. They could only have been caused by high-powered gunfire. It'd even cut through some of the structural members. Maybe shotgun slugs at close range could do that, but the sheer number of holes ruled that out. Someone had used a heavy automatic weapon on the convoy, probably a .50 caliber. Serious hardware to be lugging around within a few miles of where the president and his family slept.

"I've watched the coverage for a few hours now," Bethany said. "Until I got off the plane here in Atlanta. They're saying the victims in the motorcade were a mid-level CIA executive and his staff, and that the names may not be released. After a while they started reporting the exact time it happened. A few minutes after midnight. So the times match. And it's exactly where Paige and the others would've been after leaving the meeting, right between the White House and Andrews—"

She cut herself off and looked at him. "I'm sorry, you're hearing this all out of sequence. I'm not making any sense."

"You're fine. Just take it in order. Start at the beginning and tell me what you know."

She made a sound that was halfway between a sigh and a laugh. Equal parts weariness and frayed nerves.

"What I know won't take long," she said.

CHAPTER THREE

Bethany unzipped her backpack and opened it. Travis felt a pocket of dry heat roll out, like she'd opened the door of a toaster oven.

There was a single item in the pack. In the glow of passing streetlights Travis got a sense of the thing. A dark metal cylinder. It was the size and shape of a rolling pin without the handles. There were three buttons running down its length, with symbols engraved into them. Something like hieroglyphs, though not in any human language, Travis was sure.

Next to each of the buttons someone had taped a handwritten label. The three of them read:

ON
OFF
OFF (DETACH/DELAY—93 SEC.)

"This is the entity Paige was talking about in the call," Bethany said. "The one she had locked in her closet. There's another one identical to it, which she took to D.C. The two of them came out of the Breach together, like matching handsets for a cordless phone."

She lifted the entity free of the bag. It didn't look like it weighed much, by the way she held it.

"Whatever's going on," she said, "it all centers around the two entities."

"What do they do?" Travis said.

"I have no idea."

"All right."

"Only the top four people in Tangent know that. Paige being one of them. They're the same four people who went to D.C. They were the only ones involved in experimenting with these entities, figuring out their function. That work began this past Monday, not quite three days ago now. Paige and the others restricted the research to closed labs, and kept all their notes and video on secure servers. They must have figured out right away that these things did something big."

"Is that normal?" Travis said. "Secrecy within Tangent itself?" It didn't sound like any policy he remembered, but then he hadn't been in Border Town for very long. His entire involvement with Tangent—and with Paige—had lasted less than a week, two years ago. He hadn't wanted to leave, but in the end he'd learned something that made it unthinkable to stay. And what he'd learned, he'd kept to himself.

"The secrecy is a temporary policy," Bethany said. "Paige feels bad about it, but she and the others at the top think it's necessary for now. So much of the population there is new these days. They've had to refill the ranks almost completely in the past two years." She glanced at him. "I guess you know about that."

Travis nodded. "I know about that."

"Well, it's put a strain on the recruiting process. Tangent used to spend months vetting a single candidate, but lately they just haven't had that luxury. They needed so many people, so fast, that the process had to be truncated for most of them. It's just going to be a while before they can all be trusted like the former staff. Paige apologizes for it all the time. People understand, though. They're well aware of the risk of another Aaron Pilgrim coming along. So, yeah, when an entity shows up that's serious business, generally just the top few people are allowed to work with it. That's how it went with these two."

She set the cylinder back in her lap, half in and half out of the open backpack.

"So, Monday," she said. "The closed labs. I know Paige and the others did a safety assessment first, because they took test organisms in with them. Fruit flies. Nematode worms. Half a dozen mice. I guess the entities checked out fine, because they returned all the animals to containment by that night, and nothing was wrong with them. Then on Tuesday morning they took both entities up into the desert and did more work there. A lot of it. They stayed up there all that day and right through the night. I doubt they even slept, unless it was on the ground. They kept coming back down, one or two of them at a time, and taking communications gear up to the surface. Long-range radio equipment, every kind of frequency. Satellite stuff too. Big transmitting and receiving dishes, and the tools to take them apart and put them back together. I have no idea why. Then early Wednesday, a little less than twenty-four hours ago, they brought it all back down, and the entities too, and told us they were leaving for a while. Maybe for weeks. Maybe longer than that. Some kind of exploratory trip involving the two entities, putting them to use somehow. They wouldn't say more than that, except that their first stop was Washington, D.C."

"What were they going to do there?"

"Meet with the president."

"Did they say why?"

"Not really. I got the impression they wanted his help with what they were doing. Like going to him was the logical first step in the process."

"On the phone Paige told you not to trust the president," Travis said.

Bethany nodded. "Something changed her mind about him." She went quiet for a few seconds. She stared ahead at the pressing darkness over the freeway. "I think the president was behind the attack on the motorcade. I think he had to be."

Travis thought about the damage to the vehicles again. The kind of weapon that could do that wasn't handheld. It needed a heavy tripod. It needed setup time too. A couple minutes, at least. You could ready one inside a van, but then your firing positions would be limited to where you could park, and you'd be a lot less agile once the shooting started. You'd need to put yourself in just the right spot, well ahead of time, and to do that you'd need to know the target's exact route and schedule.

Only the president and a few aides would've had that information.

Travis thought about President Garner, a man he'd spoken to on the phone once, briefly. Like the five presidents before him, Garner had enjoyed close ties with Tangent while never making a move against its autonomy.

But Garner wasn't the president anymore. He'd resigned from office two years ago, after losing his wife to what the world believed was a heart attack. His replacement, Walter Currey, had carried on the former administration's policies to the letter, and already made it clear he had no ambition to run for another term in 2012. Currey had been a friend of Garner's for over twenty years. He'd made a speech at the First Lady's funeral and had to stop twice to keep his composure. By almost anyone's measure he was a good man.

Maybe he was just good at *looking* like a good man.

"Anyway, that was it," Bethany said. "They left for D.C. yesterday afternoon. And late last night I got the call you heard. I tried calling Paige back after it cut out. Nothing. Right to voice mail. So then I just did what she told me to do. I got the entity from her residence and I got the hell out of Border Town. I guess I understand the point of not telling anyone there. If she wants me to go underground and use this thing—whatever it does—then the fewer who know about it the better. And it was faster that way, without notifying anyone. No group decisions, no proper channels. I just called in one of the Gulfstreams we keep at Browning Air National Guard Base in Casper. Did it on Paige's authority. This was less than five minutes after the call. No one had learned of the motorcade attack yet. It took the plane ten minutes to reach Border Town, and another ten to fly me to Rapid City in South Dakota. And then Renee Turner chartered a private jet, and Bethany Stewart vanished off the grid. As far as anyone knows, I'm hitchhiking on Interstate 90. And now I'm here, and you know as much as I know."

Travis said nothing for a long moment. He considered all that she'd told him. He let the pieces fall together where they seemed ready to.

"Learn from it," Travis said. "That's how Paige phrased it in the call. Whatever you *learn from* the entity, make it public."

Bethany nodded.

Travis looked at the cylinder sticking half out of the backpack.

"Paige and the others learned something from it," he said. "Something big and important that the world would want to know about—something that should be made public. But there must have been even more they wanted to learn. That's what the exploratory trip was about. Like they'd found one piece of some puzzle, and they were going off to find the rest of it, using the entity. But before that, they went to see the president, to show him the one puzzle piece they already had. Maybe they thought he could help them make sense of it. But that plan backfired. Whatever they'd uncovered, the president didn't *want* it made public. Didn't want them digging up the rest of the pieces. Maybe Paige and the others didn't realize what they'd stumbled onto. And obviously the president did."

"They touched a nerve of some kind," Bethany said.

Travis nodded. He thought of the burning vehicles in the street.

"A big damn nerve," he said.

"Hence the instruction to go underground. Figure it out for ourselves and trust no authorities."

Travis looked at her. "But you're not going underground. You're going right to where she was attacked. Something she'd probably tell you not to do."

Bethany returned his gaze. "You don't sound like you disapprove."

"I don't."

He saw the hint of a smile in her eyes, buried under a ton of stress.

"Do you have some way of finding her?" he said. "If she's still alive?"

"I have a way of trying. It's hard to explain how it works. Easier if I just show you once we're on the plane. But I can only locate her. After that, I don't know what to do. She'll be somewhere secure." She looked down at the black cylinder. "I guess I'm hoping that whatever else this thing does, it can help us with that part, somehow. No reason to expect that, I know. It's just all I've got. After we get Paige's position, we can find someplace safe and switch this thing on, and then I guess we'll find out."

She went silent again. She watched a sign with directions to the airport slide by. Then she looked at him. "You don't *have* to help me, you know. You don't have to get involved in this at all, if you don't want to."

Travis watched the road. He thought of Paige, bound somewhere, her life in the hands of whoever had hit the motorcade. Just ahead, I–285 swung broadly to the east, toward the blood-red promise of dawn at the horizon.

"Yes I do," he said.

CHAPTER FOUR

T ravis parked in the long-term lot, a quarter mile from the private hangars.

"Do they search your bags before you board a private flight?" he said.

Bethany shook her head.

Travis turned and took hold of the upholstery of the passenger seatback just behind Bethany's left shoulder. The narrow panel of cloth that covered the side facing inward was loose at the top, a half-inch flap that would look to any observer like a sign of wear and tear. It wasn't. Travis pulled down hard on it, and the few threads binding the cloth to the seatback broke easily. The move exposed the seat's interior, a cage of spring steel and foam. He reached inside and felt his hand close around the grip of the SIG-Sauer P220 he'd hidden there two years before. He took it out and set it in Bethany's backpack alongside the black cylinder. Then he reached back in for the three spare magazines he'd stashed with it—a fourth was already loaded into the gun—and put them in the pack too.

If the sight of the weapon made Bethany more nervous than she already was, Travis couldn't tell.

*   *   *

They were in the air fifteen minutes later. The little business jet banked into its climb and gave Travis a last look at the spiderweb of highways crisscrossing Atlanta. He was sure he would never come back, unless he happened to be passing through. Rob Pullman wasn't going to show up for work tomorrow. Wasn't going to answer his door when the landlord came to ask about the rent next week. It occurred to him with a kind of sad amusement that Pullman would probably never be reported missing. Just fired and evicted in absentia. No great loss to anyone.

He and Bethany were sitting at the back of the plane, ten feet from the pilots. The engine sound was more than enough to mask their conversation if they spoke softly.

Bethany took out her phone and plugged it into a data port on her armrest.

"The plane has satellite capability that my phone doesn't have by itself," she said. She pulled up a screen that reminded Travis of computer programs from the eighties and early nineties: a black background with a simple text prompt, like an old DOS system. He was sure the program wasn't actually old; Bethany was just navigating the no-frills backwaters that ordinary users never saw.

"Will the pilots see this on their screens?" Travis said.

"Nobody will see. Not even the satellite vendors."

She typed a command string that looked like random letters and numbers to Travis, and executed it. An hourglass icon appeared for a second, and then the little screen filled with a street map of the United States, overlaid on a satellite image. The satellite layer was fractured into several distorted squares, overlapping one another to make a composite. Travis realized what he was looking at: not the static view of the world that was available on any number of websites, but a realtime image composed of multiple live satellite feeds. Most of the visible United States was still deep in the shadow of night.

Bethany used the phone's arrow buttons to center the map on Washington, D.C., and zoomed in until the city filled the frame. Even in that narrow field of view Travis could see a margin where coverage from different satellites overlapped. The margin was moving, just perceptibly, a pixel's width every few seconds. He envisioned recon satellites skimming over the Earth in low orbit, their fields of view always moving relative to the ground.

Bethany zoomed in one step further. More detail of the city emerged. Travis saw the long green belt of the National Mall running left to right across the middle of the image. Just above it was the focal point that several major streets converged toward: the White House. A mile northeast of that, an area of about three by three blocks was highlighted in bright yellow. Bethany tapped that part of the screen.

"Still there," she said. "The survivors have been somewhere in that rectangle since I first checked around two in the morning. They must have been moved right after the attack, which would've happened further south, between the White House and Andrews. The fact that I'm getting a signal means

...least one of them is still alive." She thought about it and added, "Or at least their blood hasn't congealed yet."

Travis waited for her to explain.

"They have a radioisotope in their bloodstreams," she said. "Iodine–124 doped with a signature molecule. Harmless levels of it are in the water supply in Border Town, and it stays in the body for about twenty-four hours after last ingestion. Certain satellites can pick it up, but only very, very faintly. The signal is far too weak for them to get a sharp focus on it." She touched the yellow rectangle on the map again. "What you're seeing there is the computer's best guess about where the target is. When we get on the ground in D.C. I can get the signal directly with my phone. That'll narrow it down to a building. Even a specific part of a building once we're close enough."

Travis recalled the mindset he'd adopted during his short time in Border Town. The logical flexibility that was such a necessary part of life there, like the native tongue of a foreign land. He found it coming back to him now. Radioisotopes in the water. Christ.

"I guess that's another trust thing," he said.

"The iodine? Sure. It's a precaution in case someone tries to leave Border Town with an entity, unauthorized. Other than me, the only people who know about it are inside that rectangle in D.C. right now."

"No offense," Travis said, "obviously Paige trusts you in a jam, but why would she have told you about the iodine before last night?"

"I'm sure she trusts me as much as any of the

other new blood—maybe an inch more, since she recruited me herself—but she *didn't* tell me about the iodine. I told her."

Travis waited.

"It was Paige's idea to implement the technology," Bethany said. "But only after I told her how it works."

"I take it you didn't work at a petting zoo before she recruited you."

Bethany managed a smile. "Not exactly." She looked down at her phone. Stared at the map as if she could look right through it at Paige. "I'm twenty-four years old. I finished college at nineteen. I've spent the last five years working for a company that handles data security for the biggest clients in the world. International banks. Trading firms. The Department of Homeland Security. It's hard to overstate how sensitive a job like that is. It's kind of like the companies that make the lock mechanisms for bank vaults. You know how that works? Like, there are hundreds of companies that build vaults, and vault doors, but they never build the locks. There are only two or three companies in the whole world that make those. It's just one of those things you don't want a million people to be familiar with. Better for everyone if it's limited. Data security is the same way, at the high end. The systems that protect the largest corporations and government agencies are scripted and run by just a handful of people. And until this spring I was one of them."

She looked out the window. The whole sky was pink and the landscape below was coming to life in ripples of light and shadow.

"That's the story behind Renee Turner, by the way. I'm sorry if it's bragging, but there are maybe twenty people on the planet who know information security like I do. Paige has *some* skill in that department, but it's an entirely different thing if you've specialized in it for years. I created Renee tonight, based on an old college fake ID I had in my wallet. I sat down in a booth at Burger King in the Rapid City airport and I magicked her to life in twenty minutes using this phone. She has a social security number, DMV record including a DUI and two speeding tickets, bank accounts at First National and B of A totaling three million dollars, and a paid membership with Falcon Jet. I even gave her an arrest for having sex on a park bench in Miami when she was sixteen years old. I think that's a nice authentic touch, in case anyone looks up departures out of Rapid City and digs into her background. Who'd make up sex on a park bench?"

"Renee sounds fun."

Bethany shrugged. She looked down at the phone again. The diamond-shaped coverage zone of a new satellite drifted slowly into the frame. "Anyway, I'm sure Paige recruited me because I know how to code high-end security for data networks like the one in Border Town—and how to stay ahead of new technology that threatens it. But I guess it wouldn't surprise me if she had other reasons. Like maybe in some general way she could imagine a time like right now. Some rainy-day scenario when Tangent would be up against people with very serious resources on their side. Maybe she just wanted someone on *her* side who could counter that kind of thing."

Travis considered that. For the first time he saw the situation in its broad context, beyond the danger that Paige was in. The president of the United States had made a direct, aggressive move against Tangent. Had crossed a line that no one had crossed for the three decades that Tangent had existed.

"This could get a lot worse," Travis said.

"It already has," Bethany said.

She backed out the satellite image to a full view of the country, then dragged it sideways and zoomed in again, this time into the vast darkness that made up the American west. Only the digitally generated borders and roads gave any sense of scale as she zoomed. She pushed in tight on the emptiest part of eastern Wyoming, a hundred-mile-wide square bound by I–90 to the north and I–25 to the south and west. She zoomed in until the highways disappeared off the edges of the frame, leaving the screen entirely black. Border Town was somewhere in the middle of this area, Travis knew.

"In darkness these satellites use thermal imaging," Bethany said. "But Border Town's heat signature is carefully managed. Any heat output is first stored underground, and only released during daylight hours, specifically at times when the desert surface temperature exactly matches that of the exhaust ports. The compound is thermally invisible."

She pressed the button she'd used earlier to zoom, though it was impossible to see any result on the screen. There was only more darkness.

Then Travis saw something. A bright white speck moving rapidly across the top of the frame. It trailed a line behind itself, narrow at the front, fanning out and dimming toward its end. Bethany pushed in tighter. The speck resolved into two. Two specks, two trails. Moving side-by-side in formation. They were much faster in the smaller field of view. Bethany had to keep dragging it sideways to keep up. Travis noticed a distance scale at the bottom of the screen. A thumb's width was about half a mile. The two specks were covering that much distance every few seconds.

"Fighters," Travis said.

Bethany nodded. "I first noticed them during the flight to Atlanta. I spent about twenty minutes using specialized software to identify them by the heat plumes. They're Super Hornets. Dual role, able to engage both air and ground targets. There's another pair orbiting on the far side of the same big circle, about a forty-mile radius around Border Town."

"It's a blockade," Travis said. "No one's going in or out of there."

Bethany nodded again. "President Currey probably ordered it within an hour or so after the hit on the motorcade, once he decided to go all in. I must've gotten away by a margin of minutes."

They fell into a silence for the next half hour. They listened to the whine of the engines and the soft tones of the avionics up front. Bethany stared out the window. Travis stared ahead at nothing and thought of the power that was arrayed against them.

Bethany turned to him. "Can I ask you something personal?"

"Sure."

"Why did you leave Tangent?"

Travis thought about it. He thought of how complicated the answer to a simple question could be.

"Things would've gone bad if I'd stayed," he said. "Somewhere down the road."

"What made you think that?"

"Something told me," he said. The statement was more literal than it sounded.

"If we get through all this, maybe you'll feel better. Maybe you'll feel like coming back."

"I'm never coming back. If we're alive when this is over, I'll set up another identity like Rob Pullman, and find another warehouse to work third shift in for the rest of my life."

"You do realize you could make it easier on yourself. As long as you're creating an ID from scratch, you could give yourself a few million dollars. You wouldn't have to work at all."

Travis shook his head. "Money is means. It's better if I don't have much. Better if I stay on the fringe. It's the one way I can be sure things will be okay."

She stared at him. It was clear she had no idea what he was talking about, but after a moment she let it go and looked out the window again.

CHAPTER FIVE

They landed at Dulles and took a cab into the city. Half an hour later they had the location. The survivors of the motorcade attack—whichever ones they were—were in a sixteen-story office building overlooking the traffic circle at M Street and Vermont Avenue. The building had reflective green-tinted glass. It had no corporate logo visible. Just an address in large black letters on its concrete foundation, right next to the main entrance on the east side.

The signal was coming from the ninth floor at the northeast corner, directly facing the traffic circle.

Travis and Bethany were sitting on a cafe patio on the far side of the circle, one hundred yards from the building. It was 7:30 in the morning and the city was alive and busy in the early light. Every surface glittered. It looked like it'd rained all night and only cleared in the last couple hours. The story of the motorcade attack was everywhere. There was a big LCD screen inside the cafe playing the aftermath footage on a loop. The subject dominated every conversation Travis could hear at the tables around them.

Bethany had her phone low in her lap, out of sight to others nearby. Travis watched her mouthing commands she was entering into it. He couldn't make out any of them. Probably wouldn't have understood them any better if he could see them typed on the screen.

After a minute she looked up at him. "Signal strength is pretty weak now. Fall-off is consistent with a living body gradually flushing the iodine through the kidneys and passing it out as urine. And once it's in the sewers it's way too dispersed to read." She frowned. "This signal is also consistent with just one body. Paige is the only survivor."

Travis nodded. He stared at the corner of the ninth floor. No way to see in. No way to tell if Paige could see out. Maybe it wasn't even a window. Maybe the glass exterior concealed a brick-walled holding cell on that floor.

"So what exactly are we up against, here?" Travis said. "What do we know, right now? We know Paige and the others came to D.C. to meet with the president, and show him the entity. We know they trusted him, at that point. And we know that once they were attacked, they realized they'd been wrong about him—and that he's part of this thing, whatever it is. Whatever she and the others were trying to learn about. And obviously, lots of other people are involved too. Including whoever controls this building."

Bethany continued gazing at the structure. Travis did the same. They'd seen no one enter on foot through the street entrance yet. A number of cars had pulled off of Vermont into the narrow drive that separated the building from the one next to it—a building that had its own garage entrance at the front. That meant the cars going into the drive were entering the green building by some entrance at the rear. Most of the vehicles were town cars or SUVs with tinted windows in the back, professional drivers alone up front.

"Let's see who owns the place," Bethany said.

She went to work on her phone again. Travis watched screens of data, reflected in her glasses, flashing and changing every few seconds.

After a minute she frowned.

"It's not federal property," she said. "It's not listed that way, at least. The district records have it as a corporate office structure, privately held. Built in 2006. No entry for a company name, or any shareholder's name. Maybe it's a defense contractor, or a civil-engineering firm, something like that."

She stared at the building for a long moment, eyes narrowed.

"Can you get anything more on it?" Travis said.

"I have to, if we're going to help Paige." She looked at him. "Here's what I'm thinking. If we wanted to get some help, like *official* help, it would have to be the FBI. There's really no one else who can touch something this scale. But we'd need to be careful as hell. Whatever Paige and the others stumbled onto, whatever it is that the president is protecting, we have to assume that everyone he's appointed is on the same page as him. And since Currey's taken office he's replaced both the attorney general and the FBI director. And who knows who *they've* fired and replaced since then. They've probably got all kinds of loyalists in the ranks by now. If we go in blind, we stand a good chance of just touching the same nerve Paige touched."

"How far from blind can we get?" Travis said.

Bethany looked at her phone. "It depends on the connections I can make. Names to bank accounts. Other kinds of holdings, like real estate. Connections from those back to other names. Like that. If I could get a clear enough picture of who's involved in this thing, it might tell us who's *not* involved. It would make our guess a hell of a lot more educated, anyway. The problem is that none of the names we know right now will help us. Not the president. Not anyone in his cabinet. Their names won't be on anything damning, I promise." She looked at the building again. "What I need are names from inside there. Owners. Executives. Almost anyone. It'd give me a loose end to start with."

She looked thoughtful. But not optimistic. Her eyebrows made a little shrug, up and down, and then she turned back to her phone.

"We'll see," she said, and went to work on it.

Travis said nothing for the next ten minutes. He left her to it. He stared at the high-rise and thought of how it would work if they could get the FBI's cooperation. The bulk of the Hostage Rescue Team was right across the river at Quantico. Between them and whatever local police they felt like coordinating with, there could be a sea of armed law enforcement around the green-tinted building within a few hours, like rabid fans waiting for a pop star to come out of a hotel.

At which point Paige's survival should be assured. The people holding her were corrupt and violent, but they weren't stupid. If the game was absolutely up, then their focus would shift to securing high-priced lawyers and cutting deals with authorities, turning against one another in the process. They would have nothing to gain by killing Paige at that point, and they would have plenty to lose.

But *until* that point, she might as well be kneeling in her own grave. Her captors' reasons for keeping her alive could evaporate any time. It was hard to imagine she had more than a few hours left. Maybe not even that. Travis felt a tremor in his hands on the tabletop. He made them into fists.

Bethany finished with the phone and set it in front of her.

"Nothing," she said. She didn't sound surprised. "Every transaction is routed through some middle pathway with a gap in it. Everything from the original construction costs to last month's electric bill. It's strange how it works, but a relatively small enterprise can actually have much better protection than a big international bank or a federal system like Social Security. Giant trillion-dollar organizations like that have to be widely accessible. It's the whole point of their existence. They can be secured, but they can't be secret." She nodded at the highrise. "A place like that *can* be secret. It can do its business without anyone knowing its name, or the identity of its CEO. And it does. The place is an information black hole. Someone very smart worked very hard to get it that way. Probably someone I've played tennis with."

"Can you run the license plates of these vehicles we see going in?"

She shook her head. "I'll try it, but it won't work. They'll all be registered to some service that doesn't have to keep client names on file, or something close to that. There'll be a gap in the dominoes somewhere, I'm sure of it. We could even rent a car and try to tail someone home tonight, but I'll bet you a shiny half-dollar that these drivers are trained to go through shakes along their routes."

Travis knew the term. A shake was any wide-open space, like an empty stadium parking lot or a fairground, that a driver could pass through in order to reveal a tailing vehicle. In the movies a smart hero could glance in his rearview mirror and spot a tail five cars back amid rush-hour traffic, even though the law of averages pretty much guaranteed that a few vehicles in the pack were following the same route just by chance. In real life, professional drivers used shakes.

Bethany rubbed her temples. She looked very tired. "In my old line of work there's a term for this kind of setup. Have you ever heard of an oubliette?"

"Can't say I have."

"It's a kind of prison cell. *Was* a kind of prison cell. In the middle ages. A cell with no bars, no walls, no door and no lock. The simplest kind was just a platform sticking out of a smooth castle wall a hundred feet above the ground. They lower you onto it from above, and there you are. Imprisoned by nothing but open air." She nodded at the building. "That place is a kind of oubliette for information. It's not that there are firewalls protecting its identity, or powerful encryption algorithms. I'm sure it's got all that too, but what really protects it is just open space. All the paper trails leading in have just the right breaks in them. It's the sort of thing you can only pull off if you have the right kinds of connections and a lot of money. Enough to bend the rules around yourself."

Travis watched another SUV pull into the place. The driver looked like an NFL linebacker with a Marine haircut. Maybe he'd been both of those at one time.

"It's not gonna happen with the FBI," Bethany said. "Not if we don't know who we're dealing with."

Travis nodded, his eyes still locked on the building.

"What about Tangent's hubs?" he said. "Didn't they have a couple dozen of those around the world? Secure sites staffed with their people, armed and trained to beat hell? Couldn't we get help from one of those?"

Bethany was already shaking her head. "The hubs are gone. They only existed to deal with Aaron Pilgrim. Once that threat was eliminated, there was no more need for them. Hub staff were never really members of Tangent to begin with. They were elite military units from a number of countries, cleared for some minimal knowledge of Tangent and its operations. Over the past two years they've all been let go, with nice, thick non-disclosure documents to sign on their way out."

She was looking down at her hands as she spoke. She looked about as lost as anyone Travis had ever seen.

"I don't know what to do," she said. "We're not going to get any help, and we're not getting in there by ourselves. You know that, don't you?"

Travis stared at the place. If Paige's room had a window, and if she could stand up and walk to it, she could see the two of them right now—even if she'd never recognize them at this range.

He looked away from the building. Met Bethany's gaze.

"Yes," he said. "I know. Every guard in the place will have an automatic weapon and a big red button that can lock the whole building down."

"And we're a kid armed with a slingshot."

Travis's eyes fell to Bethany's backpack lying between them on the table, and the long cylindrical shape inside it.

"We don't know what we're armed with yet," he said.

Bethany nodded. "Let's find out."

CHAPTER SIX

Paige woke in the same place where she'd fallen asleep: a hardwood-floored office eight or ten stories up, overlooking D.C. through tinted windows. The room was bare. The windows stretched from floor to ceiling. She lay in the center of the open space, her wrists and ankles bound with heavy-duty zip ties.

It was morning now, but during the night she'd lain awake here for hours, listening to footsteps coming and going in the corridor. Overhearing conversations outside the door, hushed and tense, right at the brink of her discernment. One word had jumped out at her half a dozen times, maybe the working title of some project or operation. The closest thing to context she'd gotten was a single exchange, a few decibels higher than the rest of the talk:

"They sound rattled. They're not thinking of shutting it down, are they?"

"Umbra? Not a chance."

Umbra. Paige had fallen asleep replaying the word in her mind, along with the rest of the exchange. Now she was awake, still replaying it.

Trying to fit it with the scattered knowledge she'd had before coming to D.C.

She lowered her head to the hardwood and stared out at the city in the soft yellow light.

These people were going to kill her. No doubt about that. The only question was when. Sometime today, for sure. As soon as they were certain she was of no value, it would happen. By now they'd probably spoken to the president, and figured out that she'd already told him everything she knew. *She'd* requested the meeting, after all; why *wouldn't* she tell him everything?

She tried not to think about it. There wasn't much point. She thought of Bethany instead. Wondered if she'd made it out of Border Town with the second cylinder.

It crossed her mind that she actually *hadn't* told the president everything: she hadn't said a word about the other cylinder. It simply hadn't fit into the conversation. She'd left it behind in Border Town on only the most general principles of caution and pragmatism. "Shit happens" principles. It was depressing how often those proved their worth.

If Bethany had gotten out, then she'd probably already linked up with Travis. By now they might be just seeing what the cylinder did, somewhere in Atlanta. The thing's basic function was easy enough to understand. But what about the rest of it? Would the two of them figure out what they needed to do—including the parts Paige herself hadn't nailed down?

And would they understand how damn little time they had left to do it?

CHAPTER SEVEN

There was a Ritz-Carlton halfway up the block on Vermont. Travis and Bethany got the Presidential Suite on the tenth floor—Renee Turner was paying for it, and it would've been at odds with her pattern to rent anything cheaper. The suite was 1800 square feet with views to the south and west. They could see the green-tinted building without obstruction. They could see the ninth-floor corner overlooking the traffic circle. Past the building they could see all the way down Vermont to the White House. The flag on its roof was flying full and tense in the wind.

They sat on one of the leather couches, opened the backpack on the floor, and set the black cylinder on the empty cushion between them. It bled heat into the air like a cooling engine block.

It was Travis's first good look at the thing in bright light. The object was heavily scuffed and scratched, like a power tool put to years of hard use by a carpenter. There was no way anyone at Tangent had abused it like that. Travis had seen the paranoid care they took with entities. The scuffs could've only been made by the object's original owners on the other side of the Breach. Whoever—or whatever—they were, this thing meant nothing more to them than a cordless drill or a radial saw meant to humans.

Travis studied the labels Paige or one of the others had taped beside the three buttons. He'd seen them just briefly in the Explorer.

ON
OFF
OFF (DETACH/DELAY—93 SEC.)

He spent only a few seconds trying to imagine what DETACH/DELAY meant. There was no point in thinking about it until they knew what the entity did.

Aside from the buttons, and their engraved symbols, the cylinder's only notable feature was a small lens inset in one end. It was about the size of a quarter, and deep black.

"You said this came out of the Breach along with one just like it," Travis said.

Bethany nodded.

"And that was a few days ago?"

"Oh—no. They actually egressed years ago. Sometime in 1998, I think."

He stared at her. Waited for the explanation.

"They were sealed," she said. "Do you know about sealed entities?"

Travis nodded. Paige had given him a pretty thorough tour of the Primary Lab in Border Town. She'd told him about sealed entities, and shown him a few of them. They were rare. They tended to be the more powerful ones. They emerged from the Breach in their own secure packaging, maybe the alien equivalent of the hard plastic shells that retailers used to deter shoplifters. Each sealed entity was unique, not only in the seal's color and size, but in terms of what it took to open it. Some were easy: they opened to an electric charge or a certain temperature, or even blunt impact force. Others were tricky. Lab techs might spend weeks or months running them through a battery of experiments, every one a shot in the dark. Exposure to random chemical compounds, wavelengths of light, air pressure settings in a vacuum chamber. Some of them simply never gave up their secrets. Paige had shown Travis a lemon yellow box about the size of a cinder block. Seamless. Featureless. Opaque. It'd come through the Breach on Christmas Day in 1979, and three decades later no one had a clue what the hell was inside it.

"I first came to Border Town this April," Bethany said, "and I've been rotating through all the different jobs as part of the standard training. They like everyone to be good at everything. I started in the Primary Lab two weeks ago, and I spent a couple hours the first night looking at the sealed entities. I thought they were fascinating. They're like solitaire games someone else got stumped by and left sitting out. You look at them and you think, 'Maybe I'll see something they missed.'"

Travis knew the feeling, though he hadn't felt it in any lab in Border Town. He'd experienced it years before, walking through crime scenes in the quiet hours after all the prints had been lifted and the photos shot and the bodies taken away.

"There was one seal that got my attention," Bethany said. She indicated the cylinder lying between them. "It was a little bigger than two of these side by side. A white casing shaped like a pill but flattened a little. There was a seam right around the middle, like a waistline. It looked like you could just hold the thing by each end and pull it open."

She went quiet for a moment, like she didn't know how to say the next part. Or didn't expect him to believe her.

"You've got to be kidding me," Travis said.

She shrugged. "It was such a stupid idea I was too embarrassed to try it, even if nobody was around. Obviously, it would've been the first thing someone tried back in 1998. And probably a hundred people had done the same thing since then. Like trying to twist a doorknob even when you're sure it's locked. You're compelled to give it at least one go. So finally, this past Sunday night, I did it. I grabbed the two ends and pulled. And the damn thing came apart like a plastic Easter egg."

Travis could only stare. It simply wasn't possible that no one had thought to do that in thirteen years. He saw a trace of dry amusement in her eyes at his expression.

"We figured out the trick later," she said. "After we took out the two cylinders, we put the halves of the seal back together and they automatically relocked. And everyone in the room tried pulling them apart, with no luck. Even I couldn't do it again. It was like trying to pull apart a lump of steel. Paige figured it out, though, and it only took her an hour to prove her theory. She positioned two robotic arms to recreate the way a human would pull on the seal, and she went methodically through different levels of force. At exactly 12.4 newtons, the seal came apart."

Travis thought he understood. "Any more or any less, and it wouldn't open, right?"

She nodded. "You need to apply that exact force for just over a second. If the pressure wavers up or down by even a tenth of a newton during that second, it won't open."

"High-school physics was a long time ago," Travis said. "I'm not even sure I took it. How small is a tenth of a newton?"

She thought about it for a second. "Say it took 12.4 newtons to lift a hardcover of *War and Peace.* Tear out twenty pages and it would take 12.3 to lift it. That's the sensitivity involved."

"Not very forgiving."

"You have no idea. Even after we knew what it took, how much force and how long, none of us could get it to open again. It's damn near impossible. And I opened it the first time *without* knowing. It was a one-in-a-hundred-thousand fluke." Her expression changed. It took on the tired nervousness Travis had seen outside the door of his apartment building. "Which makes all of this my fault, if you think about it. The motorcade attack. Everything. If I hadn't joined Tangent, none of this would be happening. This entity and its counterpart would've sat sealed on that shelf forever."

Travis had been staring away at nothing while she spoke. He'd been thinking it was actually pretty damn unnerving that whoever built these entities put them in something so hard to open. He thought about childproof caps on bottles of chemical cleaners, and for a second he felt a chill because he could almost get a sense of their mindset, whoever they were on the other side of the Breach. These black cylinders might only be power tools to them, but they were dangerous as hell. Dangerous even to their makers.

Travis looked at the button labeled ON. He glanced at Bethany and saw her looking down at it too.

The end of the cylinder with the inset lens was pointed outward, into the open space in front of the couch. That face of it cleared the cushion's edge by an inch. There was nothing obstructing the lens.

"Let's do it," Travis said.

Bethany nodded. "Should we count to three?"

"No," Travis said, and pushed the button.

CHAPTER EIGHT

What it did, it did instantly. Travis felt the button click under his fingertip and a cone of light shot from the lens at the end of the cylinder. The cone was long and narrow, fanning out maybe one foot in width for every five feet in length. It had a dark blue cast to it. Almost violet.

Ten feet out from the lens, the light cone simply terminated in midair, as if there were a projector screen there. What it projected in the air was a flat disc, two feet across, perfectly black. The disc was centered at about chest level, due to a slight upward tilt of the cylinder on the couch.

Travis stared at it.

He lost track of seconds.

In his peripheral vision he saw Bethany glance at him, but only briefly. Then her gaze went right back to the disc and stayed there.

More time passed.

Nothing about the disc changed.

Travis wasn't sure what he expected to happen. Maybe the projection would show them something. A video recorded on the other side of the Breach.

That fit the scale of something Paige might have been compelled to show the president. Though how it could've touched a nerve with him, Travis couldn't guess.

He watched. Bethany watched.

Nothing happened.

The black disc just hovered there at the end of the projected beam.

It wasn't reflective, Travis noticed. The way they were sitting, with large windows full of daylight spanning half the room, a reflective surface would have bounced nothing but glare at their eyes. A glass-screened television, positioned like the disc, would've been impossible to watch.

But the disc bounced nothing. It was no more reflective than cloth. And even cloth would've picked up plenty of the room's light and appeared much brighter than true black. It would've looked gray, no matter how dark it was colored.

The disc was simply and purely black.

Only one explanation came to Travis's mind.

"Holy shit," Bethany said.

Travis turned and saw that she'd drawn the same conclusion he had, and at the same moment.

For a few seconds neither spoke.

Then Travis stood from the couch. The move was almost involuntary. The couch cushion responded to the sudden loss of his weight on it, and as it rose, some of its movement transferred to the middle cushion, where the cylinder rested. Travis saw the black disc—or what looked like a disc—bob up and down a few inches as the light cone shifted and settled. It happened again a second later when Bethany stood.

Travis moved forward. He gave the cone of light a wide berth as he went. He saw Bethany do the same on her side. Then she drew a sharp breath and stopped. Travis looked at her.

Her hair was moving in a steady breeze, though none of the windows in the suite were open. She turned her face directly into the slipstream of air, which was at least as strong as a current driven by a table fan. The wind appeared to be coming from the disc itself. But that wasn't exactly true.

Because it wasn't a disc.

It was an opening.

Travis felt the rational parts of his mind gradually coming back to life after their initial freeze— seeing the impossible could have that effect. Now as the seconds drew out he found himself trying to make sense of what he was looking at. Whatever sense could be made of it.

The projection was an opening. A hole in midair. Like a doorway between rooms. On this side was the presidential suite of the Ritz-Carlton in Washington, D.C. On the other side was—what, exactly?

The wind through the opening continued blowing Bethany's hair around. It ruffled the fabric of her shirt. Her expression was nearly blank, as if she wasn't sure yet what to feel. Travis imagined his own looked similar.

He took another step forward. It put him two feet away from the opening. He could reach it from here. Could reach *through* it, if he wanted to.

Being closer to it made no difference in its appearance. Still black. Like an open window on a moonless night, seen from inside a brightly lit room.

Bethany came closer on her own side. So far neither of them had put so much as a hand into the projection beam.

The angled windstream was still mostly affecting Bethany, but Travis could feel the edge of it, too, at this distance.

Bethany spoke, just above a whisper. "What's over there?"

Travis could only shake his head.

Whatever the place was, it had to be outdoors. There was wind there. And it was nighttime, which narrowed the location down to half the Earth at any given moment.

Assuming the place on the other side was *on* Earth.

Travis wondered if the air coming through was safe to breathe. Probably too late to worry about it, if it wasn't.

And it hadn't killed the test animals in Border Town. Travis suddenly understood what they'd been used for. Paige and the others had put them through the opening, to test the safety of crossing the threshold.

He glanced at Bethany and saw her staring through into the darkness, eyes narrowed, no doubt thinking all the same things he was.

She turned to him. "Remember the end of the phone call? Paige said something like, 'You can go through and come back.' She practically screamed it."

Travis nodded.

The wind through the opening shifted a bit

toward him. He felt it tug at the arms of his T-shirt. It also gave him the scent of the place on the other side—a number of scents. Strong vegetation smells: pine boughs, dead leaves, ripe apples, all of it sharp and crisp on a wind that was maybe ten degrees cooler than the air-conditioned hotel room. The other side of the opening felt and smelled like an autumn night in the country.

"What location on Earth right now would have a climate like fall in the northern United States?" Travis said.

Bethany thought about it. She shrugged. "Maybe western Canada, a few hundred miles up the coast from Seattle. I really don't know. It would still be dark there, for what it's worth."

Travis took another breath of the chilly wind.

"It doesn't make sense," he said. "Even if it really is an opening to someplace thousands of miles away—as impressive as that is—what could Paige and the others have learned from this thing? What could *anyone* learn from it that they couldn't learn by just flying to wherever it leads?"

"There must be more to it than we're thinking," Bethany said.

Travis nodded. There had to be. And they weren't going to find out what it was by just standing here.

Travis turned and looked around. There was a leather-bound room service menu on the nearest end table. He crossed to it, picked it up and came back to where he'd been standing beside the opening.

He held the menu by one end. He put the other end into the projected cone of light. It blocked a big chunk of the beam, maybe a third or more. That portion of the light no longer reached the black opening.

But the opening was unaffected.

In a way it was the most surreal thing Travis had seen yet. It was like sticking your hand into the beam of a movie projector, seeing the shapes of your fingers cast down the length of the light—but seeing no shadow on the screen.

"It makes sense," Bethany said. "They'd have to build it so that the hole stayed open, even if part of the beam were blocked. Otherwise, think about it: you'd block the beam with your body before you could climb through the opening."

Travis wondered how much of the beam could be cut off before the opening failed. Keeping the menu in the light cone, he moved it slowly toward the couch. Toward the cylinder's lens, and the narrow part of the beam.

He watched the opening as he did it. Watched the rectangle of blocked-out light grow until it was well over half of the beam. Then three fourths. The opening showed no effect at all. It didn't so much as flicker.

It stayed that way until only a sliver of blue light reached the hole. Maybe five percent of the total. When Travis blocked it further, the opening vanished. At the same time the projected light on the leather menu began to flash symbols in the same text that was engraved on the cylinder. Maybe it said OBSTRUCTION ERROR. Maybe it said STOP BLOCKING THE LIGHT, ASSHOLE. Travis pulled the menu out of the way and the opening immediately reappeared.

He pressed his other hand to the menu. It felt as cool to the touch as when he'd picked it up. He held it close to his eyes and tilted it so that the gleam of sunlight showed him the surface in detail. It didn't appear damaged.

He went back to the opening. He still held the menu. He shared a look with Bethany: *Here goes.*

He put the menu fully into the cone of light, and then he put half of it through the hole in the air.

It met no resistance. The leading half of the menu simply went through, as if the opening were no more than a hole in a wall, with a darkened room on the far side. They could still see the entire menu. It was right there with them—even if part of it was also far, far away from them, in the night air of some rural place halfway around the world.

Travis drew it back into the room and tossed it onto an armchair a few feet away.

He turned back to Bethany. "Unless you know a place in D.C. to get lab mice, I'm out of things to try."

"I think *we're* the lab mice at this point."

CHAPTER NINE

They closed all the drapes in the suite's living room and shut the doors to the adjoining areas. The resulting near darkness allowed their eyes to adjust a little, but it made no difference as far as the opening was concerned. The place on the other side still looked pitch-black.

Travis stepped into the projected beam of light and faced the hole directly. If the blue light had any effect where it shone on his back, he couldn't feel it. Even the exposed skin on his neck and arms felt normal.

Travis stood there a moment and let the wind rush over him. He closed his eyes. He listened. Behind him he could hear the ambience of D.C., even through the closed windows of the suite. The rumble of traffic. The beeping of some kind of construction vehicle on a build site. The drone of a propeller aircraft.

But there were sounds coming from in front of him too, through the opening. Night sounds of insects and maybe frogs. They were very faint. He hadn't noticed them earlier. He tried to isolate them now. The sounds seemed to come from only a few point sources, far away in the darkness. Which made sense. If it'd been a summer night on the other side, the chorus of insect song would've been overwhelming. Literally billions of tiny noise-makers within the nearest mile, any one of them loud enough to be heard at a distance. But the location on the other side of the opening—Canada or wherever it might be—was long past its local summer. The night air called to mind the trailing edge of the living season, when most things had already gone to ground or simply died off. Travis had the sense that he was listening to the region's last few holdouts. A few nights from now, even those would probably be silenced, and there would be nothing but the dead quiet of the oncoming winter.

Travis put his hand through the opening.

In the corner of his eye he saw Bethany flinch a little, even though she'd expected the move.

His hand felt fine.

He lowered it to the bottom edge of the hole, but stopped just shy of touching it. He wondered what the margin was like. Was it a kind of blade-edge between the space on this side and the space on the other? If he ran his hand into it, would it pass right through, cutting his fingers off and dropping them away into the darkness over there? It seemed like Paige would've warned them about something like that, but she hadn't had a lot of time to go into details.

Travis was tempted to grab the bound menu again and test the edge of the hole with it. Instead he lowered his hand another inch, slowly, ready to retract it.

His fingers settled onto a smooth, rounded edge.

Like the tubing of a hula hoop. It was cool and rigid as steel. Travis applied a few pounds of force to it. It didn't budge. Strange—the cylinder's movement on the couch a few minutes earlier had made the opening bob up and down easily, but the opening itself couldn't be moved by direct force against it. It was as fixed as a hole cut into an iron wall.

Travis ducked and leaned his upper body through the hole, into the night on the other side.

At once he saw what'd been impossible to see from inside the suite: a sky shot full of stars, sharp and clear in the unhindered darkness. The hazy band of the Milky Way defined a long arc from one horizon to the other. A crescent moon hung like a blade, an hour from setting or having risen— Travis wasn't sure which. But it was definitely the same moon he'd grown up under. He was staring at a nightscape somewhere on Earth, at least.

His eyes were already adjusting to the dark, much deeper on this side of the opening than in the suite, even with the drapes closed.

As the seconds drew out he began to discern details in the night around him, both near and distant. He saw the canopy of a forest, the treetops maybe twenty feet below his viewpoint. Spires of pine trees and the rough curves of hardwoods, all of them pale in the faint light of the moon.

There were other shapes, but he couldn't make sense of them. Strange geometric forms, like huge scaffolding assemblies or bamboo towers, jutted up from the forest here and there. The light was too poor to offer any detail about them. Even their distances were hard to gauge. Travis looked down and saw the footings of one of the structures right below. Its complex form rose into the darkness just behind his position.

The only other shape he could resolve was something very tall and narrow, and solid in appearance, standing on the horizon at least a mile away. Its height was imposing even at that distance: it towered above the trees, easily five times their height. He focused on it but could perceive no detail beyond its bulk and rough size. He thought of an enormous smokestack rising from a factory complex. The problem was that there was no smoke, and no factory, either, unless all its lights were shut off.

He saw movement in his peripheral vision and then Bethany was there, leaning into the darkness beside him. He edged over a few inches to give her room.

For a moment they just stood there in silence, side by side. They listened to the night. Travis looked at the moon again and judged that it was higher than when he'd first seen it. The crescent was very narrow, which meant the sun couldn't be far below the horizon. Dawn was no more than an hour away, though there was no hint of it yet.

"I've never seen any place this dark," Bethany said. "There's not the least bit of light pollution on the horizon. We'd have to be over a hundred miles from even a mid-sized town for it to look like this. But at the same time it's a place where people have built large structures, whatever these are. And whatever *that* is." She waved a hand to indicate the towering form in the distance. "It has to be forty stories tall. Maybe taller." She was quiet for a moment and then she turned to him. "Where the hell are we?"

Travis had no answer. He had a vague notion that it could be a military installation, built in remote wilderness out of concern for public safety or—more likely—secrecy. But why would an alien-made device just happen to show them a place like that? Why would it show them *any* place in particular, as opposed to some random location? Even if the place on the other side were some fixed distance and direction from here, it should still be someplace purely random. Simple probability said they should be looking out at the ocean right now, or a wide-open prairie, or an arctic tundra, or a city street with a McDonalds and a Starbucks and half a dozen stoplights.

"I don't know," Travis said.

Bethany started to speak, but before she could, a high-pitched cry rose from the trees right below them. Bethany flinched hard and grabbed onto his arm. Travis was glad for that: it masked the fact that his own muscles had tensed pretty damn hard.

He grew calm at once, recognizing the sound: a wolf's howl. As it died away Travis cocked his head and listened. He heard the clatter of running footsteps as the pack went by right beneath their position. Their claws scrabbled on ground that sounded unusually hard. Stone, he'd have guessed—if a forest could grow from stone.

A hundred yards off, the wolves stopped and howled again, first one and then another. Seconds passed, and then a series of answering cries resonated from the trees half a mile away. The nearer set of wolves had just begun to respond when a new sound erupted somewhere between the packs, silencing both of them. Bethany didn't exactly flinch, but Travis felt her body shudder. He felt his own blood go cold, and wasn't surprised that it did. He was biologically wired to fear this sound, courtesy of a long chain of ancestors who'd survived to pass on their genes. It was the guttural bass wave of a lion's roar.

A lion. Among wolves. In a temperate forest far enough north that it felt like late fall during the month of August.

"Okay: *Where the hell are we?* is the wrong question," Bethany said. "Where the *fuck* are we?"

Ten minutes later the first glow of dawn came to the horizon. Five minutes after that there was enough light to show them everything. They saw what the scaffoldlike things around them really were. And they recognized the towering shape on the horizon. They'd seen it in movies and on television all their lives.

They knew exactly where they were.

And they knew that *where* really *was* the wrong question to ask.

CHAPTER TEN

Travis paced at the windows on the west side of the room. The drapes were open again. There was no reason to keep them closed now—the place on the other side of the opening had its own daylight, though it was dulled by cloud cover that'd come in with the dawn.

Travis wondered how Paige and the others had first reacted to what the cylinders did. They were long familiar with Breach technology. They'd been dealing with it for years. Maybe it hadn't been hard for them to get their minds around what was beyond the open circle.

It was hard for Travis.

It looked like it was hard for Bethany, too. She was sitting in the armchair Travis had tossed the menu onto earlier. She was staring at nothing in particular. Her eyes kept narrowing as she considered new angles of the situation.

Travis went to the south end of the room and stared out the windows. Not quite a mile and a half in that direction stood the Washington Monument. For height it dwarfed everything else in the city. It was over five hundred fifty feet tall. Its white marble was nearly blinding in the summer sunlight.

Travis turned and walked to the projected opening, which was aimed more or less to the south. He ducked and leaned through it and stared at the Washington Monument there, rising from the canopy of pines and brightly colored hardwoods, its marble dull and gray beneath the overcast autumn sky.

Nearer by, the rusted girder skeletons of highrises reared from the trees in various states of decay. Strangler vines had enveloped all but the tallest of them. Travis looked down at what remained of the Ritz-Carlton beneath him. Much of the southwest corner had collapsed, but otherwise the framework still held. Here and there a few sections of concrete flooring remained in place, though mostly there were just stubs of rebar where the concrete had long ago cracked and fallen away.

Through gaps in the trees Travis could see the ground ten stories below. He could see the remnant of Vermont Avenue, fractured by years of plant root invasion and ice expansion. He recalled the sound of the wolves clattering over it in the darkness.

"There's a city in Russia called Pripyat," Bethany said. "It's right next to the Chernobyl power station."

Travis drew back in from the opening and turned to her.

"The city had a population of about fifty thousand," she said. "It was evacuated within a couple days of the accident, and it's been empty ever since. Biologists are fascinated with it. It's kind of a thumbnail view of what the world would look like if we all just disappeared one day. In Pripyat there were saplings taking root in the middle of city streets within just a couple years. We can assume the same thing would happen here. Which means the age of the trees on the other side gives us an estimate of the time frame we're dealing with. It gives us a minimum, anyway."

Travis nodded. "There's a white pine out there that's got sixty-seven rings of branches, and it's about as tall as anything in sight. Branch rings equal years, more or less."

"So call it seventy years," Bethany said. "On the other side of the opening, it's seventy years after the end of the world. Whenever that is."

"The rest of it slots in easily enough," Travis said.

He was pacing at the windows again.

Bethany was still sitting in the chair. Still looking numb.

Travis continued. "Paige and the others turned on the cylinders inside Border Town. Who knows what they saw on the other side, down there. Maybe that far in the future, the place is just deserted. Whatever the case, they took the cylinders up into the desert the next morning, and spent a lot more time there. They took radio and satellite equipment through the projected opening, and set it all up in the future. They wanted to find out if there was anyone alive in that time. If there was anyone out there, on the air."

Bethany turned to him. Her eyes looked haunted.

"I wonder if they heard anyone," she said.

Travis thought about it. "One way or another,

they learned something. Something specific enough that they thought the president could help them understand it."

"The first piece of the puzzle," Bethany said.

Travis nodded. "It could have been anything. Some old military transmission broadcasting on a loop somewhere, even decades after everyone was gone. Or something else entirely. Who knows, right? But whatever it was, if they couldn't make sense of it themselves, who better to go to than the president? He could put them in touch with almost anyone who might have expertise."

Bethany considered it. Nodded slowly.

Travis stopped pacing. He returned to the opening and leaned into it. He stared at the wreck of the city beyond.

What the hell had happened? Not a nuclear war. D.C. would be an ash plain in that case. There might be trees there by now, grown up in the aftermath, but there sure as hell wouldn't be girder frames left standing.

"Paige's goal was the most obvious thing in the world," Travis said. "She and the others were going to take the cylinder to some number of sites, go through to the future, and dig through the ruins for evidence. Figure out exactly how the world ends. Figure out how to prevent it. No doubt they explained all that to the president." He leaned back into the suite and turned to Bethany. "So think about this. Suppose right now, the president is involved in something nobody's supposed to know about. Something that's happening, or maybe is *about* to happen. Paige and the others uncovered some little scrap of it in the future. Not enough that they could recognize its full meaning, but enough that the president could. And when he saw it, he understood the threat they posed to him. Because his secret is well protected in our time, but it's vulnerable as hell in the future. Someone sifting through the rubble could eventually learn all about it."

Travis went quiet. He stared at nothing. "What is he hiding?"

"Could it just be his own complicity in whatever happens to the world?" Bethany said. "Say the thing he's involved in right now is going bad. Really bad. Say it's big enough that it's over even *his* head, and when it goes off the rails it's going to take the world with it. Maybe Paige and the others could have found information in the future to help us turn it all around—something to give us a chance, anyway—but in the process they'd have discovered President Currey's role in it. Jesus, could it be that simple? Would he rather let the world end than have people find out it's his fault?"

Travis thought about it for a long time. "That should be harder to believe than it is."

Bethany made a face that was a little too unnerved to register humor.

"We're guessing until we know what Paige found," Travis said.

He stepped away from the circular opening and returned to the suite's south-facing windows. He stared down Vermont at the green-tinted high-rise in the present day.

Paige.

Lying there alone.

Waiting to die.

The cylinder, powerful as it was, seemed entirely useless as a means of getting her out of that place.

Travis leaned against the window, forearms crossed above his head. He shut his eyes and breathed out slowly.

And then it came to him.

CHAPTER ELEVEN

They worked out the logistics of the plan in a matter of minutes, and then Travis took a four-mile cab ride across the river, into Virginia, and found a sporting goods store. He used his credit card—Rob Pullman's credit card—to buy a Remington 870 twelve-gauge and a hundred shells for it, along with fifty feet of inch-thick manila rope. He bought the largest duffel bag the store sold, which easily fit the rope and the disassembled shotgun. He took another cab back into D.C. and broke probably twenty laws by carrying a firearm and ammunition into the Ritz-Carlton. He took the elevator to the third floor, where Bethany—Renee, technically—had checked into a second room.

She had the cylinder resting in an armchair, the opening projected ten feet away at chest level, as it'd been upstairs.

Travis set the duffel bag down and walked to the opening. The view through it was different from this floor of the building. They were deep among the trees now, just twenty-five feet above the weed-laced concrete of the forest floor. Down here there was no hint of the wind they'd felt earlier, from their position above the canopy.

Travis leaned through and studied the immediate space around the hole. There were no girders close by. This room, like the presidential suite, occupied the building's southwest corner, which in the future was reduced to a deadfall of rusted steel filling part of the foundation below. Travis saw plenty of sturdy branches all around, but the nearest of them were a good distance away—twenty feet, at least. The far side of the opening was surrounded by a margin of empty space in all directions.

Which was good. If lions were present in this wilderness—no doubt escaped from zoos when the world came apart—then there could be any number of other large predators here. Black bears, leopards, cougars. All of which could climb trees, and were probably curious enough to investigate a wide-open hole in midair with a hotel room on the other side. Travis was sure the Ritz's staff had seen all kinds of crazy shit in their establishment over the years, but there was no reason to go for some kind of record.

Behind him, Bethany guessed what he was thinking. "I positioned the iris so nothing out there could reach it," she said.

He leaned back in and turned to her. "Iris?"

She indicated the opening, and shrugged. "I gave it a name."

"Why iris?"

"Watch what happens when you close it."

Travis stepped away from the opening as Bethany walked to the cylinder. He hadn't seen her switch it off in the suite earlier; he'd left to get a cab by then.

Bethany pressed the OFF button and the open circle contracted shut like an image on an old model television set. Or like an iris suddenly exposed to bright light. It shrank to a singular point and then vanished.

Bethany shrugged again. "Iris."

"Okay."

She switched the cylinder back on.

"Did you try the other button?" Travis said.

"Yeah."

"What does it do?"

"Pretty much what you expect."

He nodded. As soon as they'd learned what the entity did, he'd assumed the third button, OFF (DETACH/DELAY—93 SEC.), allowed the hole to stay open for 93 seconds with the projection switched off—with the opening detached from the light that'd created it.

Bethany pressed the button.

The light cone brightened and intensified for maybe five seconds. Travis thought he understood what it was doing: it was feeding a surge of power to the opening—the iris. Enough power to sustain it for 93 seconds. Then the cone switched off, and the iris stayed open all by itself.

"Watch," Bethany said. She took hold of the black cylinder and moved it left and right. The iris didn't move with it. It stayed fixed in place.

"I wonder what the point is," Travis said. "Why would it be useful to delay the shutdown by a minute and a half?"

Bethany's eyebrows arched a little and she shook her head. She had no idea.

Travis thought about it, but let it go after a

few seconds. It was an interesting feature, but he couldn't imagine a situation in which they'd want to shut the iris slowly. He could think of all kinds of situations in which they'd want to shut it quickly, in which case the regular OFF button would work fine.

He crossed to where he'd left the duffel bag. He opened it and began assembling the shotgun.

"You don't have to go along," Travis said.

It was a few minutes later. He had the Remington put together, loaded, and slung on his back by its strap. He was standing at the iris, his hands around the thick cord of manila rope. One end of the rope was tied to the pedestal mount of a stool at the room's wet bar. The pedestal was made of steel. Travis had put a lot of pressure on it and deemed it more than strong enough. From there the rope stretched across the room, through the iris, and hung three stories down, that end trailing among the corroded ruins of the hotel's collapsed corner. The same bar stool was probably down there somewhere, rusted all to hell.

Bethany leaned beside him and stared out into the trees. Birdsong filtered through the forest from every direction. Sparrows. Red-winged blackbirds. It sounded like any average woodland in present-day America.

"Two shooters are better than one," she said.

"Have you ever shot before?"

She nodded. "My company mandated that I carry a concealed weapon and maintain proficiency with it. There were risks to my safety, given what I knew."

"Ever climb a rope before?"

"Gym class in junior high. I wasn't great at it, but then again the motivation wasn't really there."

"You're sure you want to do this?"

She watched the forest for a long time before answering. "I don't know how it is for you, but I've given up on being sure of things for a while."

Travis positioned himself two feet beneath her as they descended, so that he could stop her fall if she slipped. She didn't slip.

They touched down onto the pile of rusted girders, tentatively at first, testing whether it was stable. It turned out to be far more so than Travis had expected. He studied it for a moment and saw why: the pile had spent decades oxidizing and sagging and settling under the weight of tree limbs and snow and ice. The result was a mass of beams rusted together as solidly as the welded geodesics of a jungle gym.

That didn't make it safe to walk on. The wreckage filled the Ritz's two-story-deep foundation to a level just about even with the street. The path across the top of the pile, to the foundation's outer wall, was like a balance-beam maze above a tangle of serrated blades. What little sunlight reached the forest floor penetrated only a few feet deeper among the beams, leaving a pool of shadow beneath them. It was hard to imagine that nothing lived down there. Travis turned and saw Bethany staring down into the depths, no doubt thinking along the same lines. He offered his hand. She took it.

They crossed the mass of girders in about thirty

seconds. They stepped over a crumbled section of the foundation wall onto Vermont Avenue. Travis stared along its length to the south. Shafts of white light from the overcast were tinted green by their passage through the pine boughs. Here and there a bright red or yellow hardwood leaf spiraled down into the stillness. The street was surprisingly clear of undergrowth. There were plenty of dead weeds creeping from the mesh of cracks in the pavement, but in most places the roadbed was still visible. The pines probably had a lot to do with that. The needles they dropped had some effect on soil quality that usually killed lesser vegetation around them.

Visibility through the trees extended about as far as the sixteen-story high-rise at M Street, where in the present day Paige was being held. Travis could just see its girder skeleton past a grove of birches choking what'd once been the traffic circle.

He took the SIG-Sauer from his waistband and handed it to Bethany. He watched her appraise it, her thumb going naturally to the magazine release, getting a feel for it. She raised the weapon quickly to look down the sights, testing its target acquisition.

"Thanks," she said.

Travis handed her the three spare magazines. She pocketed them.

Then he unslung the Remington from his shoulder and racked a shell into its chamber. He had another dozen shells in his pockets. He took one out and pushed it through the weapon's loading port to replace the one he'd just chambered. It was good for five shots now.

He turned and looked at the rope, hanging with

its end just touching the pile of girders. He followed it up to the surreal image of the iris hovering twenty-five feet above. Through it, from this low angle, he could see only the hotel room's ceiling and two blades of the fan above the bed.

They moved south along Vermont at a near run. They watched the forest around them and listened for any disturbance in the trees, or any sudden lull in the birdsong that might mean something big was moving around.

The standing frames of buildings looked different from ground level than they had from the high vantage point of the presidential suite. Some of them were leaning at angles that looked impossible from below. They looked like they wanted to come down. Many had.

Travis let the inevitable question into his mind: did the breakdown of the world have anything to do with what he'd learned two summers ago, during his time with Tangent? In the two years since, he'd gotten good at not thinking about that, but there was no dodging it now. The bullet points all but lined themselves up in his head, and he considered them in careful order.

The summer before last, he'd been drawn into Tangent's business by what seemed, at the time, like chance. The organization had been in panic mode then, in the last days of a conflict over an object they called the Whisper. The Whisper was like a crystal ball out of some plague-era fairy tale. It knew things—impossible things—and shared them with anyone who held it. In the end Travis had found himself alone with the Whisper, on the deepest level of Border Town. The thing had revealed for him a few jagged edges of his future: his culpability in the deaths of 20 million people, and Paige's desire to see him killed. All of that lay waiting, somehow, along one possible track of his life to come. Somewhere out there in the darkness, years and years ahead, something was set to trip him up. To turn him into something objectively evil.

That was why he'd left Border Town and consigned himself to a life at minimum wage. It was the one way he could be sure to avoid whatever was coming. If he spent the next forty years stocking shelves, he could never cause the kind of disaster the Whisper had described. He'd be in no position to influence events on that scale, for good or bad.

And that answered the question: this was not about him. This was something else entirely. This was 6 or 7 billion deaths, not 20 million, and they'd happened without his help. Simple as that.

He and Bethany reached the junction where Vermont met the traffic circle. They halted for a moment at the cafe on the northeast quadrant, where they'd sat earlier. The patio's marble tiles lay canted and broken around the trunks of pines and sugar maples that'd punched up through them. Travis recalled the smell of sausage and the jumble of conversation as they'd studied the green building across the circle. That memory was barely an hour old, but in this place that moment was decades and decades gone.

Just off the patio, a few feet in from what remained of the curb, stood a row of corroded husks that'd once been newspaper boxes. Their tops were rusted to Swiss cheese and their doors had all fallen off. If any newspapers had been left in these containers at the end, they were long gone now. Paper wouldn't have lasted more than a few years against humidity and mildew, even when the doors had been intact.

"Wonder what the headlines were," Bethany said. "I wonder what was on the front page of the last *USA Today*."

Travis had no answer.

They stared at the scene only a few seconds longer, then turned and moved across the circle, toward the standing ruin of the sixteen-story office building.

CHAPTER TWELVE

T he plan was straightforward enough: all Bethany needed was a name. The name of someone who worked inside this building in the present day. A loose thread to start pulling on, and they might have the FBI involved within the hour.

Among these ruins, paper files and computer drives would be long lost, but an office building had other storage media that should have survived the intervening years just fine. Specifically, Travis was thinking of office door nameplates. They tended to be made of either plastic or bronze, and the names and job titles on them were usually deeply engraved—sometimes they were cut fully through the plate. A plastic nameplate could probably sit out in the elements for a million years and still be legible, and even bronze should be good for a long while. Longer than most other metals. Corrosion resistance was one of the advantages that had made bronze such a big deal, way back in the day.

A single name. It was all they needed.

They rounded the cluster of birches and got a full

view of the high-rise. It'd borne the years better than most of the other structures they'd seen. Its frame, though heavily rusted, was still standing whole and straight. A good portion of the concrete flooring at each level remained intact—maybe a third of it in all. Travis could see even the remnant of a stairwell near the building's core, thick metal risers and treads still in place. It wasn't hard to guess why the building had fared better than its neighbors along the street. It was newer. Built in 2006, it probably had a few decades on any other structure within a couple blocks. That meant it was not only younger, but that its steel had probably been of higher quality to begin with. It'd benefited from all the advances in refinement and impurity removal in the years leading up to its construction. For all that, it was still another relic waiting to fall. Its superior attributes would buy it an extra five years on its feet, at best.

They reached the building's concrete foundation wall. It stood three feet above street level and was four feet thick. They peered over the edge. The foundation was only a single story deep, but a third of that depth was filled with a compost layer of leaves and branches and probably a few dozen tons of gypsum plaster that had once made up the building's drywall. Travis stared at the layer and felt his optimism fade. He thought of looking for an eight-by-two-inch nameplate among half an acre of chest-deep biomass. He thought of needles and haystacks. Then he saw something that turned his optimism all the way off.

It was a blackened, fibrous slab of wood maybe two inches thick. A corner of it was just peeking from the mire ten feet away. There was a rusted hinge attached to it. A single, inch-long steel screw clung to the free-swinging half of the hinge. Both the screw and the hinge were deformed. They hadn't just corroded to rust and flaked away. They'd sagged and bent. They'd half melted.

Fire had ravaged the foundation pit at some point in the past. It hadn't burned hot enough, or long enough, to affect the massive footings of the girder structure, but everything else had suffered in the heat. The heavy wooden door had probably been solid oak. It looked like the carbonized remnant of a campfire log now. Travis thought of bronze again. He thought of the other thing it was celebrated for: the ease with which it could be heat-softened and reshaped. Plastic and bronze nameplates might last for millennia against rain and snow and mildew, but they wouldn't last five minutes in a fire hot enough to warp steel screws.

They walked the building's perimeter. They searched for any scraps that had fallen outside the foundation. They found a few shards of green glass and chunks of concrete from the missing floor sections above, but nothing useful. Nothing with anyone's name on it. Decades of rain and wind had scoured the exposed street of anything small enough to be carried away. Travis imagined meter-wide storm drains beneath the city clotted with every kind of refuse.

They climbed a maple growing against the girders on the west side of the building and got onto the second floor. They made their way across the level toward the intact stairwell at the center of the structure. They avoided walking on the huge pads of concrete that still held in some places among the steel framing. All of the pads showed cracks, and some were sagging. It was impossible to know the amount of weight they could hold. Sooner or later each one's capacity would reach zero and it would collapse. A day or a week or a month before that point, the capacity was probably just a few pounds. Given that most of them had already fallen, it seemed prudent to stay the hell off of them.

They reached the stairwell and found it to be solid. The treads and risers were at least an inch thick. None of the flights they could see above had collapsed or even decoupled from the structural members they were welded to.

They made their way up.

They stopped and studied each floor. A few very heavy objects from the building's interior remained atop the concrete pads here and there. One was a squat granite bookend, like a little pyramid cut in half. Travis lifted it and saw traces of carpet fiber and foam beneath it. The thing had sat there, a little too dense to be blown away, while everything had rotted around it—even out from under it. They found a pair of hexagonal iron dumbbells, twenty pounds each. Travis imagined them sitting in someone's office and not seeing much use. They'd seen even less lately.

They saw a few steel door frames still held in place against the sturdiest uprights, but there were no doors left in any of them. No doors lying flat on any of the concrete pads, either. They'd have long since rotted to fragments light enough that a once-in-a-decade storm could push them over the edge. At least half a dozen such storms would've happened over the years. No doors. No nameplates.

They saw something shiny at the north edge of the fifth floor. They crossed to it along the girders. It was the foil lid of a yogurt container, its edge pinned beneath the rim of a tipped-over trash basket—a stylish, heavy little thing carved from a cubic foot of limestone.

Travis pulled the yogurt lid free and held it up to the light. Whatever writing had once been on it had long ago faded to almost nothing in the sun.

But there was a line of text along the edge that remained legible—tiny letters and numbers that'd been stamped into the foil.

They read: EXP. DEC 23 2011.

CHAPTER THIRTEEN

For a few seconds everything was quiet, except the wind moving through the forest that'd replaced Washington, D.C. Far to the west Travis heard a crow cawing, high above the tree-tops. The weightless foil lid quivered just notice-ably in the breeze, but Travis's eyes stayed fixed on the expiration date.

"Four months from now," Bethany said. "In *our* time." The words came out as hardly more than a breath.

"I don't eat a lot of yogurt," Travis said. "How far away is the sell-by date, when you buy this stuff?"

"It's like milk. Three or four weeks. Someone would've bought this around the start of December. *This coming December*, in the present day."

Travis nodded.

"And it's not like people hang on to these lids for posterity," Bethany said. "Figure this thing goes into the trash in early to mid-December . . . and no one ever takes it back out. Jesus Christ, the world ends *four months from now?*"

"Janitors quit working four months from now, at

least," Travis said. "My guess is, so does everyone else."

He let the lid go and they watched it drift down on the air, like the colored leaves that were settling onto Vermont Avenue before them.

"Four months . . ." Bethany said again. "Everyone I know. Everyone I love. Four months . . ."

Travis found himself going back to what he'd thought of earlier: the chance of some connection between all of this and whatever the Whisper had warned him about—the dark potential of his own future.

He remained certain there *was no* connection, but now something else struck him: the Whisper had spoken of a future in which he belonged to Tangent several years from now. How could that have ever been possible if the world was going to collapse in 2011?

Well, weren't all bets simply off, after everything the Whisper had done? In a roundabout way, the thing had killed Ellen Garner, with the result that President Garner had resigned from office and allowed Currey to take power. That change alone could account for massive differences in how everything played out.

"End of the world plus seventy years, we guessed," Bethany said. "So on this side of the iris, the date is sometime around 2080."

Travis nodded, but said nothing. He looked around. From this position he could see along not only Vermont, but M Street to the east and west, a hundred yards in each direction before the tree cover obscured the way.

Something obvious occurred to him. He couldn't believe he hadn't noticed it already.

"Where are the cars?" he said.

He looked at Bethany. She looked blank for half a second and then made the same *oh yeah* expression he'd probably just made himself.

"The panels would be rusted to nothing by now," Travis said, "but the frames and the wheel rims should still be in some kind of shape, with windows and all kinds of plastic parts draped over them." He looked around. "They should be everywhere."

But there wasn't one to be seen. They hadn't passed anything that could've once been a vehicle on the walk down from the Ritz. Hadn't seen anything like that along the stretch of Vermont north of the hotel, either, when they'd first roped down. He'd have noticed and remembered.

"People must've had a reason to get out of D.C.," Bethany said, "at the end."

Travis stared at the empty streets and thought about it. He imagined a plague sweeping the world. People fleeing high-population areas in a mass panic.

It didn't work. Not entirely. First of all, not everyone would leave. Some number of people would have nowhere better to go, and would hole up in their homes. The city could still end up vacated of cars, even in that case—in the end, those without transportation would break into and hotwire whatever was available—but there was another problem, and Travis could see no way around it. The dynamics of a mass evacuation in a short period of time would've overwhelmed the city streets. It happened in every coastal metropolis in the days before a big hurricane. Traffic would condense at the primary outlets, like bridges and freeway interchanges. People would sit at the wheel for an hour or two, going nowhere, and then a few would run out of gas while idling, or get frustrated and simply abandon their vehicles, and try to get out on foot. It only took a few of those, and then each way out of the city would be stopped up like a corked bottle. And hurricane warnings matured over three to four days. Travis imagined that news of a major disease outbreak would hit at least that fast. Maybe faster. The gridlock would be absolute. There would be all kinds of cars left rotting on M Street and Vermont Avenue if the world had ended in a plague.

He turned and saw Bethany trying to work it out too.

"Everyone got in their cars and left," Travis said. "But not in a hurry."

They returned to the stairwell and continued the search of the building, floor by floor. At the ninth level they walked out to the northeast corner, where seventy years earlier Paige had been held. There was nothing special about the construction there. Just more girders, and a concrete flooring section that hadn't yet surrendered to gravity.

Travis stared at the undefined space. Irrational as he knew it was, he couldn't help thinking that Paige was right there somehow, just feet away, but impossible to reach from here. He wondered what she was thinking. Wondered if she knew they were trying to get to her—that she wasn't as alone as she must feel. He thought about it for a few seconds and then forced himself to look away. Losing time here wasn't helping her.

They continued up the stairwell. They found nothing of interest on any of the floors through the fifteenth. Only one floor remained above that point, and it had just three of its concrete pads still in place. Of all the surfaces in the building these were the most exposed to rain and wind and sunlight. Looking up at the slabs, Travis put the chance of finding anything noteworthy on top of them right around zero.

Then they climbed the last flight, and he saw at once that he'd been wrong.

CHAPTER FOURTEEN

Two of the three pads were bare and bleached and scoured smooth by the elements, as expected.

On the third, halfway between the stairwell and the building's northeast corner, stood an executive office desk.

It was made of rich cherrywood. Its work surface was three feet by six. It was centered perfectly on its slab of concrete. It looked like someone had hauled it out of a showroom five minutes ago and put it there.

For the longest moment Travis could only stare. He and Bethany shared a look. Then they walked across the girders to the desk.

At close range it became plausible. It wasn't made of cherrywood. It was made of some synthetic material that did a hell of a job of looking like cherrywood. And it was lag bolted to the pad. Ice expansion cracks had grown laterally from the bolt holes in the concrete, wide enough in places that Travis could see the exposed and rusted mesh of rebar inside. Of all the floor sections he'd seen in the building, this one looked the closest to failing. By far. And that was without factoring in the weight of the desk pressing on it. It was a wonder the slab had held this long.

There were four drawers in the desk. Two on either side of where a person would sit. Shallow tray drawers above, deep file drawers below. All four were closed. Their front panels were made of the same synthetic material that had held up so well during the desk's long reign atop the decaying building. Travis crouched low on the girder at the point nearest the desk, and studied the drawers. They were tightly closed. They would be weighted to stay shut until someone gave them a good tug. The wind had never managed to do so: there was nothing on the drawers' faces to offer it any purchase. In the early years the drawers had also had the benefit of being locked shut, but that protection was probably nominal by now: Travis saw only rust-choked circular indentations where steel keyholes had once been.

Four drawers. Not *sealed* shut, but at least shut. No sunlight would've gotten into them. Not much ice, either. A trace amount of rain would've made it through, and all the humidity and mold and mildew in the world would've gone in like there was no barrier at all. Any paper contents would be a distant memory. But people kept other things in desk drawers. Credit cards. Engraved metal items.

All they needed was a name.

Travis stood upright again. He stared at the concrete pad, sagging in its frame. There was no way to reach the desk drawers without venturing completely onto it, and not just a step or two. Not any short distance from which you could turn and grab for the girder if the concrete gave without warning. To open the drawers would require going all the way to the middle of the pad, eight feet in from the edge.

"How much do you weigh?" Bethany said.

Travis shook his head. "You're not going out there."

"I weigh a hundred ten pounds naked. Mind averting your eyes and holding onto my clothes?"

"You're not going out there. I'm going."

She looked at him. "Is this really the time for sexism masquerading as chivalry?"

"Yes."

Travis unslung the shotgun and handed it to her. He stood there a few seconds longer, eyeing the cracks. He turned around and leaned a few inches past the other side of the girder—the open side—and looked down at the fifteenth floor. There was no intact concrete directly below to slow or hinder the fall of this pad, if it collapsed. There was nothing but open space all the way to a pad down on the twelfth floor, which would do about as much good as a big sheet of tissue paper stretched between the girders there. And after that it was smooth plummeting all the way to the foundation. Travis turned and faced the desk again.

"Maybe this was the CEO's office," Bethany said. It sounded like the kind of thing a person only said to drown out the internal scream of tension. "Someone important, anyway. We didn't see any other desks bolted to the concrete."

"Maybe the concrete pads with bolt holes in them all cracked through and fell a long time ago. Maybe this is the last holdout, just waiting for a dry leaf to land on it and send it crashing down."

"You're not helping."

Travis put one foot on the concrete. He shifted a fourth of his weight onto it. The pad didn't budge. Maybe it was stronger than it looked. He transferred another fourth of his weight. Still solid. He took a breath and stepped completely onto the thing. It felt fine. He looked at Bethany. She didn't look the least bit relieved.

"I know," Travis said. "The edge would be the strong part anyway."

"Don't die."

"Okay."

He took a second step. Then another.

On his fourth step something shifted. It was barely perceptible. A settling movement of the pad, probably no more than an eighth of an inch. He heard Bethany take a sharp breath behind him, but she said nothing.

Three more steps would put him right at the front of the desk, centered where its owner had once sat.

He set a foot forward and eased onto it. He felt no response from the pad.

Two steps to go.

He took the next one. Nothing.

Maybe he was flattering himself to think his presence mattered to this five-ton chunk of material that'd weathered a couple thousand blizzards with a two-hundred-pound desk on its back. Maybe he could do jumping jacks on it for an hour and not impress it.

He eased his weight off his back foot. Guided it forward and touched it to the concrete six inches from the desk. He took a breath, let it out slowly, and let his center of gravity slide forward until it was positioned evenly above both feet.

Then a piece of rebar snapped like bone and the middle of the pad plunged six inches, throwing Travis forward against the desk.

Bethany screamed.

It was all Travis could do to keep his body from pitching right over the desktop and slamming down like a dropped anvil onto the concrete behind it. Bethany was yelling something at him, but the bloodflow ringing in his ears made it hard to tell what it was. He checked his forward momentum, both hands pressing hard onto the smooth desktop, and suddenly the world went still and silent. He heard his own breathing. He heard Bethany's breathing too.

He turned and looked at her. The word *pale* didn't quite do the job. Her breath went in and out in little jerks. Her eyes stayed with his for a few seconds, and then they dropped and went to the right. He followed her stare.

The largest of the lateral cracks had opened up all the way to the girder on one side, and the concrete had sagged free of its seat against the beam there, its hold having crumbled completely except for a single, fist-sized formation. That piece, clinging to the steel by an inch, was all that had stopped the pad's total failure. It was all that was preventing it now.

Bethany found her voice again. "Off." Her hands made little circular gestures, calling him back to the beam.

Travis still had both his hands on the desk, most of his weight distributed to its footings. He looked at the drawers. He could probably open all four from here without shifting his mass around very much.

"Travis," Bethany said.

He looked at her again.

Her eyes: *don't*.

"It's okay," he said. What else was he going to say?

He turned to the tray drawer on the top left. He raised one hand from the desk. Felt the weight that'd been on it transfer to the other hand. No real change to the pressure the desk was putting on the pad.

He pressed four fingers behind the rounded top of the drawer's face panel and put his thumb against the edge of the desktop just above it. He pushed with his thumb and pulled with his fingers. There was a moment of resistance. Then he heard the lock mechanism crumble like a pretzel, and the drawer opened smoothly on plastic rollers.

The drawer's sides and bottom were made of the same material as the rest of the desk. They'd held up perfectly. The contents of the drawer hadn't. There were three metal paperclips that'd rusted to what looked like orange chalk drawings of themselves. Travis blew on them and they vanished in a little cloud. There was a stapler that had corroded to a solid lump. Right beside it was a perfect little rectangle-shaped piece of rust that Travis couldn't identify at first. Then he understood: a box of staples, the cardboard long since eaten away by mildew and the tightly arranged staples inside fused together by oxidation. There were three nickels and a quarter. There was a pile of rubber bands that'd broken down to dried crumbs. There was a layer of dead mold coating everything. Once upon a time it'd been paper: memos, Post-its, business cards, maybe check stubs.

And that was it. There was nothing else in the drawer. Nothing with a name on it.

Travis considered the larger one below it. A file drawer. Was it even worth bothering with? What could have been in it but paper? What could be in it now but an inch-deep layer of mold dust?

He opened it.

It contained an inch-deep layer of mold dust.

He lowered his hand carefully to the mold and sifted through it. It came up in ragged tufts. They caught the wind as they cleared the top of the drawer and were scurried away. There was nothing lying concealed beneath the mold layer.

Travis pivoted carefully on his feet, trying not to move them or change the amount of weight on them. He put his free hand back on the desk, and slowly raised the other, letting the pressure transfer. He faced the other two drawers.

He tried the file drawer first. An inch of mold. Nothing under it.

He opened the tray drawer.

Empty.

Not even a dusting of long-gone paper.

He exhaled. Closed his eyes. Opened them again and began to stand upright.

And then he stopped.

Because there *was* something in the drawer.

Something narrow and black, lying against the back end. It blended with the dark cherrywood color and all but escaped notice. It was a pen. It looked expensive. He picked it up and drew it into the light. The metal parts—the clip and the point— were rusted dark, but the body looked fine. It was made of something that felt harder than ordinary plastic. Something that wasn't cheap. Its grip was ornate but not fancy. It looked serious. Like something a high-powered executive would whip out on special occasions—maybe the signing of final contracts for a hostile takeover. Travis rolled it between his fingers.

There was a name engraved on it: ELDRED WARREN.

Travis turned and held the pen up so Bethany could see the engraving.

"Very good," she said. "Now can you get the hell off there so I can start breathing again?"

Travis pocketed the pen and for a moment rested both hands on the desk. He looked at the fragment of concrete that was keeping him alive. He looked at the distance back to the girder.

Then he stood up straight and crossed the pad in five steps, ready to jump and grab for the beam if necessary. It wasn't necessary. If the concrete moved at all beneath him he didn't feel it. He saw Bethany exhale hard as soon as he was fully onto the girder, but he didn't pause to share the sentiment. They had information now. Something they could work on. Just like that, his urgency had fuel to burn. He turned atop the beam and made for the stairwell at close to a sprint.

They were six flights down when they heard the concrete fragment snap high above them. They turned in time to see the massive slab, desk and all, plunge through the channel of space defined by the girders. It blasted through the intact pad on level twelve without slowing, and the entire mass fell a hundred feet further to the foundation pit. The impact kicked up a halo of ash and dead leaves.

They stared for less than a second, then continued down the stairs as fast as they could move.

CHAPTER FIFTEEN

T hree minutes later they were on top of the pile
of girders at the southwest corner of the Ritz-
Carlton. The rope hung from the iris above,
exactly as they'd left it. Bethany went up first, and
Travis followed a few feet below. By the time he'd
climbed through the iris she was standing at the
window with her phone in hand, already going to
work.

Travis stared south at the green-tinted high-rise
while Bethany worked on the name. He looked
at the top floor and visualized the desk there in
the present, bolted to the concrete through some
expensive carpeting or hardwood. Maybe Eldred
Warren was sitting there right now, with the same
pen in his drawer that Travis now had in his pocket.
Literally the same pen. That was a hard concept to
get a grasp on.

"He's not in the federal tax records," Bethany
said. "Not too surprising, someone way up in a
company like that. We already know they're big on
secrecy. I'll try corporate registration in the Cay-
mans."

Thirty seconds later she came up empty there, too.

"There are lots of other tax shelters to try," she said, "but before I start on those I'll pull his social security file. That'll give us at least some basic info on the guy."

She navigated for twenty seconds. She pressed a last button and waited for something. She smiled.

Then she frowned.

"What?" Travis said.

"Got it. Only one Eldred Warren with a social security number in the United States."

"Must be our man, then."

"Yes and no."

"What do you mean?"

"Give me a minute."

It turned out to be ninety seconds. She spent them navigating to some other information on her phone, and reading it. Her frown deepened as she did.

"It's the right guy," she said, "but he's not going to be any help to us."

"Why not?"

"Because he doesn't work in that building yet. I'm looking at his blog right now. He graduated number two in his class from Harvard Law School . . . three months ago. He hasn't taken a job any-where yet."

"That's hard to believe," Travis said. "Wouldn't someone like that have offers waiting for him before he bought his cap and gown?"

"Tons of them, but a guy like that knows he can pick and choose. It's not unthinkable that he'd take his time. I had a dozen offers myself, and spent two months making up my mind. And this guy's degree is more versatile than mine was. He'll have everyone from movie studios to lobbying firms filling up his voice mail these days."

"All right, so maybe he doesn't work for this company yet," Travis said. "But he's probably in talks with them. We could go have a chat with him, shove a gun in his face if we have to."

"Not anytime soon, we can't. According to his last blog post, a few hours ago, he's on vacation in Japan with his girlfriend."

Travis sat on the couch and leaned back. He pressed his hands to his eyes. He was tired as hell.

They were at square zero. They had nothing at all to work with. The barrier of open space around the oubliette was as vast as it'd been when they'd first spoken of it.

He looked at his watch. Nine thirty in the morning. Paige had been captive for just shy of ten hours.

Bethany was pacing now. Holding her phone but unable to think of anything to do with it.

Travis closed his eyes again.

Paige wanted them to move on. Wanted them to leave her behind and finish what she'd meant to do herself. She'd said it in almost those words, in her phone call to Bethany. And she'd meant it. That was the way she thought. She had the ability to see the big picture. Six and a half billion lives versus her own. She was lying in that room down the street right now hoping like hell that they wouldn't risk trying to save her. Hoping they would forget about her and just get to work. And they could do that. They could climb back down the rope right now, into the ruined D.C. They could walk back down Vermont, ignore the remains of the high-rise and go another mile to the White House. They could spend days digging in the wreckage there for some kind of clue. And if that search turned up nothing, they could go across the river to the Pentagon and spend weeks. And after a while they wouldn't have to think about Paige lying in that room, because by then she'd be long gone. She'd be gone by tonight.

The people who'd hit the motorcade had taken her alive because it made sense at the time. They'd been acting on a snap decision, operating with more questions than answers. But that was probably no longer the case. Ten hours was plenty of time to take stock. Plenty of time for them to realize they didn't need her.

No doubt Paige was thinking the same thing right now. Lying bound, waiting for her captors to settle on the decision. Waiting for it to happen. When it did, she would try not to cry about it. She'd still be holding on to the logic of it all, telling herself that her life was just part of what it cost to get the job done. She would be thinking that very thing when she felt the silencer touch her temple.

"You love her."

Travis opened his eyes.

Bethany had stopped pacing. She was looking at him.

"You love her," she said again. "Paige."

"I knew her for less than a week."

"That's long enough."

"Why do you think I love her?"

"Because you stayed on that concrete pad. Stepping onto it was one thing. But *staying* on it, after what happened . . . that was another thing entirely. To do something that insane, you have to care about someone more than you care about your own life. A lot more."

Travis didn't reply. He stared ahead at nothing. "I can't do it," he said. "I can't leave her in there."

"I don't want to leave her, either. I just don't know what the next move is."

Neither of them spoke for the next minute. Travis's eyes fixed on a spot on the carpet. He stared at it and hardly blinked. He let the edges of his vision blur.

Then he turned and looked at Bethany.

"What was the last thing Paige said to you in that phone call?"

"That you can go through and come back," she said. "She was just saying it's safe to go through the opening."

Travis thought about it. "No, that's not what she said. Not *exactly* what she said anyway. Play the recording again."

CHAPTER SIXTEEN

S he played it. They listened. They heard the frantic rush of Paige's voice telling Bethany to go to her residence, to get the entity and get out of Border Town. To use it. To go public with whatever she learned. To get Travis Chase's help if necessary. Then she said, *"Shit, what else . . . ?"* and went silent for a few seconds. Travis caught the sound he remembered from the first time he'd heard the recording: running footsteps, men coming to get her. That sound was all he'd heard on the first listen, at that part of the clip. This time he focused on the other sound, right there beside it in the audio. The more important sound, by far. Paige's breathing in the absence of her voice. Two breaths, deep and fast. They didn't shudder on the way out. They seethed. Travis got the sense that however scared Paige was, she was frustrated even more. She was struggling to remember something critical, some detail she needed to tell Bethany in the few seconds she had left. Which was strange, in retrospect: if all Paige needed to say was that a person could step through the projected opening, would that have been hard to remember? Would it have even been necessary? Wouldn't Paige expect them to figure that out for themselves?

A second later they heard Bethany's voice on the recording: "*What's happening? Where are you?*"

Paige's voice came back in, louder and more intense than before. "*You can take it through and still come back! You can take it through!*"

Then it was over.

In the silence Travis looked at Bethany.

They both looked at the black cylinder, still lying in the armchair, still switched on. The iris stood open to the forest and the overcast sky above it. The manila rope lay in tangles on the carpet where they'd left it after pulling it up.

"Take it through," Bethany said, turning the phrase over like a found artifact. "Does she mean the cylinder? Take the cylinder through the iris?"

Travis stared at the thing. It was hard to imagine what else Paige could have meant.

"It would be easy to do," he said. "Switch it off with the delay, and then carry the cylinder through the iris during the minute and a half it stays open."

"You'd have to be out of your mind," Bethany said. "What happens when the iris shuts behind you? Now you're stuck seventy years in the future, with a machine that can only take you seventy years *further* into the future. You'd never get home."

"What if it doesn't work like that? What if turning it on in the future just opens the iris back to the present time? Like a toggle. Back and forth."

"How would it know to do that?" Bethany said. "How would it *know* it was in the future?"

"I don't know. Maybe it's something simple. Maybe it senses when it's taken through the iris, and switches itself into reverse. We'll never know *how* it works, but think of what we just heard. Paige said you can take it through and come back. She knew a lot more about this thing than we do."

He watched Bethany mull it over. Watched her warm to it.

"The logic adds up," she said. "Someone built this thing for a purpose. I can't see the use of something that just leapfrogs you further and further ahead in time, and never lets you come back. Forward and back makes more sense."

"It also explains why the cylinders came as a pair," Travis said. "Think about it. Who knows what this kind of machine was meant for, but we can imagine any number of things. It could be some military scouting tool. Use it to survey the aftermath of a war you haven't even fought yet. Hell, it could be farm equipment. Say there's some high-value crop that takes seven decades to mature. Sow the seeds, step through the iris and reap the rewards right away. But whatever the use, its makers had a reason to allow the delayed shutoff. That way you can take the cylinder with you when you go through the iris. Not hard to imagine why they'd want to. Leaving it behind, switched on, is a major vulnerability. Look at the precautions *we* had to take, setting it up so nothing could get at it from the other side. But here's the thing: taking it with you would be risky too. Extremely risky, in fact. Picture yourself putting this thing to casual use. Like it's a socket wrench or a screwdriver. You're using it all day long, going back and forth between two points in time, hauling food supplies or weapons or whatever. Can you think of the mistake you might make? It would be the easiest thing to do, and if you did it you'd be in a world of trouble."

Bethany's eyes narrowed. She thought about it. "You could accidentally leave the cylinder behind. Leave it on the other side of the iris when it closed."

Travis nodded. "It would happen one of two ways. Either you leave it in the future, in which case there's no way to retrieve it except to sit on your ass and wait several decades, or else you leave it in the past and trap *yourself* in the future, in which case you're absolutely screwed."

Bethany walked over to the armchair. Stared down at the cylinder.

"You'd want a backup copy," she said.

"You'd *need* a backup copy. Like a skydiver needs a reserve chute. Because some mistakes you can't afford to make even once. You'd have a duplicate cylinder, and you'd strap it to your back and never take it off, at least not while you were using the first one."

Bethany met his eyes. "It makes sense that Paige and the others would've figured this out. In the desert they had *both* cylinders. They could have tested this idea without any risk of getting stranded. Just leave one of them switched on, and use the other one to find out whether or not the iris brings you back to the present time."

Travis nodded. It all added up.

A silence drew out.

"We could be wrong about this," Bethany said.

"We could be very wrong."

"Just plain old wrong would be bad enough. If we try this and it doesn't work, we're stuck over there."

"If we try it and it *does* work," Travis said, "then we can take the cylinder into the future, carry it up to the ninth floor of that ruin on M Street, and step back into the present time right inside the room where they're holding Paige."

The idea seemed to wash over Bethany like a breeze on a spring day.

"Nice," she said.

CHAPTER SEVENTEEN

They repositioned the cylinder so that it projected the iris to a different part of the hotel
room—closer to the building's interior, and
away from the part that'd collapsed in the future.
They found a spot that would allow them to step
through onto a solid girder in the ruins. There was
a sturdy oak limb hanging over it, which would
offer easy transit to the ground.

Travis stepped through onto the beam. Bethany
stood in the room, next to the cylinder. She put her
finger over the third button and looked at him.

"Say when," she said.

Travis looked at his watch. The second hand was
ten clicks from the top of the dial. When it was
three clicks shy he said, "Now."

Bethany pressed the button. The cone of light
flared and then died. The iris stayed open. Bethany
lifted the cylinder and carried it to the opening.
She passed it through to Travis and he cradled it
tightly against himself.

Then Bethany reached through, grabbed the oak
branch, and pulled herself onto the girder.

"What are you doing?" Travis said.

"What do you mean?"

"You don't have to be over here too. We don't both have to risk this. If we're wrong, and there's no way back, you might as well be in the present."

"Why?" she said. "I'd be stuck there without the cylinder. What would I do?"

"Live the life of Renee Turner. Party like hell. Anything you want."

"Yeah. For four months. Knowing the whole time that the world's going to end."

"It's probably longer than we'd make it on this side." He looked at his watch. Sixty seconds left. "This is stupid. You should wait in the room."

"It's the broken concrete all over again."

"Yeah, it is, and you don't have to be on it."

She turned to face him, leaning on the branch between them. The overcast had thinned, and in the brighter light he saw her eyes more clearly than he had before now. He'd thought they were brown. Really they were green, but so dark they were almost black.

"You're willing to risk being left alone in the whole world, for the sake of someone you care about," she said. "And I think someone willing to do that shouldn't have to. If we get stuck here, we'll find ways to pass the time."

He held her gaze. It occurred to him that what she was doing was about as kind a gesture as a human could make to another. For a long moment he couldn't think of a single thing to say.

Then he said, "Thank you."

"You're welcome."

He glanced at his watch. "Thirty seconds."

She nodded. Swallowed hard.

They both turned and stared through the iris. Through the windows on the far side of the hotel room they could see the city in the present day. The orderly buildings and the gleam of sunlight on glass. The traffic flowing smoothly through the circle down the block. People on the sidewalks in shorts and T-shirts. Parents walking with kids in the light of a summer morning.

"For all that's wrong with the world," Travis said, "it really is something."

In the corner of his eye he saw Bethany nod.

And then the iris slipped shut in front of them, and left them staring at precisely the same angle on the ruined city. A perfect superimposition from one image to the other. From solid buildings to their leaning skeletons. From the bustling street to the decaying one. The effect was more powerful than Travis had expected. He heard Bethany exhale softly beside him and knew it'd been the same for her.

Travis moved ten feet along a girder that T-boned into the one they'd first stepped onto. He found a position from which the cylinder would project the iris to more or less the same spot it'd just vanished from. Bethany, on the first girder, stood clear.

Travis wondered what it would look like if they were wrong, and the iris opened onto a Washington, D.C. seven decades even further on. The frames of the buildings would be long gone. The roads, too. It might be hard to tell there'd been a city there at all.

He leveled the cylinder like a weapon.

He pressed the ON button.

The light cone flared.

The iris appeared.

Bethany didn't look through it. She looked at him instead.

"Tell me," she said.

PART II

UMBRA

CHAPTER EIGHTEEN

Paige lay bound, waiting for it to happen.
Waiting for the end.

Every few minutes she heard footsteps approach in the corridor, only to pass by and fade away. She waited for the footsteps that would approach but not fade, and the click of the latch that would tell her it was all over with.

She rolled onto her side and faced the windows. She could see up Vermont Avenue. Lots of people out. She saw a red convertible pull into the Ritz-Carlton. Saw a young couple get out. Impossible to see their expressions at this distance, but they had to be smiling. They left the car to a valet and disappeared into the building.

Beautiful day.

Beautiful world to be alive in.

She wished she could know that it would stay this way a lot longer than four months—even if she wouldn't be around to see it.

The street blurred a little. She blinked away the film of tears. She took a sharp breath and rolled onto her back again.

Another set of footsteps came and went. She closed her eyes and waited.

* * *

...vis sprinted full-out down the broken surface of ...e avenue, south toward the traffic circle. Bethany ..ept up with him. They weren't listening for heavy movement in the forest now. Travis had the shotgun cradled as he ran. If a lion stepped into his path it was going to get a long overdue reminder that meaner predators had once walked these streets.

He mapped out the plan as he sprinted. Visualized the ninth floor of the ruin, and the northeast corner there. They'd looked at it earlier. The concrete pad had been pretty solid, with just a few hairline fractures.

No way to know the room's layout in the present day. Not even its size. It didn't have to match the concrete. The safest place to open the iris would be near the room's outside corner. That would at least get them inside the space, whatever its size.

He pictured how the action would play out. In present time he would come through the iris facing the corner, with his back to the room. He'd lose maybe half a second turning and getting a sense of his surroundings. There was no reason to expect an armed presence in the room itself. Paige would be restrained, and the building was secured at ground level. Nobody would expect intruders to step through a hole in the air on the ninth floor.

But armed or not, anyone in the room other than Paige would have to be dealt with.

He considered the Remington. Imagined going through the iris with it. It would be bulky and slow to maneuver in the confined space of the corner. It would need to be cycled between shots, and he'd get only five of them. Anyone he hit would be dead all over the place, but if there were multiple targets, and if they *did* happen to be armed, the limited shot capacity could get him in trouble.

They reached the traffic circle. Crossed it in about twenty seconds. In another twenty they were at the base of the maple that offered access to the second floor. They climbed to the girders and headed across them toward the stairwell.

"Trade with me," Travis said. He held the shotgun out to Bethany. She took it and handed him the SIG-Sauer. It held nine .45 caliber rounds, including the one in the chamber. They wouldn't hit like twelve-gauge slugs, but they would do the job. And he could aim and fire the pistol a hell of a lot faster than a three-foot-long shotgun. Bethany handed him the three spare magazines from her pocket. He put two in his own pocket and kept the other one in his free hand. If need be, he could drop the current magazine out of the pistol and reload it in about a second.

They were on the ninth floor a minute later, moving as fast as caution allowed across the open beams. They came to the concrete pad at the corner. Travis gave it only a second's assessment and then walked onto it. Strong as hell. An intact pad directly above it had blocked at least some of the snow and ice that would've stressed it over the years.

Bethany followed him onto the pad. She shrugged off her backpack, opened it and took out the cylinder. The rest of the shotgun shells—one hundred minus those in the gun and in Travis's pockets—settled into the bottom of the pack.

She set the cylinder on the concrete and used the

backpack to prop up the front end. The iris would open just above waist level, two feet in from the corner of the room.

She knelt over the cylinder, ready to switch it on.

Travis stood next to where the beam would project the iris. He gripped the SIG. Took a breath. Looked at Bethany.

"Do it," he said.

She pressed the button.

The iris appeared, and through it Travis saw tinted glass and flowing traffic far below and he ducked through and spun as he stood upright, the SIG coming up and sweeping the room for targets.

The room was empty.

CHAPTER NINETEEN

There was one door out of the room. It was closed. There was a narrow strip of glass set into it. Travis crossed the room and looked through it. The corridor stretched away in two directions from the corner. He could see all the way down one stretch, and not far at all down the other. Just a few feet before the angle got in the way.

The corridor was tiled with either stone or ceramic. Travis heard footsteps clicking along on it, approaching from the hidden direction. Distinct clicks, one after the next. Someone alone. Travis turned the doorknob and pulled the door toward himself a quarter inch, just enough to clear the latch from the plate.

He waited. The tile amplified the footsteps and made it hard to judge their distance. He let them get louder than instinct advised, and then he yanked the door open and stepped through, bringing the SIG up to level.

A guy in his forties, short, wiry, came to a stop with the gun's barrel six inches from his face.

Travis gestured for him to stay quiet. The guy nodded. Eyes wide. Travis stepped clear of the door and waved the man through, and a second

later they were back in the room with the door
closed behind them.

"Shut your eyes," Travis said. "Tight."

The man complied.

Travis grabbed him by the back of the collar and
propelled him forward, keeping him off balance.
He shoved him to the corner, turned, dragged him
downward and pushed him through the iris. His
waist caught the bottom of the circle on the way
through and he pitched forward, sprawling onto
the concrete on the other side.

The man got himself upright, half sitting, and
opened his eyes. Bethany had the shotgun on him.
Travis was already through the iris behind him,
covering him with the SIG.

The guy looked around at the forest and the
ruins. His expression went dead slack. Disbelief
at its most literal. His brain simply did not accept
what his eyes were reporting.

"Wallet," Travis said.

The guy stared at him. Blinked. Took out his
wallet.

Travis pointed to the concrete at Bethany's feet.
"Toss it."

The guy threw the wallet. It landed, tumbled
three feet and stopped.

Travis gestured for the guy to stand up. The man
nodded, and when he was halfway through the
move, onto his feet but not yet balanced, Travis
grabbed the back of his collar again and shoved
him forward onto the girder that bound the north
edge of the concrete. He pushed him onto it and
then past it. The guy's feet stayed on the lip of
the beam but his upper body ended up two feet
beyond, above nine stories of empty space.

The man's breath caught in his throat. His body went rigid, his fear overwhelming every instinct to struggle. He took tiny breaths, in and out, as if he thought larger ones might imbalance him and send him over.

Travis stood with his own weight tilted inward from the edge to counterbalance the guy. His arm was fully extended. The guy was thirty degrees past his own natural tipping point.

"Where's the woman?" Travis said.

It took the guy a second to answer. "Woman?"

"Don't fuck with me. They brought her in last night, after they hit the motorcade."

Another few seconds passed. The guy cocked his head. He knew the answer. If he didn't, he'd be saying so already. He'd be screaming it.

Travis shifted his weight outward. He did it fast, letting his arm go slack and then snap tight again. The effect was that, for half a second, the guy believed he was falling. He didn't scream—he didn't have the breath for it—but he made a tight whimpering sound.

Then his words came out in a high monotone. "They took her to Mr. Finn's office. Just now. Few minutes ago."

"Where is that?"

"Top floor. Southwest corner."

Travis let go of his collar.

The guy's arms shot outward, spasming, his hands grabbing for anything. But there wasn't anything. He sucked in a gasp and screamed like a high-school girl in a slasher flick and then he was gone, out into the emptiness.

Travis didn't bother to watch him hit. He turned. Saw Bethany standing there, her hand to her mouth, eyes unblinking. The shotgun hung forgotten at her side.

"We didn't ask to be part of this," Travis said. "These people did."

It was all he had.

He held her eyes a moment longer and then he crossed to the cylinder and shut it off. He picked it up and headed for the stairwell, crossing exposed beams. After a few steps he picked up the pace to a run. He glanced behind him and saw Bethany shouldering the backpack, pocketing the dropped wallet, and following.

Paige sat waiting for Isaac Finn to arrive. She knew his name only from the brass plate she'd seen on his door when the two large men had carried her through it.

Finn's office was huge. Three times the size of the room they'd kept her in. There was a balcony along its southern expanse looking out on a view that could've been an educational poster of Washington, D.C. The kind of poster with tags and labels for every building that mattered. It was all there, from the White House to the Capitol to the Supreme Court, and a hundred other buildings that channeled power in ways most people would never care to know. Paige wondered how many of those buildings this high-rise outranked. Maybe all of them.

She was sitting on a leather couch. Her wrists and ankles were still zip-tied. The two large men were standing just inside the door, hands folded neatly in front of them. Each had a Beretta holstered under his suit coat—Paige had seen them there when they'd carried her from the other room.

The door opened and a man in his fifties walked in. He was trim, six feet tall, with dark hair going a little gray. He was far from what Paige had pictured—whatever she'd pictured. He looked wrong for the office. His eyes, in particular, looked wrong. There was no arrogance in them. No presumption. Paige thought of one of her father's friends, a pediatric surgeon she'd met on several occasions. She'd always been struck by his eyes: weathered by the years of suffering they'd seen, but not beaten. Isaac Finn's eyes looked almost like that—they missed by some degree Paige couldn't account for.

None of which mattered, in any case. Kind-looking eyes could be a trick of genetics or an unconscious mimicry of some long-dead parent. There were better lights by which to judge a person, and Finn didn't look good in any of them.

He had a coffee cup in one hand. In the other he held the black cylinder Paige had shown the president last night. He crossed to his desk and set down the coffee. He turned and looked at Paige. He seemed to be appraising her in some way. Coming to a decision.

"Free her legs," Finn said.

The nearest of the two guards came over. He took a jackknife from a sheath on his belt, opened it, and cut the tie binding Paige's ankles. He backed away to his original position.

Finn stared at her a moment longer. Then he tapped the cylinder. "The president told me about your demonstration of this, in detail. You told him it's safe for a person to step through the projected opening."

Paige nodded.

"You didn't do that for him, though."

"It wasn't necessary. He saw that it worked."

"I want to see you do it. I want to see for myself that a person can go through."

He strode to the long walnut table that stood behind the couch. He set the cylinder on it, braced on either side with a pair of leather-bound books that'd been lying there. He aimed it toward the southern windows, just over ten feet away.

He put his finger to the ON button, then looked at Paige and raised his eyebrows as if to verify that he was doing it right.

"I don't know how much simpler I could've labeled it," she said.

Finn pressed the button.

The light cone flared and projected the opening just shy of the windows.

Paige watched Finn's body language. It was immediately clear that he hadn't seen the cylinder in action until now. He stared at the opening. His face was perfectly blank. He stood there, not moving at all. Ten seconds passed. Then he stepped forward. He walked along the edge of the light cone, giving it space. Paige had done the same thing a few days ago, the first time she and the others switched it on.

Finn walked to within a foot of the opening, to its right. He stared through for a moment, and then abandoned his fear of the light and moved directly in front of the open circle. He gazed out at the ruins. Paige saw his head shake from side to side, just noticeably.

"Jesus, it works," he whispered, so softly that Paige almost missed it.

Then he turned to her. Waved her up off the couch.

"Do it," he said. "Step through."

She knew exactly what would happen if she did. She sat there for three seconds considering her options. She didn't have any. And it didn't matter what happened to her now. All that mattered was what Bethany was doing, if she'd gotten out of Border Town. Paige wished again that there were a way to know. It would be a comforting thought, and a comforting thought would be nice right now.

"Fine," she said.

She stood. She rounded the end of the couch and crossed to the opening. Finn moved aside for her. She rested her hands—still bound at the wrists—on the bottom of the circle, and stared out over the sprawling woodland. She could see the Washington Monument punching up from the canopy about a mile away. She couldn't identify much else. The White House was completely hidden by the trees. The Capitol Dome should've been visible, but it wasn't. Paige remembered taking a tour of the building in high school and learning that the dome was made of cast iron. She recalled hearing what it weighed, and not believing it at the time. Something like 11 million pounds. That much weight would've worked against the building's supports pretty quickly once corrosion set in.

Paige gripped the lower edge of the opening and leaned her upper body through. She looked down for a place to put her feet. The thick girder that formed the boundary of the top floor was right there, running side to side past the opening. The supports for the balcony extended outward from it, long since relieved of the concrete surface they'd once held up. They were just solitary beams now, each one about six inches wide, jutting out over the abyss like a pirate's plank. The nearest was right in front of the opening.

Paige let her eyes take in the rest of the structure beneath her, a latticework of steel plunging sixteen stories to the foundation pit. She'd never been a fan of heights. She looked left and right along the girder she was about to step onto. It took all of her control to keep from showing any reaction to what she could see.

She put one leg through the opening, and then the other. As her second foot touched the girder she felt Finn's hand close around her upper arm. He held on tightly, preventing her from making a run for it to the left or right.

"Straight ahead," he said, and shoved her by the arm.

To keep her balance against the push, she stepped forward onto the narrow balcony support.

Finn was still holding on. Through his grip Paige felt a sudden back-and-forth movement of his body. She pictured him waving with his other arm, silently calling one of the guards over. She imagined the man nodding, already briefed on this, crossing the room and drawing his Beretta as he came. Finn gave her arm another shove, forcing her to take a second step. She was three feet out on the narrow beam now, at the extent of Finn's reach. Nowhere at all for her to go.

Finn released her arm.

A second later she heard the Beretta's slide being racked behind her.

*   *   *

Finn stepped away from the projected hole and gave Boyce a clear line of sight to make the kill. Boyce paused just outside the light cone, hesitant to let it touch him. Then he shrugged, stepped into the light and faced the hole.

Finn watched him assess his prey. Watched his expression take on the fake, wired kind of calm that spoke more of testosterone than real composure.

"She's cute," Boyce said. "Sure we have to rush this? It's not like anyone's gonna find the body and swab it for DNA."

Finn took a step closer to him and spoke evenly. "If I ever hear you advocate unnecessary suffering again, you'll be the one standing out there. Do you believe me?"

Boyce looked at him. The bullshit calm receded from his eyes. "Yes, sir."

"Make it painless. Shoot her in the back of the head, centered in a line between the ears. Don't miss."

"Yes, sir."

Boyce raised his Beretta.

He extended it a foot through the opening.

He thumbed off the safety.

And then a hand came out of nowhere, from outside the opening on the right edge. It locked onto Boyce's wrist and yanked it downward. Boyce had just begun to flinch when a second hand came through, this one holding a SIG-Sauer P220. It jammed the barrel into Boyce's eye and fired, blowing his head apart. A fragment of skull hit Finn in the face. He staggered back from the opening. In his peripheral vision he saw Kaglan, still in position at the door, reaching for his own weapon—but the SIG was already coming up to level on him. A tenth of a second later it fired again, three shots in a tight pattern. Kaglan screamed and went down. He managed to return fire, but his aim was all over the place, most of his shots missing the opening and cratering the windows beyond it. The SIG shooter stepped away from the opening on the far side until Kaglan ran dry, and then the weapon came back through the hole and began rapid-firing blindly into the room.

Finn threw himself flat and crawled behind the couch, for whatever cover it could provide. He heard the SIG fire dry, and it crossed his mind to get up and hit the OFF button on the cylinder, but already he heard the metallic scrape of the SIG's magazine dropping out, and almost on top of it came the smack of a fresh one being rammed home. Half a breath after that the shooting started again, fast and wild, hitting everything. Finn counted seven shots. Then silence. Which was strange: a SIG 220's clip held eight rounds. He glanced up and saw Kaglan struggling to move, blood seeping heavily from a wound in his side. And then the eighth shot hit Kaglan in the temple and took the top half of his head off.

Finn vaulted to his feet and threw himself toward the walnut table and the black cylinder. The reload would have to be slower this time—the shooter would have to fish in his pockets for another magazine, if he had one. In the split-second before he slammed his thumb down onto the OFF button, Finn raised his eyes and caught a glimpse of the opening. The shooter had stepped aside again, but the woman, Paige Campbell, was just visible, crouching low on the narrow beam. Her eyes found Finn's at the exact instant he hit the button, and as the circle shrank to nothing, the last thing he saw through it was her hand coming up—and giving him the finger.

CHAPTER TWENTY

They ran until they reached the skeleton of the Ritz-Carlton. They stopped then, and turned, and the three of them watched the avenue to the south. Watched the framework of the high-rise, what they could see of it past the birches. Watched for the telltale burst of sunlight that would give away the opening of the other iris—from the cylinder Finn still possessed. It never came.

They climbed the oak to the Ritz's third floor girders. Bethany switched on their own cylinder, and thirty seconds later they were inside the hotel room, in the present, standing at the windows and looking south at the high-rise in the summer sun.

No unusual activity there. No one rushing in or out. No police response. Travis wasn't surprised— dialing 9-1-1 was probably not the standard procedure for emergencies in that building.

He saw Paige turn toward him. He looked at her. They were both still catching their breath from the run. Travis saw some kind of conflict in her expression. Like part of her couldn't believe what'd just happened, and another part wasn't surprised at all. After a second she just shook her head. She put one arm over Bethany's shoulder, the other over Travis's, dragged them together and squeezed them tightly. They stood that way, saying nothing, for over a minute.

Paige used Bethany's phone, encrypted against a physical trace, to call Border Town. She set it to speaker mode. A woman answered on the second ring.

"Bethany?"

"It's Paige, Evelyn."

Travis heard a sharp exhalation on the other end, a mix of surprise and relief. Then a silence.

"Are the others with you?" Evelyn said.

Paige closed her eyes. "No. They're gone."

The line stayed quiet for several seconds.

"Bethany told me there's a blockade in effect around Border Town," Paige said.

"Yes. Fighter jets. So far they're staying outside the boundary."

"Has there been any contact from the president?"

"No. No contact from anyone."

Paige thought about it. Nodded to herself. "All right."

"What's happening, Paige? What's all this about?"

"I wish I had time to explain it, but I just don't. I need to go somewhere. When this is over with, I'll tell you everything."

"One question, then," Evelyn said.

"Sure."

"If there's a move against us by the military, and we can't stop it . . . do you want us to use the fallback option?"

Paige breathed out slowly. She paced a few steps. Travis looked at Bethany and spoke quietly. "Fallback option?"

Bethany could only shrug.

Paige stopped pacing. "No," she said. "Not if it's the U.S. military. Do not use the fallback option."

"I understand," Evelyn said. Travis thought he heard another note of relief in her voice.

"Tell everyone to sit tight," Paige said. "We'll talk soon."

She ended the call. Turned to Travis and Bethany. "We need to get moving, fast."

"Where to?" Travis said.

"Yuma, Arizona. I'll explain at the airport."

They packed in less than three minutes. Travis broke down the shotgun just enough to fit it back into the duffel bag, along with the manila rope. They stowed the cylinder in Bethany's backpack and left the hotel without bothering to check out.

They hit a shop on 14th Street, where Paige bought a pair of jeans and a T-shirt to replace her outfit, which still smelled like gasoline from the motorcade attack. She changed in the restroom. Travis had a cab waiting when she came outside.

"Reagan or Dulles," Travis said.

"Baltimore International, in case they're watching both of those. We need to be paranoid at every step from now on."

She ducked into the backseat, followed by Bethany and then Travis.

None of them spoke during the forty-minute cab ride. Travis glanced across Bethany at Paige a few times. The hug in the hotel room had been a nice enough icebreaker, but there was still a tension that couldn't be helped—and wouldn't be. He had no plan to bring up anything that'd happened between them, including his departure. Neither did she, in all likelihood. And that would be fine. When this was over, he'd go back to sitting on loading docks at two in the morning and trying not to remember her. He'd just be starting from scratch, that was all.

They got out of the cab in front of the private terminal in Baltimore. They headed for the building, set back thirty yards from the drop-off lane.

"We're done with Renee Turner," Bethany said. "After what just happened in the green building, her travel pattern is too easy to zero. These people have Homeland resources at their fingertips. They can look at the timing of our attack on them, then pull up travel and lodging patterns in a radius and interval around it. They'll see Renee's check-in at the Ritz, and they'll see that she flew from Rapid City last night, just over the state line from Border Town. Taken all together, it's enough to smoke us. Renee shows ID here, the ticket agent gets a red pop-up window on her screen. We get a polite smile, and thirty seconds later we get arrested."

She thought about it as they walked. Glanced at Travis.

"Rob Pullman's a different story," she said. "They have no travel or lodging records for him. They have nothing that ties him to Renee, either. Her stopover in Atlanta can't link the two of them. Rob Pullman didn't show ID to board the flight. The only thing his name is on is a credit-card transaction: he bought a shotgun and some climbing rope in Virginia. But so what? That's a single purchase out of 10 million that happened around D.C. this morning. It's one point in the cloud. It's nothing." She looked at Paige. "Can our friends in the office building guess we're going to Yuma?"

"They can assume it."

Bethany thought it over. "Okay. If Rob Pullman flies from Baltimore to Yuma, it's almost unthinkable that their algorithms will flag it. And if he flies into the next town over from Yuma, there's not a chance." She took out her phone. "Rob's gonna need a membership with Falcon Jet."

Paige glanced at Travis. She managed a passing smile. "He'll need a better job to swing it."

"I get double time on Sundays," Travis said.

"I'll give him an oil tycoon uncle whose cholesterol intake caught up with him last spring," Bethany said.

"While you're at it," Travis said, "give him an encounter with Renee on a park bench."

Rob Pullman booked a private flight to Imperial, California, fifty miles west of Yuma. The ticket agent smiled politely, but nobody showed up to arrest them. The agent said the plane would be ready in forty-five minutes. They found an outdoor food court that was all but deserted, and ordered lunch.

Paige ate two huge slices of pizza in a few minutes. She hadn't eaten since early the night before. She washed them down with most of a large Pepsi.

The food court looked straight down the airport's busiest runway, eighty yards from its approach lights. Airliners passing overhead in the last seconds of their descent made the glass tabletop rattle.

Paige waited silently for one—a DC-10, Travis thought—to land, and then she said, "Most of what I know you've already figured out for yourselves. I'll tell you the rest. Then at least we'll have the same gaps."

She spent a few seconds considering how to begin.

"We started testing the two cylinders Monday morning, in the labs. The first time we turned one of them on, it didn't project the opening right away. Instead it made a sound. A sequence of high-pitched tones, like some kind of start-up process. We realized after a few seconds that both cylinders were making the sounds, in perfect unison, even though we'd only switched on one of them."

"Were they synchronizing with each other?" Bethany said. "Matching up so they'd open onto the same point in the future?"

"They might have been doing that," Paige said. "But there's something else they were definitely doing, which we didn't figure out until later. I'll explain it when I get to that part." She took a sip of her Pepsi. "The tone sequence lasted a little over three minutes. Then it stopped, and immediately after that, the projection appeared, from the one cylinder we'd switched on. Through the opening, all we could see was darkness. And then the smell hit us. Stale, dead air, like what it might smell like in a disused mine. We all put on ventilators. It helped a little. Then we shone flashlights into the darkness, and it didn't take us long to realize what we were looking at." Her eyes went back and forth between Travis and Bethany. "You know how it works, and you know we eventually determined that it was safe to go through, so I can skip to the relevant stuff. For starters, Border Town is empty in the future. The equipment is gone. The computers and paper records are gone." She paused. "All the entities are gone."

Travis felt the wind shift around. Felt it blow cool across the back of his neck.

"We checked out the whole place," Paige said. "We spent the better part of Monday down there, walking the empty rooms and hallways of the complex. There are no bodies. No signs of any struggle. Basic furniture is still there. Some of the beds are made, some aren't. It looks the way it would on any random afternoon, if everyone just left and shut off the power on their way out. That's how it was in every lab, every residence, every common area. And then we went to look at the thing we were most anxious to see."

"The Breach," Travis said.

Paige nodded.

"We couldn't get to it," she said. "We climbed down the elevator shaft, and three stories from the bottom we saw that it was a lost cause. Starting at Level 48 the shaft was filled in, and there was no way in the world to excavate it. It'd be impossible, even if you could move heavy equipment into the future through the projected opening, bit by bit."

"Why?" Travis said. "What's filling it?"

"Do you remember Heavy Rags?"

He nodded. Heavy Rags were the most common type of entity to emerge from the Breach. They'd been coming through almost daily since 1978.

Each one was dark green, about the size of a washcloth, and weighed over 2,800 pounds. The nature of the material had eluded all attempts at understanding, even after three decades of study by physicists within Tangent. The most they could say was that Heavy Rags weren't made of atoms. They were dense sheets of some smaller kind of particle—maybe quarks, but that was a guess at best—that were somehow stabilized in that arrangement. Handling them was a logistical chore. There was a wheeled chainfall down on Level 51 with a specially made titanium claw, there for the sole purpose of moving the rags around. They couldn't be stored anywhere in the complex but the bottom floor, and most of them weren't even kept there. Over the years, Tangent personnel had bored dozens of foot-wide shafts into the concrete floor of Level 51, all the way to the granite bedrock that lay beneath Border Town. These shafts were the final resting place for nearly all of the roughly ten thousand Heavy Rags that'd come through the Breach over the years.

"And you remember the Doubler," Paige said, not asking.

Travis nodded again. The Doubler had figured centrally in his dreams, at least one night in three, over the past two years. He often woke from those dreams pounding his knuckles bloody on the headboard, with fog-amplified voices still screaming in his head.

"Heavy Rags are one of the very few entities that can be doubled," Paige said. "In the future, the bottom three floors of Border Town have been filled solid with them, mixed with concrete to form a kind of mâché, though by volume it's probably ninety-nine percent rags. We calculated that a cubic foot of the mâché would weigh about 250,000 pounds—almost twice as much as an M1 Abrams tank."

Travis pictured three stories of the stuff, compressed into every possible crevice, filling even the dome that surrounded the Breach. The ungodly weight of the substance pushing some distance into the Breach itself, bulging in against the resistance force that made the tunnel a one-way passage. Paige had told him once that in the first year of the Breach's existence, some people had suggested filling the elevator shaft with concrete and leaving the Breach's chamber sealed off. That would've been a bad idea: in the time since then, entities had emerged that would've done very bad things to the world had they been left alone—even in a sealed cavern five hundred feet underground. But what Paige was describing now was a much more aggressive move. It amounted to shoving a million-ton cork into the mouth of the Breach itself, maybe preventing anything from truly emerging from it afterward. What would happen to the entities that were trying to come through? Would they just clot in the tunnel? Would they back up like a reservoir behind a dam?

He saw in Paige's expression that all the same questions had been troubling her for days, and that she had no answers.

"So at some point," Travis said, "probably before the collapse of the world a few months from now, someone uses the Doubler to fill the bottom of the complex with that stuff?"

Paige nodded. "It would go pretty quickly, once you had a big enough mass to double from. The Doubler could generate about a cubic yard every few seconds."

"But why the hell would someone do that?" Travis said.

Paige was silent for a moment. "Because under bad enough circumstances it would make sense," she said. "Which is why I thought of it."

Travis glanced at Bethany. She looked as uncertain as he felt. Then he understood.

"The fallback option," Travis said.

Paige nodded again. "The Heavy Rag mâché idea is my own. I dreamed it up six months ago. One more dividend of the paranoia I've felt since everything came to a head with Pilgrim. I just imagined a scenario in which we were certain someone bad was about to get control of Border Town, and that our defenses would only buy us hours. I tried to think of what we'd do with those hours. How could we secure the most dangerous entities, and the Breach itself?" She shrugged. "The fallback option was all I could come up with. Put everything down on fifty-one, and flood the bottom three floors with that stuff. No one would ever get through it. You could chip at it for a month with an industrial steam shovel and not make a dent. I think you could even detonate an H-bomb down there and all you'd do is compress the stuff a little more. The density is just unimaginable. You can calculate it on paper, but you still can't get your mind around it. Anyway, I wrote that up in a report, told a handful of people about it. Consensus was that it was risky as hell. No way to be sure it would work as intended, and no way to undo it if something went wrong. As a general means of just eliminating the Breach, nobody liked it. Neither did I. But everyone I talked to was in favor of doing it if desperate enough times came along someday." She thought about it for a moment, then spoke softly. "I guess the end of the world would suffice."

The whine of another airliner filtered in from behind them. The sound rose to a scream and then a 747 slid overhead, big as the world, its jetwash ruffling the umbrellas over the tables.

"That's a hell of a thing to have learned," Travis said. "That it actually works, I mean. That you can seal off the Breach, and that the seal would hold for several decades, at least. If we figure out what happens to the world a few months from now . . . if we learn how to prevent it . . . then you could choose to leave the Breach open, or go ahead and seal it anyway, just to get rid of it. It's something to consider."

Paige nodded slowly, her eyes far away. No doubt she *had* considered it, and at length.

"It *would* hold for decades," she said. "That much we know for sure. But after that it's still a guess. I imagine you could plug a small shield volcano, if you had enough concrete to dump in. And *that* might hold for decades, too. But the pressure would only keep building. And then what would happen? Nothing good, though at least with a volcano we understand the forces in play. With the Breach we understand almost nothing." A little tremor went through her shoulders. "No, if we manage to keep the world on track, I have no intention of sealing the Breach off. Even after seeing that it works—*especially* after seeing that it works—it just feels too dangerous."

She stared off a few seconds longer, then refocused to her hands on the table, and shrugged. "So that's what we found at the bottom of the elevator shaft. Then we climbed to the top and found *that* sealed too, though not as dramatically. There's just a metal slab across the opening on the surface, and a couple inches of regular concrete poured over it. A stranger up top could walk right by it and think it was just an old footing pad for some shed that used to be there. We saw it from above, the next day, when we took the cylinders up into the desert. And it was up there that things started to get interesting."

CHAPTER TWENTY-ONE

T he two of you probably guessed pretty quickly how far in the future it is, on the other side," Paige said. "You probably got within ten years of the right number."

"Seventy years ahead, we figured," Bethany said.

Paige nodded. "There's a lot that changes in a place like D.C. Nature reclaims its turf pretty fast, gives you evidence to base a guess on. But the desert above Border Town was *always* nature's turf. Civilization never modified it, so there was nothing for it to change back to when civilization went away. When we took the cylinders up to the surface on Tuesday, and switched one of them on, the opening we looked through might as well have been a pane of glass. Other than the blank concrete slab where the elevator housing should've been, nothing in the desert looked different. Nothing at all. So we still had no idea how far in the future the other side was. Could've been twenty years. Could've been a few thousand."

She took a sip.

"The fact was, we didn't even know whether the world had ended, at that point. Border Town being abandoned wasn't a good sign, but who knew for sure? We sure as hell didn't. And seeing the desert empty didn't tell us much, either. It *would* be empty, under almost any circumstance. I stepped through the opening up there and the first thing I did was stare at the sky for over a minute, hoping to see a jet contrail. Imagine if I had."

The notion struck Travis hard, and he wondered why he hadn't considered it until now: what if the future on the other side of the iris *hadn't* been a ruined one? What if Paige and the others had encountered a thriving world instead, decades and decades ahead of the present day? What would they have learned from a world like that? What would they have gained?

He saw in Paige's eyes a ghost of the optimism she must've felt, standing there under the desert sky Tuesday morning.

Then it faded.

"We started running the obvious tests after that," she said. "First an easy one: we switched on a handheld GPS unit, on the other side, and tried to pick up satellites with it. And we found some. But the position readings were a mess. The satellites were up there, but they weren't where they were supposed to be. One of the four of us, Pilar Guitierrez, spent about twenty years with NASA's Jet Propulsion Lab. She knew everything about orbital dynamics, drift and decay rates, that kind of thing. Orbits are a lot more fragile than most people think. Satellites get tugged around by all kinds of things. The moon's gravity. The sun's gravity. The tilt of the Earth plays hell with their inclinations. All that stuff has to be dealt with, all the time, by a process called *station-keeping*. Satellites are equipped with small rockets for corrective burns, to nudge them back onto course once in a while, and the commands for those burns come from human operators on the ground. But given what we were seeing on the handheld unit, the GPS satellites hadn't heard from anyone on the ground in a long, long time."

She exhaled slowly. "So that was that. We tried other things. We took radio equipment through. We listened to every frequency range with the most sensitive gear we had. Certain bandwidths, those that are popular with ham radio operators, we could've picked up from halfway around the world—if there were anyone out there transmitting on them. We didn't hear anything."

She finished off the Pepsi and set it aside.

"The only other thing we could do from a remote location like that was try to get through to a communication satellite. Our hope was that we might find one with some retrievable data on board. Something we could make sense of. Anything. But signals from those satellites are a lot harder to receive than GPS. You can't pick them up with a handheld unit bouncing around in your pocket. You need a dish, and you need to know exactly where to point it. Engineers handle that problem by putting comm satellites in geostationary orbit, right above the equator and matched to the spin of the Earth. That way the satellite is always in the same place, relative to the ground. But that wasn't going to help us: if those orbits had decayed much at all, the satellites would be lower, and orbiting faster. They wouldn't be stationary anymore. So when it came to aiming the dish, we'd be shooting in the dark at moving targets."

Her eyebrows went up in a shrug. "We had to try, though. So we did. We picked a spot above the equator, well below geostationary altitude, and we transmitted a maintenance ping every thirty seconds. A universal signal most satellites would respond to, if they heard it. We did that for hours and hours, all through the afternoon and into the evening, but there was no reply. We kept it going anyway. There was reason to believe it could take a while. In the meantime we tested other things. We figured out the use of the delayed shutoff button. We also figured out what the sequence of tones had been all about, the first time we'd switched on one of the cylinders."

Paige looked past Travis to the backpack lying in the empty chair next to him. She stared at the shape of the cylinder inside.

"It was locking out changes," she said.

Travis glanced at Bethany, then looked at Paige again. "Locking out changes?"

Paige nodded. "It's hard to explain. Hard to understand in the first place. In my case, I just saw it in action. While Pilar was working with the satellite gear, I had an idea I wanted to try. I took the second cylinder, and in the present time I drove one of the electric Jeeps to a little sandstone boulder about half a mile north of Border Town."

Travis recalled the rock she was talking about, though he'd only seen it a few times. It was about the size of a compact car, and it was the only thing larger than a scrub plant within miles of the elevator housing on the surface.

"The idea was pretty simple," Paige said. "I wanted to see an action in the present reflected in the future. I came up with one that should've been foolproof. I turned on the cylinder and positioned it facing the boulder. I looked at it in the present and in the future. The two versions of the rock were identical; whatever amount of erosion is going on out there, it doesn't happen fast. Anyway, I got out the Jeep's tire iron, and you can probably guess what I did with it."

Bethany's face lit up as the idea came to her. "You scratched the rock in the present time, so you could see the same scratch appear in the future."

"You'd think it would show up there, wouldn't you?" Paige said.

"How could it *not*?" Bethany said.

Paige shrugged. "I can only tell you that it didn't. I scratched the hell out of the boulder in the present. I chipped a crevice two inches deep into its surface. But in the future, the scratch wasn't there. It just wasn't. The rock was as smooth as ever."

Bethany stared. Met Travis's eyes. Looked at Paige again. She couldn't seem to find the words for her level of disbelief.

"Changes are locked out," Paige said. "I think it's that simple, however the hell it works. I think when those tones were sounding, the first time we switched these things on, the cylinders were locking onto whatever future we were on track toward *at that moment*. Independent of changes we'd make later on, once we could see the future for ourselves."

"Changes locked out . . ." Bethany said. "But you don't mean *our* future is locked . . . do you?"

Paige shook her head. "Just the future we see through the projected opening. Think of it this way. Suppose these cylinders only showed us a future ten days ahead of the present. You might look through and see yourself going about a normal day. You might also see a newspaper with next Saturday's lotto numbers in it. Suppose you jot them down, and in the present time, you run to the store and buy a ticket. You win the lotto, and now your whole future is going to change. But when you look through the opening at your future self, the one ten days ahead of you, *nothing* has changed. She's not celebrating. She hasn't quit her day job. *That* future, on the other side of the opening, is still following the original track—the one in which you *didn't* have the lotto numbers. It's locked. That's the only way I can put it. The future the cylinders show us is like a living snapshot of the future we were headed for, at the moment we first switched them on."

"So we can still save the world on *our* side of the opening," Travis said. "But the future we see on the *other* side will always be in ruins. The way it would've originally turned out."

"Exactly." Paige was quiet a moment. "Why the cylinders are designed to do that, I can only guess. It's worth keeping in mind that these things are built for some purpose. Built to be useful. Maybe a future that reacts to present changes is too fluid to make sense of. Maybe it would flicker through alternate versions like some rapid-fire slideshow right before your eyes. Think about chaos theory. Sensitivity to initial conditions. Maybe it's practical, or even necessary, to just lock these things onto one future and stick with it. That way, you can keep going back and forth between the two times, and never worry about the world transforming under your feet. And I'm sure the designers had some way to reset them, prep them to be locked again later on, whenever they wanted to, using equipment we obviously don't have. We've got the iPods but not the docks."

Bethany gazed off at nothing, thinking it over. She seemed to be accepting it, whether or not it made sense to her.

Travis didn't expect to fully understand it, but Paige's reasoning sounded right. If the iris opened onto a future that *did* react to changes in the present, it was hard to believe they weren't triggering at least *some* changes just by looking at it.

"I'm sure my expression at the time looked like each of yours does now," Paige said. "I stood there for probably half an hour trying to get a grasp on it. And then I heard Pilar and the others shouting, and waving at me to come back, because one of the satellite pings had finally gotten a response."

CHAPTER TWENTY-TWO

T he satellite was called COMTEL–3," Paige said. "In our present time it's positioned over the Atlantic as a relay for news-wire services, bouncing article text between ground stations in Europe, Africa, and the Americas. On the other side of the opening, we picked it up over the Pacific, moving east toward Ecuador, two hundred miles below its intended orbit. It answered the ping with a status screen full of critical error messages. It also had the date and time, based on its own onboard clock, which is probably accurate to within a few seconds over a thousand years. Adjusting for local time, at that moment in the other desert it was 6:31 in the evening, October 14, 2084."

A relative silence came, beyond the ambient whine of a jet powering up somewhere across the airport.

"Christ," Bethany said.

Travis felt something like a chill. They'd already known the kind of timeline they were dealing with, but to hear it specified to the minute made it real in a way he hadn't expected. He did the math. Seventy-three years and not quite two months.

"Having a known position for COMTEL–3 did a lot for us," Paige said. "After that we could rotate the dish to follow it, and stay in contact. Which was good, because Pilar believed some of the satellite's final transmissions—news stories—might still be stored in its memory buffer. She worked on it for a while, but she wasn't optimistic about actually retrieving the information. The bird was in pretty bad shape. It'd gone into some kind of safe mode after enough time passed without contact from its human controllers. Its orientation was off; its solar panels weren't angled to grab as much sunlight as it needed. It's a wonder it still worked at all. But after about half an hour, she managed to pull a number of articles from the buffer. They were corrupted all to hell. They were like fill-in-the-blank puzzles, with more blanks than words. We sat out there the rest of the day and most of the night trying to make sense of them, while we kept pinging for more satellites. We didn't find any more, but from the COMTEL–3 information we eventually narrowed down a few basic details of the event that ends the world."

She looked down at the table.

"The media gives it a name," she said. "They call it *Bleak December*. Whatever it is, it starts on December fourth of this year, and unfolds over the following weeks. We know that Yuma, Arizona, plays a key role in the event. Even a central role. But we don't know why. The city was mentioned in every article, numerous times, but the context was never intact. We also know that in the weeks *before* the event there's a major buildup of petroleum supplies in large metro areas. Gas stations with three or four tanker trucks parked outside as reserve stores. So whatever the event is, apparently people see it coming. Or at least those in power see it coming, and make preparations for some potential crisis. If that sounds vague, it is. There was just so little text to go on. We assumed they wanted the gas for electric generators, if power grids failed, but that was only a guess."

Bethany turned to Travis. "The cars," she said.

He nodded. There had to be a connection.

"What cars?" Paige said.

"All the cars in D.C. were gone," Travis said. "Everyone left at the end, but not in any kind of panic. There was no gridlock, as far as we could see. They left with cool heads."

Paige stared at the runway and tried to tie that fact in with everything else she knew. Travis watched her eyes. He saw only an echo of his own bafflement. Finally she shook her head.

"Doesn't make the image any sharper," she said. "Maybe they wanted the gas to evacuate the cities, but there was nothing in the articles to suggest why they'd need to do that."

"What *did* the articles suggest?" Bethany said. "I mean . . . beyond what you were sure of, was there anything in them that offered even a hint of what the hell happened?"

Paige thought about it for a long moment. On the far side of the airport, a 737 accelerated and lifted off.

"We had the sense that it wasn't a natural phenomenon," she said at last. "A sense that it was . . . a failure of something. Like a plan. Like a very big, very secret plan, that went *very fucking wrong* in every possible way. We couldn't pin down any one passage of text that said so . . . but it was there in general. It was sort of everywhere. And toward the end, the articles were fewer and farther between, and very short, leaving almost no text to go on. And then they just ended. The last thing anyone ever bounced through that satellite was dated December 28. Whatever the hell Bleak December is . . . was . . . *will be* . . . it takes about twenty-four days from start to finish. And then people stop writing newspaper articles, and correcting satellite orbits. And at some point, apparently, they stop doing everything."

She stared off. Shook her head. "That's why we went to the president first. If there was anyone to talk to about secret, dangerous shit that might get out of hand in the next few months, we figured it'd be him. I half expected him to just have the answer for us, once we'd shown him the cylinder and told him what we knew. Like there'd be some high-risk, black-budget program in the Defense Department, just about to go live, and he'd connect the dots just like that. And then he'd shut it down. Simple."

"Sounds like he did connect the dots," Travis said. "It's just the next part that didn't work out."

"But why *wouldn't* he shut it down?" Bethany said. "Why the hell would he *want* the world to end?"

"He probably thinks the danger can still be avoided, without stopping whatever this thing is," Paige said. "I overheard a conversation to that effect last night, tied up in that building in D.C. The project, or whatever it is, is called *Umbra*. But beyond the name, I still don't know a damn thing about it."

For almost a minute nobody spoke. Another air-liner rumbled down out of the sky and landed.

"So our best move is to get to Yuma," Travis said, "and use the cylinder to investigate the ruins there. See what we can learn from it, if it's such an important place at the end."

"We were on our way to do that last night," Paige said, "after we left the White House. Obviously, President Currey didn't want us to get there."

"I don't imagine he's had a change of heart since then," Bethany said. "And as of an hour ago, these people know we have our own cylinder."

Paige nodded. "And since they don't have to sneak around and take out-of-the-way flights—hell, they could take military flights—they may already be in Yuma with their cylinder by the time we arrive. Even if they burn some time keeping their resources here on the East Coast, waiting for us to make a mistake, we should expect them to be no more than a few hours behind us."

"And we can assume they outnumber and outgun us by a wide margin," Travis said.

"Probably wider than we want to think about."

Travis leaned back in his chair. Stared at the heat shimmers rising from the runway. Breathed a laugh. "What the hell. We've gone up against worse."

He didn't mention the fact that, strictly speaking, the *worse* they'd gone up against had won.

CHAPTER TWENTY-THREE

T he jet was the same type Travis and Bethany had flown in from Atlanta. Its rear four seats faced each other like those of a restaurant booth, without the table. They set their bags in one of them, occupied the other three, and fell asleep within the first five minutes of the flight.

When Travis opened his eyes again, he saw mountains passing below, high and glacier-capped, with vacant desert land to the east and west. He blinked and rubbed his eyes. Paige was still asleep, but Bethany was awake, working on her phone. Travis glanced at the display and saw that she was compiling information on the two names they'd gleaned from the building. One was Isaac Finn, the man whose office Paige had been taken to on the sixteenth floor. The other was the man Travis had dropped from the ninth floor, whose wallet had yielded the name Raymond Muller. Bethany appeared to be amassing a good deal of info on each of them.

Travis stared out the window again. He thought of the cylinder. Thought of the future it opened, with all changes locked out. In a very real way, that meant it wasn't *their* future anymore. If they figured out how to stop Umbra, then the world would live on, but the place on the other side of the iris wouldn't change to reflect that fact. It would never be anything but ghost country, the long echo of some terrible and all-too-human mistake.

He looked at Paige again. Watched her bangs playing on her forehead in the airstream from an A/C nozzle above.

"She'd find you, you know," Bethany said. She spoke softly, just above the drone of the jet engines.

Travis glanced at her. Waited for her to go on.

"If the world was ending, however it happens," she said, "if people were evacuating cities, if Tangent was scared enough to seal the Breach . . . if everything was coming undone . . . Paige would find you. She'd do it just to be with you at the end."

Travis returned his eyes to Paige. He didn't bother nodding agreement to Bethany; she'd already gone back to work on her phone.

Up front one of the pilots was talking to the tower at Imperial, asking for approach vectors. A few seconds later the engines began to cycle down, and Travis felt the familiar physical illusion of the aircraft coming to a dead stop at altitude.

Paige stirred. She opened her eyes and sat upright, blinking away the sleep.

"What's special about Yuma?" Travis said. "In our time, I mean. Any military presence? Any classified research going on?"

"We looked into it," Paige said. "No research labs, as far as we could tell. There are two military sites. One's a Marine Corps air station. They fly a few Harrier squadrons out of there, run lots of joint exercises, things like that. The other's the Yuma Proving Ground, out in the Sonoran northeast of the city. The Army tests every kind of ground combat system there. No doubt most of it's classified stuff, non-line-of-sight cannons, precision-guided artillery, all types of land vehicles and helicopters. But nothing you'd call an existential threat to the world." She rubbed her eyes. "That's about it."

Travis nodded.

"It's dry as hell," Bethany said. She looked up from her phone. "Friend of mine lived there for two years after college. Yuma's the driest city in the United States. Couple inches of rain a year, if that."

"Should work in our favor," Travis said. "There won't be nearly as much corrosion of materials as we saw in D.C. We might even find paper that's still intact, if it's shut away from the wind and the sun."

Bethany managed a smile. "Hey, we had to get lucky with something."

Travis wondered about that. Wondered if it was really luck, or if Yuma's climate was part of why the place had mattered when the world shut down.

Twenty minutes later they touched down in Imperial, a neat arrangement of neighborhood grids surrounded by miles of irrigated farmland and then more miles of open desert.

They walked out of the terminal into baked air—107 degrees, according to a digital sign over the parking lot.

They rented a Jeep Wrangler with an open top,

picked up Interstate 8 at the south end of town, and headed east toward Yuma. Five minutes later they passed the last of the irrigated fields and came into the emptiest landscape Travis had ever seen. At even a glance it was more desolate than the scrublands around Border Town, which was saying something. The highway bore straight ahead through it, just south of dead east. Far ahead were low hills and a line of mountains—some southern range of the Rockies—that lay probably just north of Yuma, forty-some miles away.

Travis was driving. Paige sat in the passenger seat, reassembling the twelve-gauge.

Bethany leaned forward from the backseat, her hair going crazy in the wind. "Want to hear the bios on our two friends in the green building?"

Paige glanced back at her and nodded.

Bethany looked at her phone's display as she began. "Raymond Muller. Guy on the ninth floor. Forty-two years old. Got his masters in political science from Brown, and in the next two decades he worked for half the power players in D.C."

"Doing what?" Travis said.

"Connecting them all to one another would be my guess," Bethany said. "I used to run into people like that in my field. Professional networkers. Matchmakers for senators and representatives and every kind of mega-corporation. A little closer to the vest than lobbyists. Muller worked for an Appropriations Committee chairman, two Ways and Means chairmen, Raytheon, General Dynamics, GE, Intel, FedEx, and Pfizer at one time or another."

"That's a lot to cram into twenty years," Paige said.

"Actually he crammed it into fifteen. His resume goes blank in 2006, right around the time the high-rise on M Street is built. If Muller has any income beyond that point, I can't find it. It may be that the company has made all his purchases for him these past five years. And that's it, for him."

There was a long silence as she pulled up the information on the second man.

"Isaac Finn," she said. She exhaled, the sound edged with a laugh. "You're not gonna believe this guy's background."

"Try us," Travis said.

"Relief work."

Paige turned in her seat. "What?"

"He's fifty-five. He has no formal education beyond high school. He graduated in 1973 and went straight into the Peace Corps, qualifying for it based on years of charity work in his teens. Stayed in the Corps for ten years, then came back to the States and spent a year rounding up financing to create his own organization, *For Good International*. At its peak, the group had over five thousand volunteers and paid staff, and an endowment of about seventy million dollars."

"Are you sure this isn't a different Isaac Finn?" Paige said.

Bethany double-clicked something on her phone. "Here's his passport photo." She handed the phone to Paige.

"That's him," Paige said. She stared at it a moment longer. She looked like she was trying to align the new information with what little she'd already known about the man. She gave it up after a few seconds and handed the phone back.

Bethany clicked to the bio information again. Her eyes roamed over it.

"He structured his group—and his approach—based on things he'd learned in the Corps. He'd seen that famines were generally *not* caused by weather, but by conflict, and the resulting breakdown of infrastructure. So his organization would try to re-establish stability in certain places, strengthen key communities in the hope that others around them would follow suit. He gave it a hell of a try, and he wasn't shy about using outside-the-box methods. He brought in psychological profilers to study the local leadership within villages, trying to determine which ones were cut out for actual governing, as opposed to just hoarding power. Then Finn would put his financial support behind the good guys, try to steer things onto the right track. He'd even apply that kind of thinking to entire communities. Try to exclude troublemakers, and empower those with certain basic attributes: kindness, concern for others, aversion to violence. Just anything to jump-start stability in enough places, and try to get the broader infrastructure back on its feet. Worth a shot, I guess."

"Did it work?" Travis said.

"I wouldn't say so. He tried it for a decade, in every place that seemed to need it. Ethiopia. Yugoslavia. Somalia. Then there was Rwanda. I think that was some kind of breaking point, for him. He was in the country for the first month of the genocide, April of 1994. And then he just left. He handed over control of his organization to those below him, cut all his ties to it, and walked away. For the next several years he didn't do much. He lived in D.C. Did some consulting, stateside, for humanitarian groups, but not a lot. In the late nineties he stopped doing even that, and as far as public or even private records are concerned, he more or less disappeared at that point. By the end of the decade his name was on no bank accounts, no property, no holdings of any kind. As far as I know, the next place anyone saw it written was on the door of that office on the sixteenth floor. How the hell it ended up there, I don't know."

She went silent.

"Anything else?" Travis said.

"Not about Finn. I found something interesting about his wife, but I'm not sure it's relevant." She navigated to the information. "Audra Nash Finn. Interesting background. Two doctorates: one in aerospace engineering from MIT, the other from Harvard, in philosophy."

"I build rockets, therefore I am?" Travis said.

"She didn't build much of anything for a while. She took a professorship at Harvard teaching philosophy, once she finished that degree. That was 1987. Held that position for quite a few years. Spent her summers abroad, involved in relief work. Met Finn somewhere along the way. Married him in 1990. Continued her teaching work but traveled often to help Finn in his efforts over the next four years. Then, Rwanda. That was the end of Audra's humanitarian streak too. The following year, summer of 1995, something strange happened. She co-authored an op-ed piece with Finn, and submitted it to the *Harvard Independent* for publication."

"What was it about?" Paige said.

"Nobody knows. It was rejected, and apparently before they could submit it elsewhere, certain influential people convinced them to sit on it. Mainly Audra's father, who was the governor of Massachusetts at the time. I guess he felt the piece was controversial, and could end up in attack ads against him. Everything I learned about this came from the *Independent*'s rival paper on campus, the *Crimson*. The staff over there tried like hell to get a copy of the op-ed, or a statement from someone who'd read it, but by then the fan was pretty well caked with shit, and nobody was talking."

"How bad could the thing have been?" Travis said.

"All the *Crimson* could pry out of their sources was that it was more than just an op-ed. That it was a proposal paper of some kind. Given that both Audra and Finn had just come away from Rwanda disillusioned to no end, we can guess what the subject was. Maybe not *that* crisis in particular, but it had to be some kind of policy suggestion about international relief. Some new idea. Maybe a pretty big idea. Whatever it was, it scared the hell out of her father. And to all appearances, that was the last anyone saw of the proposal. Audra resigned her position at Harvard that fall and went to work for Longbow Aerospace designing satellites. Finally decided to use her other degree, I guess. She died in a car accident two years later."

For the next minute they rode in silence. Travis was sure they were all thinking the same thing.

"The proposal paper could be unrelated to what's going on now," he said. "It could be just an interesting dot that doesn't actually connect. But if it *does* connect, then that paper was the origin of the plan Finn and his people are hiding now; in which case that proposal *was* Umbra. Maybe it was just talk back in 'ninety-five, and maybe it was small scale at the time. But if it's still in play, then it's become something bigger since then."

Paige thought it over. "Hard to believe a policy suggestion about refugee relief could lead to the end of the world."

"What if it's something that only touches on relief?" Bethany said. "Something involving food supplies, or crop growth in other parts of the world. Maybe Umbra is about genetic engineering of plants. That could go wrong on a large scale, theoretically."

"But neither of them had a background in genetics," Paige said. "And that kind of work is common now anyway, whatever the risks."

"We know this much," Travis said. "When you turned on the cylinder for the president, and he saw the ruins of D.C., he knew at a glance that Umbra was responsible. That's why he ordered the hit on the motorcade. But that only makes sense if he was already aware of the plan's potential to go wrong in some big, specific way. That could be the same risk that Audra's father saw, way back when he covered up the op-ed at Harvard. Whatever it was, it spooked him. Him and everyone on staff at the *Independent*."

Another long silence settled. The desert wind coursed through the Jeep, arid as blast-furnace exhaust.

A few miles further on, Travis heard Bethany shift around in the backseat. He heard the zipper of her backpack open. He glanced and saw her take the cylinder into her lap.

Then she stood up, holding the thing firmly in one hand and gripping the roll bar with the other. She leaned forward against the bar, braced herself, and leveled the cylinder straight ahead. She pressed the ON button.

The projection cone flared. The iris opened a few feet above and beyond the Jeep's hood. From Travis's position, looking upward at it, he could see only sky on the other side, the same washed-out blue as it was in the present. It made the iris nearly invisible. He wondered for a second if Bethany could feel the air rushing through it, then realized she wouldn't: the airflow through the iris would be no different from the air already surging over the Jeep.

He turned to ask her if she could see anything, but stopped himself before speaking. Bethany's expression had gone blank, and the color had faded from her face. She stared unblinking at whatever she was seeing through the iris. Then she slowly pivoted, swinging the opening clockwise like a searchlight, gazing through at the landscape beyond. Whatever she was looking at, it was there in every direction.

"What is it?" Travis said.

"Stop the Jeep," Bethany said. "Pull over."

"Why?"

"Because I found the cars."

CHAPTER TWENTY-FOUR

Travis pulled over. The highway was empty in both directions for all the miles they could see.

Bethany was still standing in the back. She turned around, leaned over and rested the cylinder on the Jeep's compressed soft top behind the backseat. The beam pointed sideways to the Jeep's right. The iris hung fixed in the air at chest level, just beyond the freeway's shoulder.

Travis got out at the same time as Paige. He was already looking past the Jeep at the iris. Could already see through it. Could already feel his own thoughts going as vacant as Bethany's had. A moment later all three of them were crowded at the opening, looking through. They stared for half a minute without speaking. Then Travis returned to the Jeep, shut it off, and pocketed the keys.

He took the shotgun from where Paige had left it on the passenger side. He picked up Bethany's backpack, hanging open with the SIG and all the shotgun shells inside it. Then he went to the cylinder and pushed the delayed shutoff button. He waited for the light cone to cut out, and then he secured the cylinder inside the pack. By the time he had it shouldered with the Remington, Paige and Bethany were already through the opening. He followed them.

The desert on the other side looked like a shopping-center parking lot the day after Thanksgiving, except that it had no boundaries. The cars stretched as far as Travis could see in every direction. The visible horizon was five miles out, any way that he faced. The cars extended at least that far.

They were parked grill-to-grill in double rows, each of which was separated by a lane of space just wide enough to drive down. The lanes branched out from the freeway, which itself remained clear.

The cars were in perfect condition except for their tires and window seals, which had baked to crumbs over the decades and settled in a thick layer on the desert floor. The wind had leveled the crumbs out but hadn't scattered them. Travis saw why: most of the cars were no more than an inch or two off the ground, sitting on their rims. All of them together would make a hell of a barrier against air currents at the surface.

The cars' paint jobs were faded and pitted, but not so much that the original colors couldn't be discerned.

Every kind of personal vehicle was there. Compact cars to SUVs. And they'd come from everywhere. California plates made up at least a third of them—understandably, given the state's population and short distance from Yuma—but within the first fifty cars he looked at, Travis saw two that were from New York State. He saw Texas and Florida and Pennsylvania, and a dozen others.

The cars were all empty. No bodies. No belongings. Just cracked and worn and bleached upholsteries that hadn't been sat on in seventy-three years.

Bethany climbed onto the hood of a Ford Expedition, then onto its roof. She put a hand to her forehead to shield her eyes from the sun, and turned a slow circle. She dropped her hand to her side. Looked down at Travis and Paige. Shook her head. Climbed back down.

"They came *here*?" she said. "From as far away as D.C. and New York, people emptied out of the big cities and came to *Yuma*? Why would they do that?"

Travis felt too thrown to even shrug. He had nothing approaching an answer. He stared over the sea of chrome and faded paint and tried to get a grasp of the numbers involved.

"A little over three hundred million people in America," he said. "Subtract the ones too young to drive a car, or that live in big cities and don't need one. How many cars would there be, ballpark? Couple hundred million?"

"Something like that," Paige said.

"How much space would they take up, arranged like this?" Travis said. "A parking space is about ten by twenty. So two hundred square feet. A square mile should have, what, a little over twenty-five million square feet in it?"

Bethany took out her phone, switched it on, and opened a calculator function. She pressed the buttons with both thumbs and had the answer in a few seconds.

"Just under twenty-eight million square feet in a

mile," she said. She did another calculation. "Divided by two hundred, that's one hundred forty thousand parking spaces. Cut that by a third to figure in the access lanes, you've got a little over ninety thousand cars every square mile."

"Call it a hundred thousand to make the math easier," Travis said. "Two hundred million cars would take up two thousand square miles."

Bethany's thumbs moved again. Then her eyebrows went up briefly. "Wow. Believe it or not, that's a square of only forty-four miles by forty-four. If Yuma was at the center of it, the edges would be just twenty-two miles from town. We're further out than that right now—more like thirty miles."

Travis thought about it. It made sense, in its own way. "You'd expect more of a rectangle than a square. It would grow east and west from towns along the freeway as people arrived. It would thicken north and south from there. Hard to say how far. But the point is that they could fit. Every car in the United States could park within a couple days' walk of Yuma. And that's assuming every car made it here, which they wouldn't. A good percentage would run out of gas along the way."

"A lot would be left behind to begin with," Paige said. "You didn't see any cars in D.C., but think of suburban families with two or three of them in the garage. They wouldn't take them all. They'd take one—whichever got the best mileage—and leave the others."

Travis nodded. The math worked, even if the reality it described was impossible to come to terms with.

"Yuma," Paige said. She stared east toward it, though the city—or its ruins, at least—lay well out of sight. Travis saw her eyes narrow. She was imagining three hundred million people gathering in one place.

"It's not possible," she said. "Not even close. The entire population of the United States bunched into Yuma, Arizona? Picture the Woodstock crowd. That was half a million people. The American population is six hundred times that amount. Think you could hold six hundred Woodstocks in Yuma at the same time?" She stared over the desert again. Shook her head. "This would be more than just a bad idea. This would be a lunatic idea."

"But it *was* the idea," Travis said. He swept an arm at the cars. "Somehow, this was the official response to whatever went wrong with Umbra. Everyone in the country wouldn't just spontaneously decide to come here. They'd have to be told. They *will* be told. In our own time . . . Jesus, all of this happens just a few months from now."

"But why?" Paige said. "*Why* would the government tell them that, and why would anyone listen? Whatever the hell was going wrong in the rest of the country, sending everyone here couldn't possibly help them. It would be mass suicide. There wouldn't even be housing space to get them all in out of the sun. And there'd be no food, either. They'd be dead in a week."

"Could things have just been that desperate?" Bethany said. "What if, somehow, Yuma offers temporary relief from whatever's happening in the rest of the country? Why that would be, I don't know . . . but suppose it is. Suppose the effect of

Umbra is so bad that it's *worth it* to come here, just to get away from it, even if it still means dying."

The notion chilled Travis, even in the baking sunlight. He watched it affect Paige and Bethany in the same way.

"Why Yuma?" he said. "What would it offer?" He thought of what he'd considered on the plane: that Yuma's climate might have a lot to do with its significance. "What if Umbra is worse in some places than others? What if it's worse where there's moisture, for whatever reason? Then a place like Yuma would be a kind of—" But he already saw why that thinking didn't work. He shook his head. "No. In that case there'd be lots of places people could go. Yuma might be the driest city, but there are tons of them that are *almost* as dry. Vegas is probably about the same, and it's a hell of a lot bigger. Christ, even Los Angeles would work, and you could fit all kinds of extra people there. Still no idea what they'd do for food, but it would beat the shit out of lumping everyone together here."

"Then they didn't come here for the climate," Bethany said. "So what did they come for?"

They walked among the cars for twenty minutes. Nearly all of them were unlocked. Either the owners hadn't expected anyone to steal them, or hadn't expected to ever use them again.

They opened doors, felt under seats, inspected glove boxes, popped trunks. They found several portable gasoline containers in almost every trunk or truck bed. In many cases there were one or more still full, especially in cars that'd come from neighboring states. The sealed plastic had kept the contents from evaporating.

They found random small things here and there. Fast-food wrappers. Pencils. Assorted change. There were guns in many of the trunks, alongside the leftover fuel. People had chosen to bring weapons along when they'd left their homes—or at least hadn't wanted to leave them behind—but by the time they'd reached Yuma they hadn't seen the need to hang on to them.

Many of them had left something else behind with the cars: bicycles. Not many had brought them, but those who had had left them here, bolted to trunk-mounted racks or lying in truck beds. For a moment Travis could make no sense of that. Why would anyone leave their bikes behind when they had a thirty-mile-plus walk in the desert ahead of them? Then he looked at the wide-open freeway again and thought he understood. There'd been some kind of shuttle system running here when everyone arrived. Buses or flatbeds or even pickup trucks making endless circuits along the road, taking on new arrivals wherever they found them, and ferrying them into the city. The whole thing had been massively organized.

"I found something," Bethany said.

She was two cars away, leaning in through the front passenger door of a white minivan. Paige was just raising the trunk lid of a Cadillac parked across the driving lane from it. She and Travis reached Bethany at the same time.

Bethany had found a spiral notebook inside the van's console compartment. Its cover was bright yellow, unfaded, and it had a child's stick-figure drawings all over it in blue ink. The figures were frowning and weeping teardrops half the size of their heads. Bethany opened the book. There were more drawings inside. More sad people. Some of the drawings showed specific settings. One looked like a grocery store, with oranges and apples colored in with crayon. Another might have been a school hallway. Most had simply doorways or trees for backgrounds. But in all of them the human figures were despondent, in some cases covering their faces with their hands while the tears spilled from under them. What the pictures lacked was any explanation for the tears. Any indication at all of what the hell was going on to make people feel that way.

Bleak December.

That's what the media called it.

But why?

After a dozen pages of drawings there was a final image showing the van itself. The child and an adult with long hair—presumably the child's mother—were seated in front. Still frowning, but not crying. The rest of the van was shown heaped with crudely drawn, out-of-scale household items. A toaster. A vacuum cleaner. A computer. Silverware and dishes and pots and pans. Bags crammed full of clothing.

None of that stuff was still in the van. Travis could see past the front seats to the vast cavity of space where the rear benches had been folded down into the floor. There was nothing back there.

The next page of the notebook didn't feature a drawing. It bore only a block of handwritten text—the oversized script of a child that somehow spoke of great effort, even in its sloppiness. It read:

I hope we get a tickit when we get to Yuma, but we will be happy enough just to get there. I hope Aunt Liz is there. Mom says we will probaly be there tonite.

All the remaining pages were blank. Bethany rifled through them, then came back to the written page.

"Ticket?" she said. "For what? A ride into town?"

They stared at the handwriting for another few seconds. Then Bethany let the book fall shut. She leaned back into the van and looked into the console compartment the book had come from. She gathered up the only other things inside it and held them up. A blue pen and two crayons, red and orange. The crayons had both melted to flattened shapes held together by just the paper around them.

"We might find a lot more questions out here," Travis said, "but I think the answers are going to be in the city."

Paige and Bethany looked like they agreed.

Travis unslung the backpack from his shoulder, unzipped it, and took out the cylinder.

CHAPTER TWENTY-FIVE

They opened the iris two hundred yards from the highway, in case someone happened to be driving by at that moment in 2011. Travis looked through. No cars in sight. The Jeep was just as they'd left it.

Twenty-five minutes later they reached the western outskirts of the city. It was larger than Travis had imagined, sprawled out over a patch of desert at least four miles by four. He exited the freeway and a moment later they were passing through a residential neighborhood full of low-slung homes, palm trees not quite as tall as the streetlights, and shallow front yards that were either gravel or irrigated grass.

They came to Fourth Avenue and turned south onto it. It seemed to be the main drag through town. It could've been any Main Street in America except for the arid terrain. There were gas stations and grocery stores and banks and jewelers. There was a Burger King. There was a movie theater with five screens.

If there was an army waiting for them, it wasn't showing itself. Which made sense, in a way.

"If we run into trouble," Travis said, "I think it'll be on the other side, in the ruins. On this side they don't know what we're driving, or even who we *are* except for you, Paige. But over there we'll be the only things moving around on two feet. It's a better place for them to set a watch."

Paige nodded. Weighed the possibilities. "It could be wishful thinking," she said, "but we might have a few things working in our favor. On the one hand we're up against the president of the United States, who has the military and every police force in the country at his disposal. He can make it rain brimstone on us if he wants to. On the other hand he and Finn, and whoever else they're working with, have already demonstrated a pretty severe preference for keeping their secrets intact. It's hard to imagine them grabbing a hundred soldiers or federal agents and sending them through the opening to lie in wait for us. That's a lot of people to let in on the game. My guess is Finn will stick with his own security personnel from the highrise, whatever number of them he trusts enough. No telling what that number is. A dozen if we're lucky. More if we're not."

Travis looked down a cross street going by. Considered the broad layout of the town. Imagined how it would look in moderately well-preserved ruins, with most of its structures still standing. It was a lot of area for a dozen people to watch. A lot for even several dozen.

Other advantages came to mind. As prey, the three of them had a significant edge on their potential predators: they would carry their own cylinder along with them, while Finn's people, if they were widely spaced throughout the ruins, would obviously be empty-handed in that department. There was no question that Finn himself would keep possession of his own cylinder.

That would give the three of them an easy way out of trouble, when and if they encountered it. In a pursuit, they could switch on their cylinder, hit the delayed shutoff and escape through the iris into the present day. It would stay open another minute and a half, but anyone trying to follow them through it would be committing suicide. It didn't take a West Point grad to see the tactical downside of climbing through a choke point the size of a manhole cover while defenders with a SIG 220 and a twelve-gauge were waiting on the other side. And when the 93 seconds were up, they could just run. It would take Finn a long time to transport the other cylinder across the ruins—on foot—to whatever location his men were calling him to.

That was the idea, anyway. In practice it might play out a lot differently, even if all of their assumptions were right. Which they probably weren't.

They found a six-story Holiday Inn two blocks off of Fourth Avenue. As far as they could tell, it was the tallest building in town. They didn't check in. They simply walked in with their bags— the Remington once again broken down to fit in the big duffel—and found an empty restroom on the first floor. It had three stalls, including a large, wheelchair-accessible one. Travis held its door wide and Bethany projected the iris into the middle of the broad space beside the toilet. She pressed the delayed shutoff. The beam brightened and vanished. The three of them crowded into the stall, then shut and locked its door.

The iris looked pitch-black, the way it had when Travis and Bethany had first seen it in the Ritz. It couldn't be nighttime in the ruins: it was a quarter past five in the present, and the day on the other side was offset behind by a little over an hour. That should make it just after four in the afternoon, there.

The darkness was only the unlit interior of the hotel, in the future. The building's walls must be fully intact. The place had endured the long neglect better than any of its counterparts in D.C.—or anywhere else, probably.

The air on the other side smelled stale but not rotten. Travis didn't imagine things would rot in Yuma. They would just dry out and harden.

He stepped through the iris, keeping hold of its sides until he felt his foot touch solid ground—no doubt the same ceramic tiles that were there in the present. He brought his other leg through, then turned and took the cylinder and duffel bag from Bethany. He got out of the way and let her and Paige climb through the iris. Then they stood there in a crush against the wall, staring back through the opening, taking in the glow and hum of the fluorescent lights.

Thirty seconds later the iris shut, leaving them in a silence and darkness so complete that they might as well have been blindfolded and wearing earplugs.

Travis felt his way forward. His hand bumped against the stall door, hanging inward a few inches. He found its edge and pulled on it. Its hinges offered only a dry scrape for a protest as it swung clear.

Travis stepped out of the stall. He saw a faint rectangle of light rimming the bathroom door. He moved toward it, slowly, while he heard Paige and Bethany emerge from the stall behind him.

Halfway across the room his foot came up against something lying on the floor. He stopped. Touched his foot to it again and pushed it to test its weight. It yielded to a moderate amount of force. It weighed maybe forty pounds. Travis knew what it was. He stepped over it and found the door handle in the darkness.

"Be ready not to make any noise," he said.

"Why would we?" Bethany said.

"Because you're about to see something terrible."

He pulled open the door. Sunlight from the corridor flooded the room. Centered on the bathroom tiles lay a body. A young woman, maybe twenty, with blond hair and pink-rimmed glasses. She wore a peach-colored T-shirt and jean shorts. Her skin was stretched tight over her bones and had the brittle, matte-finish look of paper mâché painted beige. She lay on her side, one forearm cushioning her face on the tiles. Her knees were drawn up, fetal. She'd died alone here and had mummified in the arid heat.

Bethany took a deep breath. It hissed through her teeth on the way out. She looked around, suddenly frantic, and at the dim edge of the light shaft coming in from the hall, she saw the bathroom's sinks. She crossed to the nearest in two running steps and reached it just as she vomited. The convulsion came in waves—two, three, four. Then she stood there getting her breath. On instinct she grabbed the faucet handle and turned it. Nothing came out.

"Fuck," she whispered.

She spat into the sink a number of times, and at last stood upright. Paige put an arm around her shoulders.

"I'm okay," Bethany said.

She didn't sound okay to Travis, but she sounded like she could stay on her feet. She'd have to cope with it later. They all would. And by then they'd have more to cope with alongside it.

A *lot* more, Travis saw, as he stepped into the corridor.

CHAPTER TWENTY-SIX

The ground-floor hallway of the hotel was filled with bodies. Cluttered so thick with them that it would require careful footsteps to avoid them. They lay in the positions they'd died in. On their sides and their stomachs and their backs, heads on folded arms or wadded articles of clothing. A few were seated against the wall, their arms crossed on bent knees and their heads bowed onto them. Their spinal columns stood out in sharp relief through the papery skin of their necks.

They were every age. There were gray-haired seniors. There were couples that might have been college students or even high-school kids, dead in each other's arms. There were children with their heads resting in parents' laps. Beside the stairwell door sat a woman who might have been thirty. She held a blanket-wrapped bundle in her arms. She'd died with her head leaned back against the wall. The dried remnant of her expression looked serene and calm. Travis wanted to believe she'd really felt that way at the end, but he didn't.

Here and there, exposed arms and legs bore ragged bite marks where scavengers had been at the bodies. The damage was small in scale: apparently, no animals larger than rats had made their way into the hotel, at least in the early days. Maybe bigger things had come along later, but by then the mummification had made these dead an unappealing food source, and they'd been left alone. It was as close as nature could come to respecting dignity.

Travis's gaze fell on a couple that'd probably been in their twenties. They'd piled a few jackets and shirts at the base of the wall and were huddled against them. The woman's arms were lying flat across the man's chest, but his were around her, holding her to him. Her forehead rested against his mouth. She'd died first, Travis realized. The man had held her body and kissed her forehead, and stayed in that position until he'd faded away himself.

Travis felt moisture rimming his eyes. He blinked it away. He glanced around and saw Paige and Bethany doing the same, just behind him at the open bathroom door.

He found himself taking in the condition of the building. It was almost pristine. The drywall in the corridor looked no different than it had in the present. The high-gloss paint on the crown molding had cracked and flaked, but only in a few places. There weren't even cobwebs. Travis imagined dust would've settled out of the air here after a while, without foot traffic kicking up carpet fibers and pillows being fluffed. He could see none drifting around in the pale sunlight that shone along the hallway.

He turned toward the source of the light: the double doors at the end of the hall, fifty feet away.

They were closed but they were mostly glass. The wall around them was also glass. All of it remained intact.

The wedge of parking lot that was visible beyond looked bleached and barren in the hard light. It was full of cars, which wasn't surprising.

Paige let the bathroom door fall shut.

The three of them stood there. They listened. The hotel was as silent as it'd no doubt been for decades.

They watched the space beyond the glass wall for over a minute. Past the parking lot the view was blocked in places by other buildings, but in the gaps between those they could see a long way— hundreds of yards in some cases. Against the bases of distant buildings they could see deep accumulations of wind-piled sand, blinding white in the sun. None of it was blowing around now.

They saw no movement anywhere.

Travis set the cylinder and the large duffel bag on the floor. He took the shotgun from the bag, reassembled it, and slung it on his shoulder. Then he opened the bathroom door again and slid the duffel bag far to the left inside, near the sinks. It was too much to haul around the ruins with them. If they came back this way, they could get it later.

Bethany took the SIG from her backpack, considered it, and then handed it to Paige. "You're probably a better shot than me. I'll carry the cylinder. Better to have it in hand than in the pack. If we need to use it fast, seconds will count."

She zipped and shouldered the backpack again—it held only shotgun shells now—and picked up the cylinder from where Travis had set it.

Travis studied the parking lot another few seconds, then turned and made his way through the bodies to the stairwell door.

There was a vague light shining in the stairwell. It came from somewhere high above. Even on the lowest flights it was enough to reveal the few bodies that lay in this space.

They found the light source on the fourth-floor landing. The husk of a balding man in his forties lay sprawled across the threshold leading to the hallway, the door forever propped open at forty-five degrees. It let in sunlight from the same kind of glass wall that capped the ground floor corridor.

They continued to the sixth floor. The bodies in the hallway there were as densely strewn as downstairs. Some of the guestroom doors they passed stood open. More bodies inside, on beds and in chairs. Travis stared at the shapes of bones beneath drawn skin. All the bodies were shriveled to that degree. He didn't think mummification alone had done that to them. More likely starvation and dehydration had done it before they'd died.

They came to the glass wall at the end, looking out over Yuma from six stories up.

They stared.

"Jesus Christ," Paige said softly.

It was the last thing any of them said for several minutes.

Every building in Yuma looked exactly as it had when they'd driven through it in the present day, except that the colors were baked to pastel versions of themselves. Like soft-drink cans left in the sun for weeks. Every parking lot was filled to capacity with cars and trucks. Every curb space was taken too. The vehicles had endured just as those in the open desert had: faded paint and no tires or window seals. Beyond the edges of the city, the mad but organized sprawl of cars extended out of sight in all directions. From this height it looked dramatically more absurd than it had from the shoulder of I–8, since the horizon was much farther away.

The three of them noticed all of that within seconds, and then disregarded it. Something else had taken their full attention.

The city of Yuma was drifted with human bones. Seven decades of wind had scurried them into piles against all available obstructions. Cars, buildings, landscaping walls, planter boxes. They were everywhere except for open stretches of flat ground—like the section of parking lot immediately below, which had been visible from the first floor. From down there they'd seen the bones only at a distance, and mistaken them for sand.

Travis let his eyes roam the nearest pile, seventy feet left of the exterior door. The bones had massed there against a different wing of the hotel. He could see them with enough clarity to discern adult skulls from those of children, and large ribs from small ones. The bones were scoured clean and white. Everyone who'd died outdoors had been quickly discovered by coyotes and foxes and desert cats, and whatever they'd left behind, the sun and wind had eventually taken care of.

"It's everyone, isn't it?" Bethany said. "They really did it. They all came here and just . . . died."

Travis looked at her. Saw her eyes suddenly haunted by a new thought.

"Maybe we were with them," she said. "Maybe our bones are out there somewhere."

They watched the city for another five minutes, for any sign of movement. If Finn's people were there, they were already hidden in ideal vantage points. Travis considered that. Realized something obvious.

"I think we're here ahead of them," he said.

"How can you know?" Paige said.

"Because if they'd gotten here first, some of them would be standing at this window."

There were three other floor-to-ceiling windows on the sixth floor, at the ends of other wings. They spent a few minutes at each of them, scrutinizing the city. They saw bones everywhere, but no sign of recent disturbance.

They also saw no indication that Yuma had been modified to handle any kind of crowd. No trailers or temporary shelters had been set up. If there'd been tents erected about the place, they were long gone in the wind.

Then they came to the last window, facing southeast, and understood where they needed to go next.

A mile away lay the broad expanse of the airport. The runways were clear, flawless. They probably looked no better even in the present. The terminals stood glittering and vacant. There were no aircraft docked at any of the gates. Travis studied the scene and wondered why it looked odd to him. Then it hit him: there were no parked cars filling the airport's space. It was open ground—the only open ground for miles.

"There's something written there," Bethany said. She pointed to the south end of the longest runway.

Travis saw what she meant. A few hundred feet in from the runway's identification numbers, someone had written a message in huge white letters—probably using the same paint the airport used for the runway lines. Travis had missed it at first; it was hard to read the letters from a long side angle. The message seemed to be intended for someone looking straight down on it from a plane.

Travis put it together one letter at a time, and had it after a few seconds.

It read: COME BACK.

CHAPTER TWENTY-SEVEN

They were outside the hotel a minute later. The quiet of the city was unnerving. The bone drifts looked bigger from ground level than they had from the sixth floor.

The air temperature was about the same as it'd been in the present. Somewhere between 105 and 110.

They crossed the parking lot and made their way to a residential district three blocks beyond. Moving among the houses felt safer than crossing the wide-open lots of commercial and industrial zones. They'd seen from the hotel that they could follow the houses all the way to the airport if they went straight east and then south to its perimeter.

They saw leathery bodies in every home they passed. After the first block they stopped looking.

Bones were scattered everywhere outside the houses. In fenced yards where the wind had never picked up momentum, some of the skeletons were partially intact. A tiny skull and ribcage lay half submerged in a sandbox among faded toy tractors and steam shovels.

Travis brought up the rear. He looked back every

twenty yards. Whenever they crossed a space that offered a view of the hotel behind them, he studied the big corridor windows on the high floors. Even through the glare of reflected sky, he could see through them well enough to spot a person, if one were standing there. So far, he saw nobody.

He heard Bethany taking sharp, quick breaths ahead of him, and realized she was trying not to cry.

Paige gave her shoulder a squeeze. "You don't have to hold it back. No one who sees this can be unaffected by it."

"I know," Bethany said.

But she held it back anyway. After another minute she was breathing normally again.

At the next street they came to, they looked south and saw the northern edge of the airport half a mile away, its chain-link boundary fence still standing.

They crossed into the next block and followed the sheltered path among backyards southward. They were moving against a light breeze now. It wasn't much, but it was enough to perturb the air around their ears and make it hard to listen for movement. Travis kept turning his head to counter the effect.

They were a hundred feet from the airport fence when the breeze died for a few seconds.

Travis heard something.

He grabbed Paige and Bethany and pulled them almost off their feet, into a narrow channel between houses. They flinched and stared at him. He put a finger to his lips.

They stood in silence.

The breeze moaned under the eaves of the houses.

Then it faded again, and all three of them heard the sound.

It came from somewhere south of them, maybe within the airport grounds.

It was a woman's voice, speaking calmly, saying something they couldn't quite make out.

It took them only a few seconds to realize what they were hearing. The woman's voice was pleasant and monotone and had a distinct reverb to it. It was a recording, playing over some kind of PA system on the airport grounds.

They cocked their heads but couldn't discern any of the words.

Then the breeze picked up again and they lost the sound altogether.

They stepped out from between the houses and continued south. They stopped at the corner of the last home before the fence line, twenty yards farther on. Beyond the fence there was easily a quarter mile of open space before the nearest terminal building. Anyone watching from a high perch in the city would see them. There was no shorter path across the space on any side. There was nothing for it but to run.

The fence was ten feet high. Simple chain-link. No razorwire looped across its top. All it offered as deterrents were signs every dozen yards threatening harsh legal penalties for trespassing.

Travis tried to resolve the recording again. It was no good. It was still too far away, coming from somewhere near or within the terminal.

They traded looks. They nodded.

They ran.

They crossed the fence with no difficulty, and a few seconds later they were sprinting as hard as they could across the vast reach of the airport. Travis wondered if the distance had played with his eyes. Wondered if it was a lot more than a quarter mile to the buildings. It didn't matter now. He ran. The wind streamed past his ears. It was impossible to hear the recording, even though he was much closer to it now than before. His own pulse against his eardrums became loud enough to match the wind after the first thirty seconds.

He was fifty yards from the terminal, with Paige and Bethany matching his speed, when he began hearing the monotone voice again. He still couldn't make out what it was saying.

The three of them reached the corner of the building. Its long side planed away to the east, three hundred yards or more. Its short side was maybe fifty yards in length, leading south to another corner. They followed the short side, sprinting along it without stopping. Travis was acutely aware that they were still visible from town. More visible than ever, in fact—against the blazing white metal of the terminal's outer wall, they'd stand out like ants on china to anyone even glancing this way from downtown.

They reached the south corner and rounded it. They stopped and stood hunched over catching their breath. For the first time since leaving the hotel they were visually shielded. The entire bulk of the town lay north and west of the airport. Their position on the south side of the terminal building, even a few feet in from the corner, hid them completely.

Travis walked off the pain in his legs. Took a last deep breath and felt his heart rate begin to fall off. As it did, he finally heard the message in all its clarity—which wasn't a lot.

The woman's voice sounded like it was coming through a cardboard tube with wax paper over the end. It took some concentration to piece the words together. Travis looked up and saw the speakers, tucked far under the ten-foot overhang of the building's roof. They had to be wired to solar panels up top. The recording itself must be stored on some kind of solid-state media—a flash drive, probably. The whole system might have no moving parts except the electrons passing through the wires, and the vibrating diaphragms of the speakers themselves. For all that, it was amazing that it still worked, even in a place like Yuma.

Travis saw Paige and Bethany straining to catch the words along with him. He realized the message was repeating every twenty seconds or so. By the fourth pass all three of them had deciphered it:

PLEASE BE PATIENT. PLEASE DO NOT LEAVE THE YUMA GATHERING SITE. ALL ERICA FLIGHTS WILL RESUME SHORTLY. BE SURE TO HAVE YOUR TICKET AND PHOTO I.D. WITH YOU FOR BOARDING. INBOUND FLIGHTS WILL BRING FOOD AND EXTRA WATER PURIFIERS FOR THOSE WHO CONTINUE TO WAIT. PLEASE BE PATIENT . . .

They listened to it one more time. Travis was certain he hadn't misheard any part of it.

"Erica flights," Paige said. She looked at Bethany. "I wonder if those are anything like the Janet flights out of Vegas."

"I was wondering the same thing," Bethany said.

Travis looked from one of them to the other. "Pretend I don't know what the hell you're talking about."

"The Janet flights are something like a private airline," Paige said. "They're run by one of the big defense contractors. I forget which."

"EG&G," Bethany said.

Paige nodded. "They fly out of McCarran Airport in Vegas to airstrips in the Nevada Test Site. Mostly Groom Lake, I'm sure. They're basically commuter flights for military and civilian personnel who work out there." She gazed out over the empty airfield in the searing light. "Maybe the similar naming convention tells us something. Maybe the Erica flights were military, or close to it."

Overhead, the message finished another iteration and began again.

"We know they were departures from here," Travis said. "Which means Yuma wasn't really the final stop. At least not for some."

"Tickets," Bethany said. "That's what the kid meant, in the notebook. People came to Yuma hoping to get aboard one of these flights, wherever they were going."

Travis stared at the southern face of the terminal rising above them. The lowest portion of the wall, from the ground to a height of fifteen feet, was white metal like the other sides of the building. Above that it was all glass. Jetways extended from boarding gates every hundred feet or so. Like everything else in Yuma they were in nearly mint condition. All they'd lost were the heavy-duty tires that'd once given their free ends mobility. Not even rubber crumbs remained around the bare rims. The unimpeded wind at this location had long-since taken them away.

Travis focused on the windows. From below all he could see was the terminal's ceiling. No way to see anything at floor-level inside, though he imagined the space was full of bodies, each with a ticket and ID in its pocket. He turned and looked at the far end of the runway. He could see the rough shape of the words painted there, illegible at this angle but easy to recall.

Come back.

He listened to the recording blaring its neverending promise, and wondered what it'd been like to sit here dying, waiting for it to come true.

"The message says the flights will resume," Travis said. "They must have actually been taking place at some point, when everyone was first coming to Yuma. And then they stopped."

He thought of the bodies in the hotel. In the houses they'd passed. He thought of the bone drifts.

He shook his head. "We don't need a calculator to see that the math doesn't work on this one. How many people could they have possibly airlifted out of here, even if they were cycling the planes through with pit-crew efficiency? Say the Erica flights were 747s departing every ten minutes with five hundred people aboard. Probably impossible, but let's be generous. That's three thousand people an hour. It'd take a thousand hours to move three million people. A hundred thousand hours to move three hundred million."

He saw Bethany and Paige doing the math in their heads.

"About eight thousand hours in a year," Bethany said. "To fly everyone out would take more than a decade, even running at peak efficiency, day and night."

"The people who came to Yuma would've known that," Travis said. "They'd have had all the time in the world to figure it out. They'd know that this place couldn't keep them alive, and that their only chance to survive was to get picked for one of those flights in the first week or so. And what would be the chances of that? Close to zero. Coming to Yuma would be Russian roulette meets the Super-Lotto. But knowing all that, they still came. They played the odds. What could have made them desperate enough to do that?"

They stared at one another. Thought about it from every angle. Came no closer to making sense of it.

There were ground-level doors under each jetway, leading into the terminal. Travis tried the knob of the first one. It turned easily, but the door wouldn't open. The white paint coating the door and the frame had fused together over the decades. Travis braced a foot against the frame and pulled with both hands. The seam gave with a dry crackle, and then they were in.

The place was noticeably warmer inside than outside—120 degrees instead of 105. It had the greenhouse effect in play because of the big southern windows, and no breeze to transfer the heat away.

They'd entered some kind of maintenance space one level below the concourse. It was close to pitch-black inside once they'd shut the door behind themselves, but they'd already seen the stairs ahead of them. Travis found the bottom tread and the handrail and started up. Fifteen steps later he touched the handle of the upper door. He opened it, stepped through, and held it for Paige and Bethany.

Five seconds earlier Travis had been sure—without even thinking of it—that he'd already seen the worst Yuma could show him. That he was sufficiently hardened to face whatever they might find here.

He wasn't.

The three of them stood there, staring at the cavernous and brightly lit interior of the concourse.

The door fell shut behind them with a soft click.

Bethany inhaled slowly—Travis heard her throat constricting as she did. She put a hand to the wall beside the door, and then her knees gave and she sat down on the spot. She made no attempt to hold back the sobs now. Paige sat beside her and held on to her.

Travis took a few steps forward into the space. In the giant sunbeam that filled it he saw hundreds of padded seats, most of them facing out toward the runways and the open ground. On the chairs and on the floor and on the flat benches here and there, bodies lay as densely packed as they had in the hotel corridors.

In this place they were all children.

None looked older than twelve.

They stretched to the end of the concourse, at least a third of a mile away. Thousands and thousands of them.

Everywhere among them were discarded food

containers. Foil chip bags, cracker boxes, candy-bar wrappers, pickle jars, bread bags. All of them lay empty among the bodies, which were as gaunt as any Travis had seen elsewhere in the city.

It was clear enough what'd happened. In the end, when the survivors in the town had dwindled to thousands, the adults had made a decision. Maybe the last big decision any humans ever made. They'd put all the kids here and consolidated the remaining food with them. The grownups had sacrificed themselves to give the kids a few extra days, in the guttering hope that the planes might come back in time for them.

Nothing Travis had seen in Yuma had brought him close to losing control. His eyes had moistened in the hotel, but his breathing hadn't so much as hitched.

It didn't hitch now, either.

He didn't get even that much warning.

He simply found himself sitting down hard in the middle of the floor, his hands pressed to his eyes as they flooded, his chest heaving beyond his ability to stop it.

Time went by. Ten or fifteen minutes. The emotions passed and left a kind of vacuum in their wake.

They stood.

They glanced around.

They had no desire to search the concourse. It was hard to imagine what it could show them except more suffering.

Travis tried to think of what part of the city they might investigate next. He was thinking about that when they heard the exterior door open downstairs.

CHAPTER TWENTY-EIGHT

The concourse offered very few hiding places. Even fewer that could be reached within seconds.

The wall opposite the windows was lined with shops that'd once sold tourist items and sandwiches and sunglasses. The shops didn't have doorways—they simply lacked front walls. They offered concealment from only one sight line—that of someone approaching along the row.

They were also the only option.

Travis waited for Paige and Bethany to move past him. They went forward along the row of shops, avoiding the bodies. He followed, keeping an ear toward the door atop the stairs. The metal treads would give away the newcomer's approach easily enough, but the monotone recording—much louder inside the terminal—would make it tough to listen for it.

He heard it when they were four shops along. Heavy thuds coming up, echoing in the space beyond the door.

Paige ducked into the fifth shop, which seemed to be a bookstore with all its shelves empty. Bethany and Travis followed. They heard the door open a second later.

Five seconds passed.

The door clicked shut.

A man exhaled.

Then, footsteps. Slow and careful. Coming toward them. Distinct, individual steps. The man was alone.

Travis clicked off the Remington's safety. He had a shell in the chamber already. He had his back to the shop's wall on the side the footsteps were coming from. He was two feet in from the edge. He leveled the shotgun and pulled the stock against his shoulder.

The footsteps halted. It was hard to say where. Maybe ten feet short of where the man would've come into view. Not much further away than that, Travis was sure. Part of him wanted the guy to continue forward. Wanted a reason to start shooting, even if the sound might draw more trouble onto them.

Then he heard a crackle of static. A walkie-talkie. The only form of long-range communication that would work on this side of the iris.

The static cut out and the man spoke. "Lambert here. Inside the terminal. Copy?"

The static came back. Then a man's voice spoke through it, just clear enough to be discerned.

"This is Finn. Go ahead Lambert."

"They were here. There's paint flakes outside an exterior door. Gotta be recent, or else the wind would've blown them away."

Travis clenched his teeth. Fuck. Careless.

"Any sign they're still inside?" Finn said.

"No way to tell. I just came in."

The static hissed for a long time. Then Finn spoke again. "All right. Get out of there. You've already found out what we need to know. Come back and help with the camera mast."

"Copy."

The static flared again and then clicked off for good. Travis waited for the footsteps to retreat, but for a moment they didn't. Lambert was just standing there, no doubt gazing around at the spectacle of the concourse. Whatever the man felt about it, it didn't reduce him to tears. After a few seconds he retreated to the door, and then he was gone.

Travis relaxed his grip on the shotgun. He turned to look at Paige. She was looking in his direction, but past him. Staring at the big windows, thinking about something.

"It's probably about five o'clock here," she said. "I don't know when the sun sets in Arizona during October, but eyeballing it I'd say we've got an hour."

Travis followed her stare. He looked at the angle of sunlight coming into the terminal. It shone as harshly as it would have at midday, but it fell at a long slant. An hour was probably about right.

"We need to get out of here right now," Paige said. She sounded on edge. "We need to get out into the desert and go back through the iris to the present. We can walk to the Jeep from there."

Travis had an idea of what was spooking her.

"This camera mast they were talking about—"

Paige cut him off. "Yes. We need to be scared shitless of it. And we need to get moving. I'll explain on the way."

She stepped past him, out of the shop. He took a step to follow and then realized Bethany hadn't moved yet. He stopped, turned back to her. Saw what she was staring at.

In a little wastebasket just visible behind the shop's counter, there was a scrap of newspaper. Maybe the top third of the front page, torn roughly from left to right. It was stained with ancient blotches of mustard, like it'd been used to clean up the remnants of a sandwich on the counter. Glancing around, Travis saw no sign of the paper it'd been torn from. For that matter, there were no newspapers of any kind in the shop. A tower of wire shelves in the corner had clearly once been stocked with them, but it was empty now, like every bookshelf in the place. Except the scrap in the trash can, not a single piece of paper remained in the store. Travis turned his eyes to the concourse and saw the reason within seconds: the kids had burned the paper to stay warm. Ash piles remained in various stone planters among the bodies. As hot as this place would get during the day, it would cool down fast at night. The big glass wall would bleed away the heat in no time—especially in December.

Bethany stooped and took the piece of newspaper from the trash. Filling most of the space was the paper's title: *The Arizona Republic*. Below that was the date: December 15, 2011. And beneath that was the lead headline and the top few rows of the story's text—a single column beside a giant photo—before the torn bottom edge cut it off.

The photo was impossible to make out. Only the top inch of it showed: a defocused background of a crowd somewhere.

The headline read, FORMER PRESIDENT GARNER ASSASSINATED IN NEW YORK CITY.

Paige let her urgency fade for the moment. She stepped back into the shop.

Bethany spread the paper on the counter so all three of them could see it. Despite age yellowing and the mustard stain, the fragment of article text was easily readable:

New York (AP)—Former United States President Richard Garner was shot to death at a gathering in Central Park yesterday evening, Wednesday, December 14. Garner had for several days spoken publicly against the mass relocation to

That was it. It reached the bottom edge and there was no more. Bethany flipped the scrap over, but the other side featured only an advertisement for a local restaurant. She turned it back over to the headline.

Travis stared at it. Read the story text again. Thought about what it implied.

"We think bringing everyone to Yuma was some kind of panic move," he said. "The official response by those in power—those behind Umbra—even if they knew it couldn't actually save everyone. And Richard Garner called them on it, at the end. Even opposed it, publicly. Any question that's why he was killed?"

Paige's eyes narrowed. She saw where he was going. So did Bethany.

"Garner's not in on it," Paige said.

Bethany looked back and forth between them, hope rising in her eyes. "But he probably knows a hell of a lot about this stuff, right now in the present day. He only resigned the presidency two years ago. Up until that point, he had all the top security clearances. He had to have known about Umbra, whatever the hell it is."

For a moment none of them spoke. The recording droned over the concourse.

"We should pay him a visit," Travis said.

Paige nodded again. Then she blinked and looked around. "We need to get the hell out of Yuma first. Come on."

She turned and led the way out of the shop, back toward the door they'd entered through.

They came out through the exterior door with the SIG and the Remington leveled. There was no one in sight.

Travis looked down and saw the paint chips he'd left earlier. He shook his head.

They moved east across the southern span of the building, out of view of anyone in town. They ran at nearly full speed and reached the southeast corner in a little under a minute.

The donut of open space surrounding the terminal was a quarter mile on every side. They'd first come into the airport from the north, with the city at their backs. They were facing south and east now, with nothing ahead of them but a few pole barns at the edge of town and then a tundra of cars covering miles and miles of flat desert.

Finn and his people were in town. Probably toward the middle. A sprint from this corner of the terminal toward the southeast would be largely hidden by the building itself, at least for the first half of the run. After that they would probably be visible to someone high up in the city, like a watcher on the top floor of the hotel.

Travis saw Paige judging the distance, running through the same logistics.

"I don't imagine they'll have a watch posted anymore," she said. "They'll have everyone working on the camera mast. They'll want it raised as soon as possible, and once it's up they won't need a watch at all."

She looked toward the sun. Couldn't look right at it. The arid sky did nothing to filter its glare, even though it was shining from low in the west. Their guess inside the book shop had been right: it was an hour above the horizon.

Travis suddenly understood Paige's concern.

"Thermal cameras," he said.

She looked at him. Nodded. "Eight FLIR cameras, seventy-five meters up. The kind of mast they'll use is lightweight, guywire stabilized, rapid-deployable. What the military uses for forward operating bases in open country. A skilled team can put one up in an hour."

Travis looked around at the tarmac. Looked at the scrubland past the perimeter fence, and the sprawl of cars beyond. Every outdoor surface in Yuma was still baking at over one hundred degrees.

But not for long.

All of it would cool quickly once the sun set. It might be cooling already. And once the background was cooler than ninety-eight degrees, the three of them would be the warmest things within a hundred miles of Yuma. Even if they got far out among the cars and army-crawled into the desert all night long, the cameras atop the mast might see them. Infrared light from body heat radiated and reflected like any other kind. It could bounce off metal and glass. FLIR cameras watching from a height of seventy-five meters would have an effective horizon dozens of miles out.

If they were still in Yuma an hour from now, they might as well be wearing neon body suits.

They ran.

They reached the perimeter, crossed the fence and made their way among the cars.

They ducked low and zigzagged south and east for over half an hour, until even the terminal building was at least a mile away.

They stared through the cab of a pickup toward the center of town. They could see the mast going up, rising meter by meter as unseen workers added sections to it at the bottom. The camera assembly was already mounted on top. The mast seemed to hold itself perfectly straight as it rose. Travis pictured four men holding onto guywires—invisible against the sky at this distance—that they would stake into the ground once the mast was complete.

Travis studied the nearest edge of town. On this side of the airport there were only a few outbuildings, all of them tucked in close to the fence line. The zigzagging had put the three of them well beyond the bounds of the city, in what should be empty desert in the present day. There would be little risk of any bystander seeing them appear through the iris.

"Let's do it," Paige said.

Travis nodded.

Bethany was still carrying the cylinder. She settled onto one knee and aimed it at almost ground level between the rows of cars. She switched it on.

The iris opened to vacant land under the same kind of long sunlight they were crouching in now, maybe half an hour before dusk. For a second, that seemed wrong to Travis: the present was shifted an hour ahead of this side. It should already be dark over there. Then he remembered. The present was an hour later in the day, but two months earlier in the year. August instead of October. The sunset would be a lot later in August, about enough to offset the difference. It occurred to him that rival armies using this technology against each other would have a lot of abstract thinking to do.

He crawled to the iris and looked through at the broad sweep of present-day Yuma.

He felt the back of his neck go cold.

"Shit," he whispered.

Paige was beside him a second later. Bethany remained ten feet away, holding the cylinder.

"What is it?" Bethany said.

For a few seconds neither Travis nor Paige answered. They just stared through the iris at the living version of the city—which was filled with police and federal and even military vehicles. Flashers stabbed at the evening air from a hundred places, and at a glance Travis saw at least three helicopters circling high above.

"I had it wrong," Travis said. "They *did* set a trap for us in the present. They just waited until we were on this side to spring it."

CHAPTER TWENTY-NINE

Bethany closed the iris.

They lay there on the hard ground, silent.

The breeze played over the tops of the cars. It dipped among them in weakened breaths, noticeably cooler than it'd been even ten minutes ago.

"It's probably a Homeland response," Bethany said. "The president can initiate one without anyone's approval. They'll have every road into the city blocked off. The residents will be locked down under curfew. Anyone moving around in the open within ten or fifteen miles of town will be stopped and questioned. Our chances of escape are better on this side."

"Our chances of escape are near zero on this side," Paige said.

"I know," Bethany said.

Travis got up into a crouch, and looked through the truck's cab again at the rising mast. It was impossible to accurately judge its height, but it was a lot taller than the six-story hotel a few blocks from it. It wouldn't be long before it was completed, and in fact the cameras on top were probably already functional, even if the desert was still blinding them. And that protection might only last another twenty or thirty minutes.

"What's working in our favor?" Paige said. "What can be *made* to work in our favor?"

Travis thought about it, but for at least a minute nothing came to him.

Then he smiled.

Finn watched the mast take shape. Lambert and the other specialist, Miller, were quick and efficient in their moves. The tech, Grayling, had the camera feeds already routed to a line of eight laptops, arrayed on the pavement of Fourth Avenue in the lengthening storefront shadows.

So far the cameras could resolve nothing. The laptop screens were fully white, overwhelmed by the desert's background heat. But that would change very soon.

Finn had brought fifteen men through the opening. Three were assembling and configuring the mast, four were holding the guywires, and eight were just standing there, HK MP5s in hand, ready to run. Ready to make the kills.

If the condition of the ruins had affected any of the men, they weren't showing it. Finn wished they would, at least to some small degree. Wished he could see some human reaction in them—a respect for the suffering that'd happened in this place. He was sure they felt it, deep inside—maybe not even so deep inside. It was only human for them to stifle their empathy in the presence of others, but Finn had to believe that any one of them, walking these ruins alone, would have been brought to his knees. It helped to think so anyway.

"We're not going to make it painful for them," he said. He turned his eyes on the eight who were armed. "Miss Campbell and her friends aren't bad people. From their point of view they're in the right. There's no call to make them suffer. We make it fast, as soon as we're on them."

Travis, Paige, and Bethany covered distance among the cars as quickly as possible, moving straight west from their earlier position, from one lower corner of the town toward the other.

The wide driving lanes between the cars ran north and south, but the going was just as easy from east to west. The cars had the same natural channels between them that existed in any parking lot: the spaces their drivers had needed in which to open their doors that final time, long ago.

They slipped through the channels, every few seconds crossing the wider lanes. They were acting on a risky assumption: that Finn's people weren't standing lookout at all, but were just waiting for the cameras to do it for them. The assumption was as necessary as it was dangerous: they needed to move quickly in order for Travis's plan to work, and they couldn't do that while staying low among the vehicles.

They moved upright at half the speed of a sprint. They'd have gone faster, but the plan required stopping at vehicles every few hundred feet—among other things.

For Travis there were two other reasons to slow up. Two specific items he was looking for, that he hoped to find in glove boxes along the way. He found the first within minutes. The second took longer, but only a little. He pocketed both things and continued along at a quicker pace.

If they were lucky they might cover two miles before the cameras could see them. Maybe even three. But either way it was going to be close. The plan would succeed or fail by minutes. Seconds, even.

If it worked at all.

The first thing that showed on the laptops were the broad lanes between the cars, stretching away to a vanishing point like rows of corn. Finn had expected that. The ground between the cars had lain in shadow for at least an hour now.

Humans still wouldn't be discernible in the lanes: the lanes were reading a hundred degrees, while the tops of the cars were reading five degrees higher. But it was progress.

It crossed Finn's mind that Paige Campbell and her associates, however many she had with her, might be hiding in one of the structures within the city. That would be problematic, short term. Every building's interior had been superheated all day long by the greenhouse effect. It was probably a hundred twenty or higher in each of them, and that heat would take time to bleed out through closed windows and plaster walls.

But long term it was no problem at all. How long could Campbell and the others stay hidden in those conditions? It was unlikely they'd brought much food and water of their own, if any, and they sure as hell weren't going to find any left sitting around in Yuma.

If it came to simply waiting them out, that would

be fine. They weren't going anywhere on the present side, and they weren't going anywhere on this side either. It was going to end here, sometime in the next twenty-four hours.

But every instinct told Finn that they were out among the cars, making whatever run for it they could, and that this would be over very, very soon.

He stared at the laptops again. Watched the contrast of the lanes deepen. Some portions of them were taking on a new shade now. Ninety-nine degrees.

Moving quickly. Not quite running. Stopping at intervals. They were dead south of town now, two miles west of where they'd begun their sideways move.

Not far enough, Travis thought. Not nearly far enough. The plan had a giant drawback built into it: it was going to give away their position the instant they executed it. Which might be okay, as long as the plan worked. As long as its effect was immediate and overwhelming for Finn's people.

But for that to happen, they needed to cover a certain amount of distance first. The path they'd taken so far was a line from east to west, south of Yuma. Like they were underlining the city on a map, right to left. The longer they could make the line before everything happened, the more likely the plan was to succeed.

Distance and time. They needed more of one. They were running out of the other.

Nearly straight ahead of them, the sun's lower rim touched the horizon.

* * *

The mast was finished. Lambert and Miller stood armed with the others now, while the four with the guywires staked them into the ground.

Grayling was moving back and forth over his laptops, hunched, looking excited.

Finn could see sparse portions of the open lanes reading ninety-seven degrees now. Even the cars themselves were reading down around one hundred.

Two and a half miles. Still probably not enough. It was impossible to guess exactly what *would be* enough. The plan would work or it wouldn't.

The sun was gone. The desert felt immediately cooler, though Travis was sure that was a psychological effect. It'd been cooling steadily for a long time now. He let his hand press on the hood of a truck as he passed it. Warm, but not hot.

"There!" Grayling said. His hand shot out to indicate the fifth laptop's screen. "South of southwest, a mile and a half away." He dropped to one knee and studied the monitor. "I see three of them. Christ, they're not even hiding. I've got direct line of sight. They're moving—straight west through the cars. I wouldn't say they're running. I don't know what the hell they're doing. It's like a fast walk, hunched over. Maybe they're tired."

"Then it won't be hard to catch them," Finn said.

He turned and picked up the cylinder from where he'd set it on the curb. A second later he was running, holding the cylinder with both hands and tucking it against himself. Lambert and Miller and the other eight fell in behind him.

This would be simple. Straight south out of town along one of the broad lanes among the cars, until they were level with the east-west line the others were fleeing along. Then just catch up to them from behind—maybe stick to a parallel path ten yards north of theirs until the last minute, to stay clear of the sightlines between the cars.

Finn freed a hand from the cylinder and took from his vest pocket the FLIR goggles he'd brought along. He hung them around his neck by their strap. They weren't necessary yet, but in another ten minutes the desert would be an ink-black void without them. His men each had them too.

Paige Campbell and her friends almost certainly didn't.

Finn really did feel bad for them. It wasn't even going to be a contest.

CHAPTER THIRTY

Three miles. Three fourths of the town under-lined. The going was harder now: their mus-cles were sore and the channels between the cars lay deep in shadow.

Yuma looked strange in the twilight with no lights coming on. Just low, black rectangles against the dying sky. Nearer, the sea of cars made a single, undefined field of darkness.

The wind was much cooler. Under any other cir-cumstances it would've felt soothing.

Travis stopped. There was no question that Finn and his people had seen them by now. No question that they were coming, that they were out there somewhere among the cars, threading this way.

Paige and Bethany stopped too.

The three of them met one another's eyes.

Finn found the desert surprisingly easy to traverse. The inch-thick layer of rubber crumbs, the rem-nant of a few hundred million tires, made for a soft—and silent—running surface. Finn had in-corporated running into his exercise regimen years ago, not long after settling down in D.C. His mile time varied between 6:30 and 6:50. His men, most of them with twenty years on him, were all at least that fast.

They'd completed the southern arm of the sprint and were well along the westbound track now. They had their FLIR goggles on. The desert looked spectral through them. The cars were bluish white, while the passageways between them were shrouded in deep indigo and black. It was like running through a photo negative.

Finn held up a hand and brought the men to a stop.

He set the cylinder down beside a pickup, then climbed onto the sidewall of the truck's bed. He balanced himself against the cab and surveyed the desert.

Christ, they were right there. Six cars west and four cars south. They were crouched low; Finn could see only the reflection of their heat signature against the side of a minivan.

Were they hiding because they'd heard the approach? Finn ruled it out. They couldn't have heard.

The answer was simpler than that. They could no longer find their way in the dark. There was no moon. No light glow bleeding into the sky from distant cities. There was starlight, but starlight was worthless. Human eyes, even dark-adjusted for hours, couldn't see a thing by it. Finn had faced that fact a number of times, in remote places all over the world.

Miss Campbell and the others had stopped because they simply couldn't go on. They were crouched as low as they could get, hoping it was enough.

Finn considered waiting for them to go to sleep. Then they could be executed without even knowing it, and spared the jolt of animal terror that would otherwise mark their final seconds as the shooting started.

He thought of it and then discarded it. They would probably post a watch. That person would sit awake for hours, anxious and miserable, listening for footsteps in the dark. And that was its own kind of pain. No need to prolong it.

He turned to step down from the truck—but stopped.

He'd smelled something. Just briefly. It'd come to him on the breeze, blowing northward over the cars.

He tilted his head up and inhaled. Couldn't detect it again, whatever it was. He tried to place it, based on the trace of it he'd gotten. Somehow it made him think of gun lubricant, but that wasn't quite it.

He took another breath, still couldn't reacquire it, and let it go. Maybe it was the natural odor of tens of millions of cars, mothballed in the desert for all time. It occurred to him only for a second to question that idea—to wonder how any smell at all would still be around after seven decades of sun and wind—and then he stepped down from the pickup and waved the men forward again.

They rounded the truck's front end and went south. Finn stopped them again one channel north of the row the others were crouched in, and led them west. They would drop down into the same pathway as Miss Campbell when they were two cars shy, and simply rush them. It would begin and end in seconds. As close to painless as circumstances afforded.

Travis took the first glove box item from his pocket. He shook it next to his ear. Empty as expected. Even though it was nearly a sealed container, its trace contents would've no doubt evaporated long ago, even in the sun-sheltered interior of a dashboard.

It didn't matter. The item should serve its purpose here, regardless.

He lowered it until it was nearly touching the bed of tire crumbs.

Finn brought the men to a halt at the near edge of one of the broad north-south lanes. He could see the victims' heat signature against the minivan, one channel south and two cars past the far side of the lane. He was sure all the men could see them too. No need to plan the final move. They knew what to do now. Finn stepped forward into the lane, and simply got out of their way. He sidestepped to the left. Waved them on.

They advanced, single file, angling across the lane toward the channel in which the victims were crouched.

Lambert took point as Finn moved aside. He moved slowly, silently, one step per second. No need to rush.

He came even with the open channel between the last few cars and saw the three targets easily. Two were dead right now if he pulled the trigger. The third—someone small, slender-framed—was crouched at the back corner of the van, halfway around it. That one might create a problem if the shooting started too soon. Might get clear and lead a pursuit among the cars, however brief. Might even return fire—Finn had said these people were armed. Better to take them all in a single action.

Lambert raised his foot to take another step, and heard a faint suction noise from the ground beneath it. He looked down. Saw nothing there in his thermal vision. Looked up again at the targets, still a good thirty feet away. The largest of them had his hand to the ground. Looked like he was holding something with it.

Finn took another step aside as the men filed past him. As he did, his heel struck something in the darkness. It made a light, hollow thud. Something big and empty, made of plastic. It spun aside easily under the impact of his foot. He looked but couldn't see anything. Whatever it was, it was the same temperature as the ground.

He stooped, felt for it, found it. A smooth container with a handle.

And a spout.

He drew it toward his face, and his next breath told him exactly what it was, and what he'd smelled from atop the truck bed twenty seconds earlier.

Travis was sure the Bic would work—would spark, anyway. Flint and steel shouldn't have changed at all in Yuma, these past seventy-three years.

He was less sure that the spark would be big enough, or long-lived enough, to ignite the fuel-soaked tire crumbs.

He flicked the sparkwheel with his thumb. It generated a tiny flash that barely escaped the lighter's windscreen—and had no effect on the fuel.

He flicked it again.

Same result.

Lambert pressed forward between the cars. Twenty feet from the targets now. Still no clean angle on the little one behind the van.

What the hell was the big one holding?

Lambert could see the guy's thumb moving. Snapping across whatever it was. Each time there was a tiny pinprick of light in his FLIR-enhanced vision.

The third spark did nothing, either. It wasn't working. Not this way.

Travis pressed the end of the lighter directly into the soft tire crumbs. He put the tip of his index finger to the sparkwheel and dropped his shoulder, allowing plenty of slack into his arm. Then he pivoted, swung his entire upper body clockwise, and kept his finger pressed to the wheel until the last instant, so that every ounce of his momentum would come to bear on it. When his fingertip jerked across the wheel, he felt the steel dig into his skin almost hard enough to draw blood.

In the same instant he heard a man shouting, somewhere close by in the darkness. He was saying, "Fall back!"

Lambert heard Finn start to shout just as the big target lowered its shoulder and wrenched its torso around.

It was the last thing his FLIR goggles showed him.

A tenth of a second later his vision was washed out by blazing white light, and he felt a wave of heat engulf his legs and waist.

Travis had expected Finn's men to be close. Maybe within a hundred feet. Maybe closer than that.

When the trail of gasoline ignited, revealing the men in a line formation just over a car length away, it was visually startling but not so surprising. Travis threw himself backward, still in his crouch, slamming into Paige and pushing her back with him.

He got his left hand beneath himself on the ground to keep his body from sprawling. He brought his right arm up and around, getting his hand on Paige's shoulder, and the moment they'd cleared the back of the van, he shoved her sideways, propelling her and Bethany behind the vehicle's bulk.

At no point did he take his eyes off of the men in the flames. They may have caught him off guard, but it was clear they'd gotten the worse end of the encounter. They flinched backward, their left hands coming off of the forward grips of their weapons, reaching instinctively for their eyes. The top halves of their faces were hidden by some kind of night-vision goggles, but the lower halves said more than enough about the sudden panic they felt. They were blinded and confused, and a second from now their clothing would be on fire. They were in every kind of trouble.

But they weren't the whole story. Beyond the five who were trapped between the vehicles, Travis could see as many as five more who hadn't yet filed into the narrow space. They were disoriented too, but they weren't immobilized.

They were going to be a problem.

Travis understood all that, even as he shoved Paige, while his own body's momentum continued backward. A millisecond later it shifted beyond the balance point of his left arm beneath him. His feet kicked out of place on the rubber crumbs, and he went down hard on his back, landing on the shotgun he'd slung on his shoulder.

Finn had already torn his FLIR headset off by the time the flames erupted, his second shouted word still clearing his mouth. He saw the burst of light forty feet away, and a fraction of a second later the fire was rushing toward him. It didn't just spread along its pathway: it screamed. It looked like a bullet train emerging in flames from a tunnel. Finn only just managed to step clear of it, even with plenty of distance to see it coming.

Lambert and Miller and the three behind them were almost immediately ablaze. Finn saw why. It wasn't just the ground beneath them that was burning—the sides of the vehicles had been doused with gasoline, too. The men were walled in by the inferno.

Even the five who hadn't yet entered the space were flailing, impulsively trying to cover their eyes instead of the FLIR lenses five inches in front of their foreheads.

Finn lunged at them. He swatted their headsets up and off, one after another, and shoved them toward the next channel through the cars.

"It's a fucking diversion!" he screamed. "Take them before they can move on it!"

Paige saw Travis land on the Remington, even as she and Bethany fell to the ground behind the van. Paige landed on her ass, twisted hard to the side, slammed both hands to the ground and pushed herself up into another crouch, all in one fluid move. Then she was rising, uncoiling like a spring to full height, her right hand automatically drawing the SIG-Sauer from her waistband.

She heard Finn yelling something about a diversion.

She came out from behind the van, leveling the SIG across the roof of the compact car next to it. She was vaguely aware of Travis right beneath her, trying to roll over and get his hands onto the shotgun, but other things took greater command of her attention.

The fire trail. Surging away across the desert like the exhaust wash of a rocket.

The five men in the flames, their clothing ablaze, their hands grabbing at zippers and buttons, their bodies running into one another and into the cars that boxed them in on the sides.

The other five men. Not on fire. Not even wearing their headsets anymore. Turning and running in this direction, through the nearest free pathway between the vehicles. Finn urging them on.

Finn.

Right there. Just beyond the compact car and the lowrider that faced it. He was thirty feet away, and holding the other cylinder.

For a moment Paige met his eyes. She had the

SIG leveled in the neutral space between the charging men and Finn himself. It was like an intersection in time. The last point at which all options remained open.

She felt her training begin to exert itself. The world didn't exactly slow down for her. It just became simple. Very, very simple.

There were targets.

Some of the targets were threats, and some weren't.

Some of the threats were more immediate than others.

The most immediate was the man leading the pack between the cars. Twenty feet away and closing. His MP5 coming up. His eyes on her chest, where the first shots were going to go about a third of a second from now.

Paige made a slight adjustment with her wrist. It took a fourth of a second. She pulled the trigger. The bullet punched into the pack leader's forehead like a finger into stale piecrust, collapsing it inward in big bony shards. His head snapped back but his body continued forward, already dropping, obeying simple laws of physics now instead of whatever was left between his ears.

Four men left. Two of them still plowing forward between the cars.

But not the other two. They were checking their movement. Falling back. Turning their attention on Finn now, defensive. They understood the danger he was in—probably better than he understood it himself.

Finn was still in her field of fire. Still a target.

But there were still threats. Immediate threats.

Paige retargeted from the falling corpse of the

first man to the second, five feet behind him. She fired again. Caught him right in front of the ear. The entry wound was small, but in the firelight she saw what had to be the full contents of his head come out the back in a ragged cloud.

Then things began to change very quickly.

The two men closest to Finn got ahold of him. Dragged him down and away. Paige saw their heads whip around, their eyes tracking over their surroundings, looking for the best route to safety—to distance and cover.

At the same time, the third man between the cars was dropping. Dropping faster than the corpses of his friends. Getting down out of her line of fire. He hadn't reached the compact car yet. He was still passing the lowrider. The chasm between it and the next vehicle was shallow, but as Paige lowered the SIG to follow him into it, the compact car's roof slid up into her gunsights, blocking the angle.

She fired anyway. Three shots, as fast as she could pull the trigger. She saw them hit the car's roof, punching through but deflecting wildly as they did. Past the roof's edges she saw the man still coming on, unhindered.

She also saw that she was out of time to try again.

She threw her body sideways in the same quarter second that his return fire cut open the darkness. The windows of the compact car imploded. Paige hit the ground, landing near Bethany again. She hit harder than she wanted to. She'd been forced to put speed before control when she threw herself out of the way, but that was going to cost her now.

Because she wasn't going to get up in time. Wasn't even going to roll herself over into a firing position in time. That would take her a good second and a half, and by then the man would be rounding the back end of the car.

She saw it all play out like a nightmare. Still not slowed down. Just clear. Agonizingly clear. She managed to turn her head, her eyes going all the way to their corners.

The gunman was already there. Clearing the car's rear window and then its trunk. Shouldering the machine gun for the easy kill.

And then his head came apart.

It happened so suddenly that Paige almost missed the muzzle burst from the twelve-gauge, in the darkness behind the car's bumper.

A second later Travis was on his feet, racking another shell into the shotgun's chamber, raising it and sweeping it through an arc above the car. Looking for Finn.

But Finn was long gone. Paige could see it in Travis's eyes.

She became aware of screaming voices—realized she'd been hearing them for seconds already, but hadn't focused on them. They hadn't been part of the simple picture.

She saw Travis turn his eyes to the side of the van, and she realized what the screaming was. The men in the fire. Still alive. Travis swung the Remington their way and emptied its remaining shells into them, its broad pattern allowing for five kills with four shots—two or three shots could've almost done the job.

The screaming stopped.

Travis slung the shotgun. He turned, held out his hands to Paige and Bethany, helped them up.

Paige stared around at the aftermath. The bodies in the flames. The bodies alongside the lowrider. The empty space where Finn and the other two had been.

She looked at the fire trail. No more than fifteen seconds had passed since Travis had lit it, but already it extended hundreds of yards. Paige could see its far end still racing toward its conclusion: the place where the three of them had first begun dumping fuel containers in a thick line between the cars.

Already the flames were spreading away from the original trail. The cars flanking it were becoming engulfed. They were well primed to burn. Engines and tanks and fuel lines caked with long-hardened gas and oil sludge. Interiors of parched foam and cloth.

And then there was the desert floor itself. A thick carpet of crumbled tire rubber, dried and seasoned by seven decades of sun. The blaze was expanding outward through it, mostly north from the fire line in the direction of the breeze, moving at maybe a fourth the speed a person could walk.

But that was deceptive, Paige knew. The fire was going to spread a lot faster than that, once it got going. She could already see the mechanism that would drive it. From the empty window frames of the compact car, burning scraps of upholstery were being channeled up into the night, riding high on thermals and wind, touching down again hundreds of feet to the north. A single glance along the line of burning vehicles showed her the same thing happening everywhere, as windows buckled in the intense heat.

Travis scanned the darkness to the north one last time, cupping his eyes against the glare of the flames.

No sign of Finn or his men.

The crumb-scattered ground around the compact car was beginning to ignite. It was time to get moving.

The three of them shared a look, and a few seconds later they were running south, with the growing fire to light their way.

CHAPTER THIRTY-ONE

The plan had been meant to have a much simpler execution. Certainly the idea had been straightforward enough: create a long line of flame south of town and let the wind carry it north, hopefully with enough speed to disrupt Finn's makeshift base of operations—especially the camera mast.

A very long fire trail had been necessary for two reasons. First, to maximize the chances of setting the entire city ablaze, and second, to give the three of them a broad curtain of heat behind which to hide, once Finn's people came after them.

That was how Travis had imagined it, anyway, even assuming Finn and his men were already moving toward them. Had the wall of flame gone up when the pursuers were still a quarter mile north, they'd have spotted the ignition source immediately and sprinted toward it to make the kill. Someone back at the camera mast would've guided them over their radios—would've tried to, anyway. But the sheet of flame would've made that impossible. The cameras couldn't have seen a thing to the south of it.

The three of them could've simply run like hell for any random place south of the fire line, then dug in and waited for the fire to consume the town. After that they'd be free to make their escape.

It probably would've worked well enough.

But Travis was much happier with how it'd actually played out.

Finn was down eight men, while their own casualties amounted to a sore spot on Travis's back where he'd landed on the Remington. All told, the face-off had shaken out pretty well in their favor.

They still picked out a spot south of the fire line to dig in, two hundred yards down from where the shooting had happened. They reached it, then turned and stared north at the flames.

"Jesus," Travis said.

The height of the blaze surprised him the most. A minute earlier, when they'd been right next to it, it'd just cleared the tops of the tallest vehicles.

It was twice that height now.

From this angle they could see the entire line, extending three miles to the east. The whole length was burning. Every vehicle that immediately bordered it had thick tongues of flame seething from its windows.

From this position it was impossible to see the fire's northward progress. The three of them began moving to the west for a better perspective. Travis was hesitant to go too far—they might step out from behind the fire's thermal curtain and become visible to anyone watching the camera mast's feeds. Assuming whoever was up there didn't have bigger concerns now, like getting the hell out of the fire's way.

They'd gone only a few hundred feet west before

they stopped and simply stared again. They had their answer.

The fire was advancing north faster than any of them could have hoped. The falling embers had triggered spot fires as far as half a mile north of the line. Each of these had already grown to bonfire size, massive cones of flame standing atop a dozen cars each, and blossoming outward through the tire crumbs. The bonfires were venting thousands of their own embers into the darkness toward Yuma.

The city would be an inferno in another five minutes.

That was the good news.

Travis could see the bad news just as easily.

The fire wasn't only spreading north.

He'd expected that problem to an extent—it was unavoidable—but he'd hoped the fire's progress in the other directions would be nominal.

It didn't look nominal.

The original fire line had spread south by at least four rows of cars, and from its starting point it'd expanded west by several rows as well, even crossing the wide driving lanes that ran north and south. The hotter the fire burned, the more rapidly it spread through the rubber crumbs.

Suddenly, about fifty feet along the original line, a bright fireball erupted with a heavy concussion sound. A still-sealed gasoline container in someone's trunk had burst in the heat. The blast sent burning fuel out in a fifty-foot radius.

It happened again five seconds later, this time at the southern edge of the advance. Just like that, there were half a dozen more vehicles burning.

"We'd better get the hell out of here," Paige said.

* * *

They went west. It was as safe as south or east, and it was familiar. They'd seen it on the way into town. They weren't going to run up against the edge of a canyon or a mountain ridge unexpectedly.

They ran for only a few minutes before they stopped to get what they needed for the last part of the plan.

Bikes.

Though they were everywhere—from almost any point in the expanse of cars it was possible to see one or two—in most cases they were children's. Or they were adult bikes with leather seats that'd long since baked off in the sun, leaving only exposed springs and foam.

The three they settled on—two on a car's trunk-rack and another in a pickup bed twenty yards away—were adult mountain bikes with fabric seats that hadn't been worn off.

The bikes' tires were long gone, but the desert's surface was essentially one big tire now, so Travis hoped the going would be about the same, or close enough.

He took from his pocket the second thing he'd searched for among the glove boxes earlier: a narrow canister of WD-40.

The desert air had preserved the bikes just fine, but the sun would have burned away any trace of their lubrication. They spent a minute thoroughly dousing the chains and gears and bearings with the oil. Then Travis lifted one of the bikes' back ends and gave its pedal a turn. It creaked for two seconds and then everything spun silently, smoothly.

Yuma was an uncannily good place to store

things for a long time. Travis found himself wondering if that figured in somehow—the place's capacity to keep metals and other things unchanged. If it *was* part of the puzzle, he couldn't see how it fit. But nothing else fit either, so far.

They mounted the bikes, then stared back at the city. The fire was gargantuan now. A hurricane of flame. No sense of the original line remained. It was simply a massive, misshapen oval, broadly curved along the three miles of its southern sweep, and radically extended northward, in branches and separate blazing islands that now reached well into the downtown area. In the deepest parts of the firestorm the flames towered three hundred feet up, and above them rose a column of smoke that looked like something from the last pages of the New Testament. The inferno churned upward into the smoke, merged with it, lit it from inside and out. The firelight shone out over the vast plain of cars. Millions of windshields caught it and reflected it upward, lighting the column of smoke to a height of three or four miles above the desert.

The edges of the fire zone were still growing quickly. Without the bikes, the three of them would probably be in trouble.

"I'm relatively new to Tangent," Bethany said. "Do you guys do stuff like this a lot?"

"Not so much," Paige said.

"It mostly seems to happen when I'm around," Travis said.

They watched for another thirty seconds. Then they turned, put up their kickstands and rode like hell.

* * *

Long before he reached the southern edge of town, Finn understood that the math was against him. Not linear math, either. Exponential math.

Flaming pieces of vehicle upholstery, some of them as big as handkerchiefs, were raining into the desert on every side, and far ahead of him.

He ran. His surviving men, Reyes and Hunt, ran with him. They were going north along one of the broad driving lanes. Ahead, just visible above the obstacle course of spot fires, the camera mast was still standing. Its aluminum framework glinted in the yellow light.

Grayling and the other four might still be there. If they weren't, he didn't know where the hell to find them. He wished he'd brought along one of the fucking two-ways. But even if he'd thought to do so, he probably would've elected not to, out of fear the static would tip off Paige Campbell and the others. Nowhere on his list of what-ifs had the present situation appeared.

Straight ahead, two broad patches of flame crept toward each other, closing the gap between them. To go around the far end of either one would cost half a minute. The way through the middle, right up the lane he and the others were running in, was the shortest. But the gap was shrinking. Rapidly.

Finn tried to pick up his speed. He found it nearly impossible. It was all he could do to keep his breathing under control as fumes from the burning rubber drenched the air. He could feel it covering his skin in a film. Could feel it in his eyes and his hair, too. No question the stuff was flammable as hell, and saturating his clothes by the second.

Thirty yards from the gap now. It was only the

width of the lane itself. The cars that defined it on both sides were fully engulfed.

Twenty yards.

Ten.

They were passing through the gap, three abreast, when something exploded in one of the vehicles' trunks. A shower of burning fuel sprayed everywhere. Finn stayed ahead of it. He was sure the others had too. Then he heard Reyes screaming. He stopped hard, his feet sliding on the rubber-coated soil—it'd taken on a greasy feel as the heat intensified—and looked back. Reyes was down, every inch of his clothing on fire. He was rolling, but it was no good. Instead of the ground putting him out, he was igniting the ground wherever he touched it. The tire crumbs, in their half-melted state, were releasing the oils they'd been made from. They were ready to burn on contact.

At the edge of his vision Finn saw Hunt sprinting back to help Reyes. There wasn't even time to scream the warning. Half a second later the fire had both of them.

Finn took a step toward them anyway. An involuntary move. Not even a gesture. A wish, at best.

He could do nothing. He didn't even have a gun with which to put them out of their suffering.

Another trunk exploded. Close by. He couldn't stay here. Grayling and the others might still be possible to save. He turned and sprinted north again.

A minute later he rounded another fire and came to the south end of Fourth Avenue. He saw that it was hopeless. The whole city was burning. Every building. Every car in the streets. Far ahead he could see Grayling's laptops melting in the inferno. He couldn't see Grayling. Or any of the other four. They'd run for it. They weren't going to make it. There was no escape in any direction.

Finn stared at the bone drifts heaped against the buildings. Flames from first-story windows twisted and writhed through them. Blackened them. Flickered between ribs. Darted like snake tongues from the mouths and eyes of skulls.

He leveled the cylinder and switched it on.

The rubber surface of the desert didn't make up for the lack of bike tires, but riding was still a hell of a lot better than walking.

Travis, Paige, and Bethany circled north to the west side of town, keeping well beyond the outskirts. They found I–8 near the spot where they'd pulled off of it earlier—technically seventy-three years and a couple months earlier—and headed west toward whatever was left of Imperial, California.

They rode for half the night. They made ten miles an hour, riding on the hardened ground just off the freeway. The freeway itself, cleared of tire crumbs by the wind, was too rough on the bike rims.

Every time they stopped to rest they stared at the fire. It grew by miles each hour, even as it fell increasingly far behind them. It was the most absorbing thing Travis had ever seen. The central mass of the firestorm had to be well over a thousand feet high now. Like a campfire you could fit a mountain into.

Ten miles shy of Imperial they found the edge of the mass of parked cars. It ended in a more-or-less straight line, vanishing into the darkness north and south of I–8.

They rode into the town. The irrigated fields that'd once surrounded it were long gone. There was no way to even tell where the fields had met the desert. It was *all* desert now.

Imperial was as well preserved as Yuma, but it was empty. No cars. No bones. No bodies. They rode through its silent streets in the half-light from the distant fire. They scared up a barn owl among the crates of a shipping yard. They caught a glimpse of its pale face and deep black eyes and then it was gone, flapping away into the night.

They rode out to the middle of what they judged to have been cropland and ditched the bikes. They opened the iris and stepped through into moist rows of cotton plants, thirty yards from a massive wheeled sprinkler line trundling slowly across the field.

Travis surveyed the surrounding landscape for any sign of police flashers, or the beacon lights of helicopters. He saw nothing. The Homeland Security response must be concentrated on Yuma, fifty miles back east.

They walked into town and a found a motel just off the freeway that didn't require ID. They got a room with two queen-sized beds. The nightstand clock showed two thirty in the morning. Paige and Bethany took the first bed and Travis took the second. They collapsed fully dressed atop the bedcovers and were asleep within a minute.

CHAPTER THIRTY-TWO

Finn had been on the phone for hours. The entire flight back from Yuma and better than ninety minutes in his office. He was standing on his balcony now, staring across D.C. at all the places that'd been on the other ends of his calls. Dark silhouettes of buildings with a few lights on, half an hour before sunrise.

He had one call left to make.

He leaned on the rail. He dialed. Three rings and then a voice answered. "Isaac?"

"Yes," Finn said. "I've spoken with President Currey. I've spoken with everyone who matters. We've come to an agreement. We're not happy with it, but there's no other option in play. Paige Campbell and her friends were in Yuma for several hours, and now they're long gone. We don't know what they saw there, and we don't know who they're talking to right now. We have most of the big dogs in our camp, but we don't have everyone, and given time . . . these people could hurt us. They could pull the whole plan apart."

He took a breath. Let it out slowly. "We can't

wait as long as we meant to," he said. "Umbra needs to happen now. Right now."

He heard a sharp inhalation on the line. "But it's not ready. Entire segments of the plan—"

"The fundamentals are ready," Finn said. "In principle it can work. And in one sense we have an advantage now. We have the cylinder. We can go to the final location and see what's there in 2084. Who knows what we can learn from that."

"Are you going there now?"

"I'll stay in D.C. for the next twenty-four hours. I expect Campbell to come back here and try to contact people she hopes she can trust. I doubt she and the others really appreciate the extent of our connections, in which case there's every chance they'll trip a wire somewhere."

There was a long silence on the line. The sound of uncertainty. Reluctance. Acceptance.

"Currey is already getting started on his end," Finn said. "How long will it take on yours? How long to actually set the plan in motion?"

Another silence. Then: "A day or two. Maybe less. Christ, are we really doing this?"

Finn heard as much excitement as anxiety in the voice.

"Yes, we're really doing this. None of us would've chosen to rush it, but if it's that or never do it at all . . ."

"I agree. I'm scared as hell, but I agree."

"I knew you would. Get started on it right away. I'll talk to you soon."

"I love you."

"I love you too, Audra."

PART III

ARICA

CHAPTER THIRTY-THREE

Richard Garner woke to his alarm at five in the morning. He exercised for thirty minutes. He showered, dressed in khakis and a gray cotton tennis shirt, and went to his den. Beyond the windows Central Park lay in amber light and long, early shadows, thirty stories below.

He switched on the computer. While the operating system loaded, he left the room and crossed the broad stone hallway to the kitchen. He toasted two slices of wheat bread and poured a glass of orange juice. He took the plate and glass back to the den, sat at the computer, and clicked open his work in progress. The book was still only an outline. It'd begun as a study of Ulysses S. Grant's time in office, with a focus on the difference between overseeing a war and overseeing a nation, but the research had led elsewhere. Now the book was shaping up into a broader examination of every president who'd held a position of military authority before taking office. An analysis of the pros and cons regarding what that kind of experience brought to a president's perspective. He wasn't sure yet on which side he would ultimately come down—whether generals tended to make good presidents or not. The evidence pointed to a number of conclusions, each conditional to time and place and political climate, and he'd only just begun digging through it. He hoped his own military background—he hadn't made general, but he'd commanded a SEAL team for the bulk of the seventies—would provide him more insight than bias.

It was involving work.

Which he needed right now.

Would almost certainly need for the rest of his life.

He stayed in the den all morning and into the early afternoon. Mostly he sat at the computer, but at times he paced before the windows, looking out over the park and the city.

He took a break at one o'clock. He had a sandwich and a 7UP. He plugged his iPod into the sound system, piped the music through the residence and did some random work around the place. Though he'd been here for two years, some part of him still felt like he hadn't settled in yet. Like he was still getting used to it. Still getting used to living *anywhere* on his own.

The residence took up an entire floor of the building, though only two thirds of it made up his own living space. The other third comprised the living and working quarters of the Secret Service detail that guarded him. He played poker with them, most nights.

He quit the chores at four o'clock. Turned off the music. Went back to the den. He opened a heavy box of yellowed, sleeve-protected documents that'd come from the archives of the New York Public Library. The pages were by no means a part of the library's lending collection. Even as non-circulating reference material they were pretty hard to gain access to. Garner felt a bit of guilt over the privilege his resume afforded him, but not enough to lose sleep over. It was just much easier for the library to send the stuff to him than to have him and his security footprint dropping in every time he needed to verify a quote. Besides, he was an old friend of the place. He'd worked there in his college years. He'd probably walked past this very box a hundred times.

The day was clear and bright, but by five o'clock the sunlight in the room had diminished a bit. He turned on the lamp beside his reading chair. George Washington's handwriting was hard enough to make out as it was.

At a quarter past five a cool breeze filtered into the room from the hallway. It stirred the papers on the table beside him. It took him two or three seconds to realize that a breeze should be impossible. None of the residence's windows were open.

For a moment he only stared at the doorway. Tried to make sense of it. There was an intake for the HVAC system just out in the hall. No reason air should be coming *out* of it, but maybe some kind of maintenance was going on. It was all he could think of.

All he could think of that was benign, anyway. In recent years he'd grown used to considering more threatening scenarios for given situations.

He set aside the page he was reading. He stood, curious but not afraid. He could clap his hands and have six agents with submachine guns coming in through separate access points in quite a bit less than ten seconds. They didn't normally monitor video feeds of the residence, but any sharp sound above 85 decibels would trip the acoustic alarm and bring them running.

He crossed the room and stepped into the hallway. The main entry was still closed and locked. The kitchen was empty. He turned toward the living room—and flinched.

People.

Three of them.

Right there.

Garner was an instant from shouting to trigger the alarm when he realized he recognized one of them. Paige Campbell.

Tangent.

He felt his fear turn to anger. He advanced on her and the others. It occurred to him only in passing to wonder why all three of them had damp hair and clothing.

"We're sorry to intrude—" Paige said.

Garner cut her off. "Leave. Right now. However the hell you came—"

Paige stepped aside, and in the gap between her and the other two, Garner saw where the wind was coming from.

He stopped. His anger faded. He didn't know what to feel, suddenly. All he could do was stare.

Travis watched Garner's reaction. The initial anger made sense. The man's wife had died because of her work with Tangent; he couldn't have been ecstatic to see them here.

Now as Garner stared at the iris, Travis stepped

aside, along with Bethany, to give him an unbroken view.

Garner moved toward it. Started to say something. Stopped.

Then it contracted shut in front of him, and he blinked, confused.

"Sorry," Bethany said. "Hang on."

She was holding the cylinder. She looked around for a place to set it. Pointed to a narrow table along the nearest wall, and looked at Garner.

"Is this okay?"

The guy could barely process what the hell she was asking him. He stared at her for a second and then his eyes went back to the spot where the iris had vanished.

Bethany took his silence for a *yes*. She set the cylinder on the table and found a heavy bookend to brace it with.

Travis glanced at the floor-to-ceiling windows on the south wall, facing down Central Park West toward Midtown. The park itself filled the left half of the view. The right half was full of the varied architecture of the Upper West Side. Travis guessed the buildings ranged in age from a few years to well over a hundred. The day was beautiful, with huge, slow clouds dragging their shadows across the sweep of the city.

Then Bethany switched on the cylinder and the iris appeared again, and Travis saw the other Manhattan. The one they'd been looking at for the past several minutes as they ascended the ruins of Garner's building.

That version of the borough was in the same condition as D.C. for the most part. The entire island was carpeted with dense boreal forest, from which rose the corroded remains of the city skyline.

What set it apart from D.C.—more so than Travis had imagined until he'd seen it for himself—was simply the scale of the ruins. In D.C. the sixteen-story office building had looked enormous. It would've been lost among the ankles of the giants that stood rusting here. The remnants of skyscrapers below Central Park formed a solid visual screen standing eight hundred feet high—higher still in some places. The October wind sighed through it, finding odd angles and rivet holes whichever way it blew. It sounded like a chorus of a million reed flutes, playing soft and low in the dead framework of the city.

All of it lay cold and misty under bruised knots of cloud cover. Each time the wind gusted through the iris it blew a wisp of moisture into the room.

Garner remained where he'd been standing.

"It won't shut again," Bethany said. "You can go close to it. You can lean right through."

He looked at her. Looked at each of them in turn. He managed a nod, and crossed the room to the iris. He stared through. For more than three minutes he said nothing. Then he closed his eyes. He shook his head and lowered it.

"Tell me everything," he said.

CHAPTER THIRTY-FOUR

It took just over an hour. They sat around a coffee table in the den and relayed the story in detail. All that had happened. All that they knew. All that they didn't know.

When they'd finished, Garner sat in silence for a moment.

"You must know something about this, sir," Bethany said. "If President Currey knows about Umbra, I can't imagine you don't."

"I've met Isaac Finn on two or three occasions," Garner said. "Just brief conversations, each time. I wanted to like him, given the work he'd done. But I didn't. There was something about him that seemed . . . contrived, I guess. I had the feeling that the small talk wasn't really small talk. That it was something else. Like a test. Like it was some kind of psych exam, and my answers meant something to him. I saw it when he spoke to others, too. That was my sense of the man. But I was the outlier. Finn's made a lot of close friends in Washington over the years. Currey's one of them. That's why Currey's in on Umbra, whatever it is. It's sure as hell not something you learn about by just having a high enough security clearance. I had the highest kind you can have, and I never heard a thing about it."

He stood from his chair. Went to the window.

"What I *can* tell you I didn't learn as president. I learned it on the Senate Select Committee on Intelligence, years earlier. And it's not about Finn. It's about his wife, before she was his wife. When she was a grad student at MIT named Audra Nash."

He was quiet a moment, thinking, his back to the room. Travis looked past him out the windows. He could see the evening shadows of the Upper West Side easing across the park.

Garner dropped his hand to a huge globe next to the window, resting in an ornate walnut floor mount. He spun it absently. Travis imagined it was something he did often, an unconscious habit.

"Audra came before the committee behind closed doors, with an unusual request. She wanted clearance to review certain restricted military documents, as part of the research for her doctoral thesis. In exchange, the thesis itself would be classified and available only to certain people. Our people."

"What was she doing her doctoral work on?" Paige said.

"ELF radio transmissions. Extremely Low Frequency. What we use for communicating with submarines."

"That doesn't sound like something an aerospace candidate would be working on," Paige said.

"It was, in her case. She was researching ways to transmit ELF signals using satellites."

Paige looked somewhat thrown by that.

Bethany looked floored. Like she could almost laugh. "That's ridiculous. ELF transmitters are over thirty miles long. How could you put something like that in orbit?"

"And why would you want to, anyway?" Paige said. "ELF has worked fine for half a century, just the way it is."

Travis could see just enough of Garner's reflection to make out a vague smile. Then the man finally turned from the window.

"There's a bit more to it than that," he said. "Audra wasn't interested in using it for submarines. She was looking to use it on people."

None of the vacant expressions in the room changed.

Garner crossed to the big chair before his desk. He swiveled it to face the coffee table and sank into it.

"We started working on ELF in the fifties, when it was becoming obvious that subs were going to play a major role in the Cold War. We built the transmitters in remote places. One well-known site in the Upper Peninsula of Michigan. Another in northern Canada, not so well known. The technical hurdles to building the damn things were significant. Consider what they had to do: broadcast in all directions with enough signal strength to reach submarines anywhere in the world, hundreds of feet down in conductive saltwater. It's amazing they worked at all. But even once they *did* work, there were . . . other problems. Health effects for personnel that worked and lived close to the transmitters, where the signals were highly concentrated. Cognitive issues in a few rare cases, but the most common problems by far were mood disruptions. Conditions that mimicked the symptoms of bipolar disorder, though with greater severity. Much greater, at times. There were personnel who had to be subdued because they were—for lack of a better word—*high*. That was how they described it themselves, after the fact. At the other end there was severe depression. There were suicides. Lots of them."

"We still use ELF," Bethany said. "Are those problems still going on?"

Garner shook his head. "They got a handle on it within the first decade. Isolated the causes. At high enough doses, certain wavelengths were trouble. Certain distances from the transmitter were trouble, because of harmonics. Like that. The engineers worked around it." He offered something like a smile, though nothing about it looked happy. "But by then, certain people were thinking about the side effects in very different ways. Thinking about how to enhance them instead of eliminate them. How to control them. How to use them as weapons in their own right."

"Christ," Travis said. But he could already see the obvious appeal of that kind of technology. A tank battle or a naval engagement would be a hell of a lot easier to win if everyone on the other side was suddenly experiencing what felt like a crack high.

"They actually built systems like that?" Paige said.

"They tried. We tried, the Brits tried, Russia tried. Everyone worked out the useful frequencies easily enough. Even found ways to heighten the effects with on-off modulation, or rapid oscillation between frequencies. Scary stuff. Even test subjects, who were well aware of what was happening to them and who were exposed for as little as an hour, had severe reactions. It was a hell of a weapon. Two big problems, though: you couldn't move it, and you couldn't point it." He nodded at Bethany. "Like you said, an ELF transmitter is huge. It's not some dish you can swivel around toward a target. It's a straight-line antenna between leads, dozens of miles apart. You basically just have an effective zone around the signal source. So unless you can talk your enemy into lining up right there, nice and neat, there's not a hell of a lot you can do with a weapon like that. And that was about the extent of it. We kicked it around for a while in the sixties and seventies, looked for ways to make it selective, directional. Probably threw half a billion dollars at it. I'm sure the other guys did the same. But at some point, when you're not seeing any results, you have to cut your losses. There are better things to spend the defense budget on."

He glanced out at the city, shrugged with his eyebrows, looked at the three of them again.

"So you might imagine it got our attention when Audra Nash came to us in 1986 and said she had an idea. A way to broadcast ELF using satellites. If it were almost any other person—much less a student—the committee wouldn't have even taken the meeting. But Miss Nash had some credibility to back up her claim. Her work as a grad student had already influenced the design of next-gen communications satellites. She was smart as hell, and she knew the field better than probably anyone.

What she wanted from us was access to the results of all the ELF research over the years, all the raw data from the experiments in directing it, focusing it. We barely had to think about it. First, the data wasn't all that sensitive. It was just a detailed list of all the things that didn't work. And all the countries out there who could possibly want to steal it didn't need to: they already had the same data, based on their own failures. Second, we thought her idea might actually have merit. She was brilliant, she had a track record, and she was coming to this problem with fresh eyes. The concept she had in mind was certainly different enough. We hadn't tried anything like it in all our efforts."

"But how could it work at all?" Bethany said. "Just basic physics should make it impossible for a satellite. A transmitter has to be big enough to handle the wavelengths it generates, and ELF waves are huge. Hundreds of miles long."

Garner nodded. "Her idea was radical. I don't pretend to have understood it in detail, but essentially it was this: ELF waves occur naturally in the Earth's atmosphere. The sun radiates them, and lightning strikes produce them, too. It's all random, of course. All noise, no signal. And even if the frequencies that affect people happen to appear, they're drowned out in the clutter and nothing happens. Audra Nash believed a satellite, transmitting much shorter wavelengths with the right precision, could cancel out certain frequencies of natural ELF over a given target area. Could allow us to pick and choose *which* frequencies to cancel out . . . and which to leave intact." He looked at Bethany. "So you're right. A satellite can't broadcast ELF, but in theory it could disrupt it where it naturally occurs, and whittle away everything but the useful ranges. At which point, they would certainly affect people. And it would be precisely targetable. You could influence a few blocks. Or a whole city. Or an area much, much larger than that."

No one said anything. They waited.

"So we gave her the go-ahead," Garner said. "Gave her access to everything we had. She dove into it. Lived and breathed it. She came back before the committee six months later. With a blueprint."

"Did anyone build it?" Paige said.

"Nope."

Paige looked confused. "Why not?"

"Because it was still a long shot. Even with a good blueprint there's trial and error, details to hammer out in the prototype. That can be expensive even if you're modifying a Humvee. For a satellite, tack on a couple zeroes."

"Come on," Travis said. "The hubcaps on the stealth bomber probably cost a million apiece. Since when does the Pentagon get sticker shock?"

Garner smiled. "There's another reason, but it's even less believable." He considered how to frame it. "It's like this. In the early days, when everyone was looking for a straightforward way to weaponize this technology, there was an urgency to figure it out. Get it before the other guys. That makes sense if you think there's some big, obvious solution out there, the kind that everyone will eventually stumble onto. But Audra's idea wasn't like that. It was obscure as hell, based on an overlap of knowledge probably no one but she had. There was a good chance that nobody else in the world would ever come up with it. But they'd be more than happy to copy ours, if we went ahead with the project. You hear people talk about the atomic genie coming out of the bottle in 1945. Like if we didn't let it out, nobody ever would have. It's probably not true. Fission's not exactly an unheard-of concept. But Audra's satellite design *was*. And we just thought . . . why do it? Why bring the world into an age defined by something like this? So we sat on it. Locked the design away. Audra understood, though I'm sure she was disappointed. She got out of the design game after that. Went off to Harvard, got her other doctorate in philosophy, got into relief work. Married Finn. I didn't hear about her again until 1995, when that little dustup happened with the paper those two tried to publish."

Paige had been looking at the floor. She looked up now. "Did you see a copy of it?"

Garner shook his head. "Shredded and burned before it could make the rounds. I had a pretty good guess what it said, though. Maybe you can guess it, now."

Travis thought of what they'd just learned. Tried to put it in the context of Finn and Audra's lives, in 1995—just back from Rwanda, permanently burned out on their life's work.

"Holy shit," Travis said. "They wanted to use that kind of satellite technology on places like Rwanda. That's it, isn't it? If you had control over how strongly it affected people, you could do that. Target the whole region with some minimal exposure, something that creates the effect of a mild high, euphoria, whatever, just to quiet everything down. Sedate the hell out of the place until—what, a peacekeeping force could go in and get control? The peacekeepers would be affected too, but maybe with the right training to anticipate it . . ."

He trailed off, thinking it over. Considering the implications. He saw Garner nodding.

"My assumption at the time," Garner said. "Point for point. I'm sure they glossed over the specifics of how it worked—revealing those would be treason—but yes, I imagine they advocated something very close to what you're talking about."

Travis looked again at Paige and Bethany. Wondered if they were thinking the same thing he was. He guessed they were.

"It doesn't actually sound like a bad idea," Travis said.

Garner offered another smile. "No. It doesn't. Not if all you did with it was stop genocides. But how long would that last? And think about it from a human-rights perspective. A right-to-privacy perspective. A global superpower using satellites to screw with people's heads. It's right out of Orwell. Is it any wonder Audra's father saw his career flash before his eyes when he heard about it? What politician wants his name within a mile of a thing like that?"

"So that's it, then," Paige said. She looked around at each person in the room, as if surprised the answer had dropped so neatly into their laps. "That's Umbra. This technology must actually exist by now, and in a few months something's going to go wrong with it. Catastrophically wrong."

Bethany was nodding. "We know Audra left Harvard in 'ninety-five and went to work for Longbow Aerospace, designing satellites. Somehow that company must have agreed to build her ELF design, and keep the work secret. And even after she died, Finn could've kept the project going. Jesus . . . if Umbra happens four months from now, these satellites must be in orbit as we speak. A whole constellation of them, with global coverage like GPS."

Garner looked thoughtful. "I know about the Longbow satellites in some detail—at least the details the company chose to put forward. The system was supposed to be a low-orbit network for satellite phones, meant to compete with the cellular market in the nineties. As the story went, Audra worked on the project for the last two years of her life. By the time they actually launched the things, in 'ninety-nine, it was a lost cause. Cell phone transmission was getting dirt cheap, and Longbow couldn't match it. We ended up subsidizing the whole damn thing and using it for some military voice traffic. The sats actually work for that, but only just. Which makes sense, I guess, if their main purpose is something else entirely."

"All the pieces of this thing fit," Paige said. "Even the long delay since 1999, when they launched the satellites. Finn's had to do years of political work on the ground before he can use them. Suppose he wants to demonstrate this technology on a current conflict zone, someplace like Darfur. If it works, it's proof of concept, and then he can begin publicly arguing for it as policy. But he'd need all kinds of powerful friends on board to actually pull that off. He'd at least need them not standing in his way. If at all possible, he'd want the president on his side." She looked at Garner. "As you said, no politician would want to be tied to this, especially not early on, when it's just an untried, terrifying idea. It makes sense that President Currey would make a drastic move to keep it secret. Like the attack on our motorcade." She nodded, tying it all up in her mind. "This is the answer. Umbra is the plan to finally go live with these satellites, some trial run somewhere, in the next few months. And apparently, it goes pretty fucking badly. Unintended consequences on a global scale, however the hell that would happen. Some critical loss of control, and then . . . then I guess what happened to a few ELF engineers in the fifties happens to the whole damn world, and all that's left are panic options. How Yuma figures in, I don't know. Maybe *they* won't know, at the time. Maybe it's nothing but a distraction to give people purpose at the end, keep them from rioting in the streets. Maybe there never *were* any Erica flights."

Silence came to the room. Travis listened to the groan of traffic far below, dampened by the heavy glass.

"I've been mulling that explanation for the better part of an hour," Garner said, "as I've listened to your story. It seems obvious, and it covers almost everything. But where it breaks, it breaks completely."

Paige waited for him to go on.

"The failure itself," Garner said. "I don't see how it can happen. It'd be one thing if we were talking about a bacterial agent, or a virus, or even a computer worm—something that can get away from you and wreak havoc. But if satellites malfunction, we can shut them down. It's a few keystrokes and a transmission. It's easy."

"Could an error on board the satellites block receipt of the signal?" Paige said. There was a lost-cause note in her voice, like she already agreed with Garner and was just exhausting possibilities.

"I guess," Garner said. "But we're talking about dozens of satellites. If there's a glitch, it's probably not with all of them. Probably just one. In which case we'd shoot it down. Strap an ASAT missile under an F-15, launch it from seventy or eighty thousand feet up. It's not easy, but we've done it. We could do it again if we had to. If it came to it, we could shoot down every single one of them. Enlist Russia's and China's help if it's a time-critical thing. Give them the satellites' positions and vectors, sing a few rounds of 'Kumbaya,' and start shooting until the job's done. We'd do it. It wouldn't take long. Days, not weeks." He made a face. Almost apologetic. Rested his hands in his lap. "So I still don't see how Bleak December happens, playing out over a month or more."

"But everything else fits," Paige said. "The child's notebook we told you about, in the desert near Yuma. If you saw it for yourself . . . if you saw what this kid drew . . . it was just page after page of misery, with no visible cause—"

"I agree it fits," Garner said. "I'm sure these satellites are at the heart of this thing. And clearly someone makes a colossal fuckup somewhere along the line. But I can't for the life of me see what it is."

"Do we even need to know?" Travis said. "We know enough right now to make a move against them. With your connections, sir, there must be channels we can go through."

Garner nodded. "Absolutely. From this point

forward we take it slow and deliberate. Start with outsiders Finn would have no reason to be tied to. Figure out who we can trust, from there. Build our support until it's overwhelming and then, yes, we move. It'll work if we're careful. Hell, we've got a few months to play with."

CHAPTER THIRTY-FIVE

Rudy Dyer was the newest man on the protective detail. He'd been on board only three weeks. By no stretch was he green—he'd served four years with the Foreign Missions Branch and two with the Naval Observatory—but there were aspects of this new role that he was still getting used to. As Secret Service work went, protecting a former president was maybe a tick more relaxed than protecting a sitting one. The job was more relaxed, anyway—the agents weren't.

What Dyer had the hardest time adjusting to was the added familiarity here, between the agents and the focus of their work—Richard Garner. The poker games seemed a little out of line. No protocols were broken, of course—the agents playing the game were always off duty at the time, while the standard minimum of six on-duty agents remained in the watch-room. Still, it wasn't the sort of thing that would've happened in the White House, off-duty or otherwise.

Dyer was getting a feel for it, though. It was just a different fit, that was all. These were still the most professional and disciplined security personnel in the world, and he got on well with them. He got on well with Garner, too. He just didn't plan to sit in on the poker games anytime soon.

It was 6:44 in the evening. Sunlight shone through the west-side windows in long, tinted shafts. The watch-room—actually a good-sized suite of rooms—occupied the southwest quadrant of the building's floor, including the stairs and elevator accesses. From the terminal at his desk, Dyer could cycle through the feeds from every security camera in and around Garner's residence. Protocol allowed for respecting the man's privacy, however, which meant that the residence's interior feeds were set aside in a separate batch and ignored under normal circumstances.

Every fifteen minutes Dyer clicked through all of the other feeds: those covering the corridors, elevators, stairwells, and even a few angles looking across the outer face of the building at this height— even the remote possibility of someone rappelling down from the rooftop had to be allowed for.

Dyer's watched ticked to 6:45.

He opened the camera feeds. Skipped through them with precise keystrokes. Studied each one for exactly three seconds. Corridors clear. Elevators clear. Stairwells clear.

On the third exterior feed, which looked across the east side of the building past the windows of Garner's den, he stopped.

There was a young woman sitting in a chair a few feet in from the windows. Dark hair and eyes. Maybe thirty. Very attractive. Garner himself was just visible at the edge of the frame, sitting at his desk chair. Looking casual. Staring off through the window at nothing.

Who was the woman?

Dyer minimized the feed and clicked open the logbook for the security checkpoint. No one could enter or exit the residence—not even Garner himself—without passing through it and being logged with a time stamp.

There was no entry in the file for anyone coming or going today.

Or yesterday.

The day before that, Garner had logged out to have lunch with the governor in Midtown, and logged back in three hours later, alone.

Dyer quickly skipped through the past five days' entries. Nothing but Garner coming and going by himself.

He minimized the logbook and opened the exterior feed again. The woman was still sitting there.

How the hell had she gotten in without it being noted?

Dyer could think of only one explanation. He hated to believe it. But what else was there?

He looked around. One other agent had a desk in this room. The other four were stationed elsewhere in the suite, the better to rush Garner's residence from multiple angles if the need arose.

The other agent in the room wasn't looking Dyer's way.

Dyer took out his cell phone, set it in its dock next to the terminal and waited for it to sync up. When it did, he captured a single frame of the video feed, clearly showing the woman's face, and sent it to the phone. He took it back out of the dock, then stood and left the room.

He stepped into the bathroom across the hall,

turned on the vent fan and the water for masking noise, and dialed a number on his phone. It was answered on the second ring.

"Greer."

"It's Dyer. Do you have a minute?"

"Sure."

Dyer explained about the woman, and sent the image to Greer's phone. He also relayed his hunch. Greer didn't like it any more than he did.

"I find that very, very hard to believe," Greer said.

"I'd prefer another theory myself," Dyer said. "Got one?"

The line was silent for a moment.

"I don't get the motive," Greer said. "Garner's a single man. If he wants to entertain a guest, it's his business. Why would he feel the need to hide it?"

"Maybe *she* wants to hide it. Maybe she's somebody. Or somebody's wife."

Another silence on the line.

Then Greer said, "If Garner's asking these guys to keep someone out of the logbook, and they're actually doing it, their balls are gonna be hanging from the director's trailer hitch before the week's out."

"Which is why I called you," Dyer said. "I'd rather keep mine hanging where they are."

Greer was quiet again. Dyer could hear a pen or pencil tapping on his desk. A fast, tense rhythm.

"Fuck," Greer said. "All right. Let me run it up to a few guys at the top, and a couple friends at Justice. See if there's a precedent for handling something like this. And I'll see if anyone recognizes her. I'll get back to you."

CHAPTER THIRTY-SIX

Garner spent the rest of the evening compiling a list of names, drawn from records on his computer as well as paper documents. He came up with close to a hundred, and then began going through them systematically, using his computer to pull up detailed information on each of them. To Travis they appeared to be mostly military and FBI personnel. Garner made shorthand marks next to some of the names. Others he simply crossed out.

Bethany offered to help. Garner looked puzzled as to what she could do. She rattled off her credentials in about thirty seconds, and he told her to pull up a chair.

Night settled on the city. The skyline lit up in random bits and fragments until the whole thing was blazing. Travis stood at the living-room windows and looked down over the park. From beneath the forested expanses, warm light from footpaths streamed up into the darkness.

Paige came up beside him. They stood there for a while, silent.

"Never been here before," Travis said.

"Beautiful, isn't it?"

He nodded.

"My mom lived here for a long time when I was a kid," Paige said. "That building right over there. The brick one with the blue light on the roof." She pointed across the park. Leaned against him so he could sight down her arm.

He felt her skin against his. After a second she seemed to notice it too. Seemed to notice that he noticed. She didn't say anything, just shifted back to her own balance, putting a few inches between them.

It occurred to him that they hadn't been alone with each other at any point since she'd stepped through the iris from Finn's office yesterday. It'd been the three of them, hardly more than an arm's length from one another, every minute of the way. Until now.

The silence was suddenly harder to take.

"So you spent a lot of time here?" he said.

"Yeah. Every summer. And Thanksgiving or Christmas, every other year, that kind of thing."

"That must've been fun. Hanging out here as a kid."

She shrugged. "I liked it. Plenty to do."

It felt like talking to someone's sister-in-law at a graduation party. Like he didn't know that she liked to sleep on her side, naked, and that she preferred someone's shoulder to a pillow. Like he didn't know what her earlobes tasted like, among other things. Like none of it had ever happened.

It would've been better if it hadn't. The past two years would've been easier. He would've gotten more sleep.

She turned from the window. Met his eyes. Looked away again.

"Obviously, this won't take anything like four months to resolve," she said.

Travis nodded.

"A few weeks at most," Paige said. "Finn might have a lot of the top people, but Garner will get everyone else. However it shakes out after that, whatever it looks like on the news, that'll be the end of it. I'm sure Tangent will be involved, but as far as the three of us shouldering the whole thing . . . I guess that's over with, now."

"My part is, for sure," Travis said.

She looked at him again. "If you want, we can set you up with another identity, wherever you want to live, whoever you want to be."

"Anything like the last one will do," he said.

"Okay."

Neither spoke for a while. They watched the city. Far below on the opposite sidewalk, a college-aged couple went by. The girl turned to face the guy, grabbed each of his hands in hers and drew his arms up overhead, bouncing up and down on her feet. Happy as hell about something.

"You could come back," Paige said. "You know that."

For a moment Travis didn't answer. He turned and found her staring at him. Saw in her eyes everything she wasn't saying. Saw an invitation back to more than just Border Town.

"I'm sorry," he said.

She held the stare a second longer. Whatever hurt she felt, it was buried deep.

"Okay," she said.

She turned from the window. Went to a big leather chair and sat. She leaned back and closed her eyes.

"If I could explain it, I would," Travis said.

"I didn't ask you to."

"I would anyway."

She said nothing more.

Travis crossed to the couch. He set Bethany's backpack on the floor. Heard the clink of the SIG 220 inside, among all the shotgun shells. He'd left the shotgun itself on the other side of the iris, a couple stories down in the skeleton of the building. He'd leaned it out of the rain under an intact metal panel a few yards from the stairwell. It hadn't seemed like a good idea to step into the president's living room with a twelve-gauge in his hands.

He lay on his back on the couch. Sank into it. Shut his eyes. Listened to the keystrokes of the computer in the next room, and the murmur of the city.

He wondered what it would be like to just tell her. He could do it right now. He even had the note folded up in his wallet. A message from some future version of Paige, which she'd bounced in and out of the Breach so that it would emerge in the past—Tangent didn't know how to do that yet, but clearly they would, someday. Paige's message to herself had arrived two summers ago, with a specific instruction: *kill Travis Chase.*

Some future Travis had countered that move. Had created the Whisper—that wasn't its real name, of course—using Breach technology, and bounced it much further back: to 1989. The Whisper had then gone to work rearranging everything, stacking the deck to put Travis—his present self—in place to intercept Paige's message when it emerged.

Even now Travis could only make passing sense of it. It was like watching a snake eat its own tail. Why hadn't there been a counter-counter-move from the future Paige? And then the future Travis? Could those versions of themselves even exist anymore? Wasn't everything on a different track now? He didn't expect to ever understand it.

But he could tell her.

He could sit up right now and look her in the eyes and say it all. He could show her the note.

He'd feel better then, though it wouldn't mean he could accept her invitation. However she responded, he was never returning to Tangent. It simply wasn't an option, so long as he remained in the dark about what had corrupted the other Travis there, along the track of that original future.

And he would always be in the dark about that.

He didn't sit up.

He lay there and listened to her breathing. Remembered what it'd sounded like from an inch away.

"You want to know the real reason I'm against sealing the Breach?" Paige said.

Travis opened his eyes and looked at her. Hers were still closed.

"Yes," he said.

"It's that every morning I wake up and wonder if, that day, something good will finally come through. Something *really* good, that we could use to help the whole world. Why shouldn't that happen? We've seen all kinds of things that could've *hurt* the whole world. And we've seen small-scale good things. Like the Medic. Any emergency room could do miracles with it, but you could only give it to one of them. And how would you explain where it came from? It's always like that with the good ones. Did you ever hear of an entity called a Poker Chip?"

"No."

"It's bright red, about the size of a quarter. Not quite unique but very rare—only five of them have egressed over the years. You pick one up and it attaches itself to your skin by tendril extensions you can barely see. Scary at first, so we tested them on animals. It took a while to realize that their function is to slow down aging. They cut the speed to about one third, and they work on everything—bugs, mice, rats. So I guess if any five people really wanted to, they could wear them twenty-four/seven and outlive all their friends. Nice, right?"

She opened her eyes and met his.

"I have to believe," she said, "that someday, something will come through that's good on the scale of the world. Something we'd pop the champagne corks and break into tears over. Something history would pivot on. That thought gets me through all the rest of it."

A silence passed. Not quite as awkward as before. Paige looked down at her hands in her lap.

"I understand that there's something you really, really cannot tell me," she said. "And I understand that it has nothing to do with how you feel about me. Because I *know* how you feel about me. Yesterday morning, when I stepped out of Finn's office onto that girder and saw you standing five feet away, it didn't surprise me in the least. I hadn't expected it—but when I saw you, it seemed like the most normal thing in the world that you'd be standing there. That you'd be there for me. So I know. And I understand . . . even if I *don't* understand. That's an ability the Breach trained into me a long time ago. Getting it without getting it. I get that whatever this is, it just *is*, and that you wish like hell it wasn't."

She looked at him again, and he held her stare.

"Thank you," he said.

"You're welcome."

She managed something like a smile. He tried to return it. Then he sank into the couch again, eyes on the ceiling.

He heard her stand, and then she was there, climbing onto the couch, squeezing into the space between him and the backrest. Neither of them spoke. A second later they were pressed together as tightly as they could get, his mouth on her forehead, kissing it. Everything about her filling up his world, warm and soft and vulnerable and alive, her breath against his throat, her arms tense as she held on.

His sense of time was gone. This close to her, he could lose hours and not notice. That in itself was excruciating, because this little time was all they were ever going to get. He could already feel it going away.

He thought of what she'd said earlier, about seeing him on top of the office building in D.C. He thought of how close he'd come to *not* being there. A minute's delay would've done it. The timing had actually been closer than that, even. He and Bethany had been maybe ten seconds from opening their own iris when Finn opened his. The gunfight—if it could be called that—wouldn't have played out half as favorably without that turn of events. Without the element of surprise, there would've been real crossfire, and Paige would have been stuck without cover at the center of it. Her chances would've been close to zero.

He kissed her hairline. Held her tighter. Tried not to think of how it might've gone. Shit happened, that was all. Some of it had to be good.

He shut his eyes and breathed in the smell of her hair.

Five seconds later he opened them again.

A thought had come to him. A memory. Sharp and insistent. Something that'd happened just after Finn opened the iris from his office. Paige had come out, but not right away. First Finn himself had come to the opening and stared out through it—Travis had stayed beyond his peripheral vision. Then the guy had ordered Paige out onto the beam. That part Travis remembered clearly. But there was something else. Something before that. Something Finn had whispered right at the beginning, seconds after stepping up to the iris. Travis had been just close enough to hear it. It'd escaped his notice at the time—there'd been more pressing things to focus on—and it hadn't sounded like anything important.

Now he tried to call it back, because something told him it was important, after all.

What'd Finn said?

He thought about it.

Seconds passed.

He remembered.

"Holy shit," Travis said.

Paige stirred in his arms, tilted her head back to meet his eyes.

"What?" she said.

For a long moment he couldn't answer. He was thinking back over every aspect of the past two days, seeing it all as it'd really been. Seeing what everything meant. It was like watching a film of a shattering wineglass being run in reverse. Every jagged piece of the thing twisting and tumbling, pulled inward toward its proper place by some logical gravity. From the first moment they'd looked through the iris, they'd been wrong about what they were seeing. Their biggest mistake had been right there at the outset, and every conclusion they'd built on it had been way off the mark.

"Travis, what is it?"

He blinked. Looked at her.

"I'll show you," he said.

And then against his every inclination, he let go of her and stood from the couch. He waited for her to get up, and they crossed the living room to the hallway and then the den.

Loose paper files were stacked everywhere in the room—on the desk, the coffee table, the chairs, the floor—in some kind of improvised Dewey decimal system.

"We've narrowed it to five people we're certain we trust," Garner said. "I've e-mailed them and set up a secure conference call—"

He cut himself off, having glanced up and seen Travis's expression.

Bethany looked up too.

They stared. Waited for Travis to speak.

But he didn't. Instead he made his way through the stacked files to the giant globe by the window. He knelt before it and rotated it until he was looking at the United States.

"Where could they go?" he said, more to himself than the others. "Where's the best place for it?"

At the edge of his vision he saw the others trading looks.

He rolled the globe upward, pulling South America fully into view.

"Anyone know a place almost as dry as Yuma?" he said. "Maybe in Central or South America?"

Garner chuckled. "I know a place that makes Yuma look like Seattle. NASA uses it to test Mars rovers. Every year I was in office they wanted more money for research sites down there."

Travis waited for him to go on.

"The Atacama Desert," Garner said. "Northern stretch of Chile. Great big sweeps of it have had no observed rainfall in recorded history. Those parts are biologically sterile. No plants or animals. Not even bacteria."

Travis leaned closer to the globe. Only three of Chile's cities were labeled on it. One was the capital, Santiago. He hardly noticed it. His gaze had already locked onto one of the other two.

The last shard of the wineglass slipped into place.

"Unbelievable," Travis said.

But before he could say more, the stacked papers in the room began to scatter. A cold breeze had blown in from the hall.

CHAPTER THIRTY-SEVEN

It was over before they could make any move. Just like that, there were men in the doorway—two standing and one crouched between them—with silencer-equipped pistols leveled. No one even spoke. There was no need.

The gunmen motioned for them to exit the den, and pulled back from the doorway to make room. Garner led the way, and a moment later everyone was standing in the living room.

There were six gunmen in all. Each had the same weapon: a Beretta 92F with a silencer that nearly doubled its length. There were narrow LED flashlights mounted atop each gun, switched off at the moment. Each of the men also wore a FLIR headset, identical to what they'd had in Yuma, though at the moment they hung from their necks on elongated straps.

Finn was there too. Holding both cylinders. Behind him, the disconnected iris from his own cylinder was still open. Moist October wind blew in from the pitch-black New York on the other side. Then the iris closed and the air stabilized again.

Bethany's backpack, with the SIG inside, still lay

where Travis had set it near the couch. He didn't look at it. Just got a sense of it, and judged the distance to it. It wasn't an option at the moment. It would take an ice age to reach it, and another ice age to unzip the pack. Time enough for every weapon in the room to acquire him and hit him half a dozen times.

Finn pointed to a bare stretch of wall. "There. All four of you."

They hesitated, but only for a moment. There was no other move they could make. The geometry of the situation was what it was. They went to the wall. Stood there in a row, facing the room. The gunmen arranged themselves in a broad arc before the four of them, no shooter in any other's line of fire.

"I need all of you to understand that the following isn't bluster," Finn said. "If you give us a reason to start shooting, we're just going to kill all four of you. We can do that and still get away, and each of you knows it. Clear so far?"

None of them answered, even with a nod.

Finn shrugged, took it as an affirmative. Then he set the cylinders in one of the big leather chairs, strode to the hall and disappeared into the den. Twenty seconds passed. They heard keystrokes and a few mouse clicks. Travis pictured the computer screen as it'd been when they left the room. Garner's e-mail program was open, all passwords already entered. Finn could access everything.

They heard him curse softly, and a second later he came back out, holding the cordless phone from the cradle on the computer desk. He looked at Garner.

"The e-mail you sent to coordinate the conference call mentions me by name."

"Does it?" Garner said.

Finn stared at him for a long time, then turned and looked at nothing, and Travis could see him putting together the implications. He didn't look happy about them. He glanced at his watch.

"The call starts in six minutes," Finn said. He looked at Garner again. "When it does, you're going to join it and tell everyone to disregard the message you sent them. Tell them the situation is already being handled higher up, and not to worry about it."

Garner didn't reply. Five seconds passed.

"Do you understand?" Finn said.

Garner exhaled, the sound almost a laugh. "If you think I'm going to do that just because you say so, you're high. Go ahead and shoot us. I'm sure the five people on that conference call, and all their secretaries and staffs, won't think it's the least bit suspicious when they read that I got killed a few minutes before it was scheduled to happen. I'm sure your name being in the e-mail won't bring any unwanted attention onto you, either."

Finn didn't blink, but his eyes drew a third of the way closed. He was thinking again. Visualizing moves and countermoves on the chessboard.

Then he nodded. "Fair enough."

He looked at Garner's phone and punched in a number. Put it to his ear. Waited. When the other party answered, Finn said, "We're here," and described the situation regarding the conference call. He wandered away down the hall as he spoke. Travis heard him say, "No, the e-mail doesn't go into detail, but it names both you and me, which isn't helpful." The conversation continued in low tones Travis couldn't make out.

The nearby wall clock showed four minutes left before the conference call.

Finn came back into the room. He was holding the phone down away from his ear now. Its power light was still on. He looked at Garner.

"It's on speaker," Finn said, and then spoke toward the phone's mouthpiece. "Go ahead."

A man on the phone cleared his throat softly. Even by that sound Travis recognized his voice.

"President Garner," the man said.

"President Currey," Garner said.

Travis heard Currey exhale. He sounded tired. "Rich, what are you trying to do?"

"I'd like to hear your own answer to that question."

"That would take more time than we have. Why don't you take some advice from an old friend and fall in line here, all right? Get on the conference call and say you jumped the gun, and that it's all good. It's the only move you've got, anyway."

"I don't know about that," Garner said. "I was thinking I might just stand here and watch the minute hand tick a few times. If I don't show up on the call, that in itself raises a few flags. I don't imagine you and your people want any flags going up, if you expect to keep whatever you're doing secret for another four months."

Travis saw something flicker through Finn's expression at that line. Something like amusement. It vanished as quickly as it'd appeared.

"Here's your problem," Currey said. "From this

point forward, your goal is to build a base of support against us. To do that, you need to convince rational people of something no rational person can believe without proof. If you had one of the cylinders, it'd be easy for you. You could show people what's on the other side. But you've lost that advantage now. So who's going to believe you? It won't carry much weight that you're a former president, when the people contradicting your claim include the *sitting* president and his entire cabinet, among many others."

Travis watched the resolve fade from Garner's eyes. Watched something darker take its place.

"It's over, Rich," Currey said. "All that's left is to acknowledge it. And the sooner, the better—at least for you. We'd be happy to leave you alone, once you've cooperated. It's not in our interests to stir up any headlines just now."

Garner looked at Paige, right beside him, then at Bethany and Travis.

"What happens to the others?" Garner said. "And don't bullshit me, Walter. I'll be able to tell."

"I know it," Currey said. There was a long pause, and then he said, "All right, fine. They die. They go to Rockport Army Depot on Long Island, they get interrogated by some friends of ours there, and then they get a bullet to the temple each. Sound like the truth? The thing is, that part happens regardless of the outcome. You can't help them. You need to take care of yourself, now. So do it. Get on the call and make it right. I'll get out of the way so you can."

The line clicked dead.

Finn pressed the button to hang up the phone, then held it out to Garner.

The wall clock showed thirty seconds left. In all likelihood, Travis knew, the other parties had already called in and were waiting.

Garner didn't take the phone. He looked at the three of them again, beside him along the wall. His eyes stayed on each one for a few seconds. Then he looked down, straight in front of himself. Travis saw his eyes track across the floor in an arc, just below the feet of the six gunmen. It almost seemed that he was getting a sense of the men, without appearing to do so. Travis wondered why. He did the same himself. He took in their posture. They were alert but not poised. Their weapons had dropped to their sides over the past couple minutes—but they could be aimed again in a quarter second, so Travis couldn't see how it mattered. Maybe Garner's assessment was only the manifestation of a wish that he could do something. Nothing more than that. Already he was staring down at his hands, folded before him. Looking hopeless. Looking like he'd made up his mind.

He took the phone from Finn.

"Keep it on speaker," Finn said.

Garner nodded.

"Sir, don't do this," Paige said.

She looked at Garner, but the man could no longer meet her eyes. He punched a number into the phone. It began to ring.

"Mr. President . . ." Paige said. Travis heard her voice crack. It had nothing to do with fear, he knew. It was simply disappointment to a crushing degree. Paige had known Garner for some time, and couldn't believe what she was seeing. Or didn't want to, at least.

The ringing stopped and a recording came on. It told Garner to enter something called a bridge code. He entered it. There was a tone and a series of clicks. Travis guessed the same recorded voice was letting the others on the call know that Garner had joined.

A tear overran one of Paige's eyes and drew a long track down her cheek.

Then the line opened and several voices were speaking at once, saying *hello* and asking if everyone was on.

"Gentlemen," Garner said.

The voices went quiet.

Garner took a breath. Continued avoiding Paige's stare. He let the breath out slowly.

"Gentlemen, I seem to have inconvenienced you for nothing. I've just spoken at length with President Currey, and I'm now confident that he has control of what I planned to discuss with you. It's not something any of us needs to worry about. And I'm sorry to cut it short, but that'll be it."

He turned the phone off. Lowered his head.

Finn looked more relieved than happy. Travis could almost see sympathy for Garner in his expression.

"You're a realist," Finn said. "I could always see that in you. There's no shame in it. You're a man who understands his options, that's all."

He took the phone from Garner.

Garner didn't look at him, but after a second he finally met Paige's eyes.

"You probably want to slap my face as hard as you can," Garner said.

"Don't tempt me," Paige said.

"No, I think you should do it. You'll feel better. So will I."

For a moment she only stared at him. His face was devoid of anything but pity, maybe for himself more than the three of them.

And then Paige slapped him. It had to be the hardest open-handed hit Travis had ever seen. The sound of it, loud and sharp as a whip-crack, echoed off the windows, the opposite wall, the stone floor of the hallway nearby. It rocked Garner's head sideways, throwing his balance off enough to make him take a step.

When he looked back at Paige, there was blood on his lip.

But he was smiling.

A strange kind of smile. Like he was in on a joke no one else understood yet. He turned to Finn. The smile hardened. Became colder.

Finn looked puzzled for maybe half a second.

And then he looked scared.

"I understand my options better than you do," Garner said.

If he'd said another word it would've been lost under the sound of the hallway door slamming inward. Travis snapped his head to the side and saw two men in crisp black suits coming through, with MP5 submachine guns shouldered. In almost the same instant he heard similar crashing impacts from elsewhere in the residence—two other teams coming in somewhere.

He understood at once why Garner had taken note of the six gunmen and their relaxed postures. They were plenty prepared to raise their silenced Berettas if any of their four captives made a move—but the sudden arrival of armed Secret Service agents was a very different matter.

The effect on the six men—not to mention Finn—was immediate. Their heads turned toward the sounds of the various doors breaking in. From where they stood—the six of them in their long arc—they couldn't see directly down the entry hall. Travis and the other three could: the living-room wall they stood against was an extension of one side of the hall.

But Finn's gunmen knew exactly who was coming. The part of their brains that would've told them to drop a hot potato had figured it out in about a hundredth of a second. The result, Travis saw, was a kind of neural tug-of-war between all possible reactions: killing the captives, finding cover, getting the hell out of this place. Not the kind of decision they could make in the almost comically small amount of time they had to work with.

At least one of the six opted for the first choice. The man nearest to Travis. The guy's Beretta began to come up toward the four of them, even as the Secret Service men in the hallway advanced at a sprint. They'd reach the living room soon, but not soon enough.

Travis threw himself forward at the man bringing up his gun. The two of them were lined up in a perfect face-off. Travis crossed the five-foot reach of space between them in the time it took the gun to come up to chest level. He got his left hand around the silencer, yanked the weapon down and away from pointing at the others, and punched the guy in the throat with all the force his weight and momentum could provide. Which turned out to be enough. The guy's hand came off the gun with a reflexive jerk. And then Travis was twisting, holding the pistol, going right past the guy and beyond the arc of the others. Not trying to check his speed. Not even trying to stay on his feet.

He took one more step before his balance outran him, and then he was falling, completing his spin as he dropped. Still holding the Beretta in his left hand by its silencer. He brought his right hand up and took the weapon by the grip. Raised it to sight in on one of the still-armed gunmen. His angle of fire, as he fell, was tilted radically upward. If he missed, the bullet would hit only the ceiling—there was no more of the building above this floor.

He fired. He didn't miss. The shot hit the man at the base of his skull and blew it open.

Then Travis's ass hit the floor painfully and his gun arm dropped beyond his control.

By then, everyone was moving. Things were happening too quickly for him to keep track of. He saw Paige and Bethany ducking and running toward him, getting out of the kill zone that was about to open up between the gunmen and the oncoming agents in the hall. He could hear the agents' footsteps, as well as those of the other teams, still out of sight somewhere behind him. He could see the gunmen scattering, ducking—no doubt they could see the agents now. One man slammed into the leather chair that held the two cylinders. The chair pitched forward, spilling the cylinders onto the carpet. They rolled in different directions— neither one toward Travis.

Travis raised the Beretta again, looking for a

target, when it occurred to him what he was doing. He was holding a pistol, in a room containing a former president, into which Secret Service agents were about to flood.

Not a good way to stay alive.

He cocked his wrist and threw the gun sideways, saw it hit the carpet and spin into the gap beneath the couch. At the same time he saw Paige and Bethany diving toward him, and even as they hit the ground the shooting started.

CHAPTER THIRTY-EIGHT

Travis saw within seconds that it wasn't going to shake out in their favor. Finn and his men had fallen back to defensive positions in adjoining rooms, leaving Garner alone where he stood. The Secret Service agents were already converging on him, unloading suppressing fire at the doorways through which the others had retreated.

But not engaging them.

Not attacking.

That wasn't their job.

Their job was to get Garner out of harm's way, and they would do it in probably fifteen seconds. Twenty at the most. They would surround him and hustle him out, down the entry hall and out into the larger corridor. Probably right out of the building after that. They would maintain fire to cover the retreat from the residence, but that would be it. Not even Garner could order them to do otherwise. In the heat of it all, they wouldn't even be listening to him.

Well under half a minute from right now, Travis knew, the three of them would be left alone with

Finn's remaining people—nearly all of them still
alive.

Travis was lying facedown on the floor now,
hands outstretched and empty. Paige and Bethany,
right beside him, were in the same position.

Travis turned his head and saw two agents pass
by on the inside wall of the living room. They were
firing three-shot bursts.

The rest of the action was going on where Travis
couldn't see it. He couldn't tell if Finn's people
were shooting. Their silenced fire would've been
impossible to make out against the other shots.

Paige turned to him, her eyes intense. She understood the trouble they were in as well as he did.
Then she looked past him. He turned to follow her
gaze, and saw one of the cylinders.

It was ten feet away, under the coffee table.

He looked for the other one. Couldn't see it anywhere. Given the direction it'd rolled, it had to be
closer to Finn's position now. It wasn't even worth
thinking about.

Travis looked at the nearer one. If he could get
to it and get the iris open, no special care would
be needed to position it. The ruin of this building
had thick steel gridwork for subflooring instead
of concrete and rebar. The grids were completely
rusted, but because they were such a heavy gauge—
inch-thick steel rods crisscrossing at three-inch
intervals—they were still very strong. No matter
where he opened the iris, there would be a solid
surface to crawl onto on the other side.

It would take him two seconds to reach the cylinder, starting from his prone position.

Paige saw what he was thinking. "You can't!"

Her voice was just audible under the shooting. "The agents will think you're going for a weapon!"

He craned his neck around to look at them. They'd reached Garner. They'd boxed him in. Two or three of them, with their free hands, had grabbed hold of the man's arms. They were dragging him toward the hall. Garner *was* shouting something at them, as Travis had imagined. It was about as effective as he'd imagined, too. Ten more seconds and they'd be gone. They were still shooting at the doorways through which Finn and his people had ducked. Sporadic fire, meant only for deterrence.

One of the agents had his eyes fixed on Travis and Paige and Bethany, even as his MP5 stayed trained on the doorways. He could swing the weapon toward the three of them, where they lay, about as quickly as he could decide they were a threat.

Travis wouldn't get halfway to the cylinder if he went for it.

He judged the agents' progress toward the mouth of the entry hall, beyond which they wouldn't be able to see him anymore. Five seconds now, at most.

He looked at the doorways. Finn and the others were somewhere beyond them. Travis had no doubt that Finn, at least, was running the same calculation he was: gauging the straight-razor margin of time between the agents' departure from the suite and the earliest moment that Travis could reach the cylinder and trigger the iris.

It would take some number of seconds, and some number of seconds would be available. One of those numbers would turn out to be larger than the other. In the end it would be that simple.

In the last few feet before the mouth of the hallway, the Secret Service agents began to run. They hauled Garner along, barely on his feet.

And then they were gone, out of Travis's view, into the hall.

Travis moved. Drew his legs up under him, dug his feet into the carpet and lunged. Even as he did, he heard—even felt—the suite go silent as the shooting stopped. The agents were simply hauling ass now, transiting the length of the entry hall as fast as they could physically go. Their footsteps were the only sound—for a second. And then there were other footsteps, nearer by.

Travis hit the coffee table with both hands. Slammed it aside like it weighed nothing, though it was made of solid walnut.

Finn and the others were coming fast. Maybe not through the doorways yet, but close.

Travis got his hands on the cylinder. He landed on his shoulder, twisted and aimed the thing toward Paige and Bethany. He hit the ON button and the OFF (DETACH/DELAY—93 SEC.) button a fraction of a second apart.

The iris opened a few inches above the floor. The night beyond it was dark and depthless except for streaks of rain at the opening, silvery in the light-bleed from the suite. The projection beam was already intensifying, charging the iris to stay open on its own. Travis had never measured exactly how long that part took. It'd always seemed like just a few seconds. It seemed longer now.

The footsteps were closer. Definitely in the living room. Travis didn't bother turning to look. Whatever he might see, there was nothing he could do any faster.

Paige was up on all fours and moving. Throwing herself into the beam of light, but not toward the iris. Instead she passed through the light, hit the floor and rolled, and came to a stop with her hand clutching Bethany's backpack. She twisted back toward the iris and threw the pack with all her force. It went through into the darkness. Travis heard the clatter of the SIG and the shotgun shells as the pack landed on the gridwork.

At the same instant the beam finally vanished, leaving the iris alone.

Paige was waving for Bethany to go through, but Bethany was already moving, fast and lithe. She got her limbs beneath her without rising more than a foot from the floor, and went through the iris in a single movement. No part of her even touched the circle.

Paige was right behind her, and when she was two thirds through the iris, Travis gripped the cylinder in his right hand and tossed it at her backside in an underhand spiral. He was betting it all that she would turn toward him once she'd crossed the threshold. Would turn and have time to catch the thing. He had no choice. His ears told him he was out of time.

Paige spun on her knee the moment she was through the iris—and flinched, her hands coming up just in time to keep the cylinder from smashing into her face. She blocked it and then got hold of it, pulling it against herself, already forgetting it entirely.

Because Finn and two of his men were right there. Ten feet from Travis. Just passing the visual barrier of the overturned leather chair and the up-right one beside it. Their guns already coming up to level.

But Travis was coming up, too. Not with a gun of his own. The Beretta was close by, somewhere under the couch, but the gap was too narrow to easily reach into.

What Travis had instead was the coffee table. He had it right by the middle with both hands, rais-ing it over his head, and he was heaving himself upright from a crouch.

Finn and his men faltered. Whatever they'd ex-pected, this wasn't it.

Travis extended his arms violently as he stood, and hurled the coffee table at them like a two-handed shot put.

Finn ducked. The man to his left brought his forearms up. The man to his right did nothing at all, and Paige saw the leading edge of the table con-nect dead-on with his nose. There was an explo-sion of blood across the bottom half of his face.

Paige missed whatever came next. She could see Travis diving toward the opening now, and pitched herself sideways to clear the way. He came through headfirst, landed on his forearms, twisted and pulled his legs the rest of the way across the margin.

It occurred to Paige that they were nowhere near safe yet. Just the opposite. They were sprawled out in the darkness before the opening, in no position to move quickly or take cover—if there'd been any cover. Finn and his people had been slowed by no more than a few seconds. There was still all the time in the world before the iris slipped shut.

She could see two sets of feet and shins coming

already. Rounding the chairs. Pivoting. Crossing the open space. The men wouldn't even need to look through the iris for their targets. They could simply shove their pistols through and start shooting. They couldn't miss.

The SIG.

Where the hell was the backpack? When Paige had tossed it through, she'd been thinking only of getting out of the room fast. She spun, trying to guess where—and how far away—it could have ended up on this side.

But she saw the SIG the moment she turned. A small hand was gripping it. And centering it on the iris.

Bethany fired.

Paige looked in time to see a kneecap, five feet beyond the opening, burst inside its pant leg. A man screamed and fell bodily into view. Not Finn. The guy still had his Beretta, but he wasn't aiming yet. Bethany's next shot went right through the bridge of his nose. He flopped forward onto the carpet. The second pair of legs dug in to a hard stop. The man vaulted sideways, just missing Bethany's next round. It cratered one of the suite's bulletproof windows instead.

By then Paige could see Travis getting to his feet. Reaching to help her up. Bethany was rising too, but staying bent at the waist, keeping the SIG positioned to fire again.

Ten seconds later they settled into a safer position, several yards from the iris at a random angle. The opening looked strange hovering there in the darkness, lighting up the intermittent rain a few feet around it.

Bethany kept the SIG leveled. Nobody appeared at the opening.

The next minute went by like ten, and then the iris slipped shut, and there was nothing but the rain and the chill and the darkness of the ruined city.

CHAPTER THIRTY-NINE

Almost at once the rain provided a form of guidance. They could hear it hissing where it passed through the rusted bars of the steel grid, but somewhere close by it was making another sound. A hard pinging against something solid, resonant.

The stairs.

Just as in the office building in D.C., the heavy treads of the stairs in this structure had survived the decades of neglect. The three of them had climbed the full thirty flights earlier in the day.

Travis stood. "Let's go."

They made their way across the gridwork, stopping a few times to reassess the direction of the pinging. They took careful steps, placing each one tentatively before shifting any weight forward. There were other things than the stairwell that they might encounter. The elevator shaft, for one.

Travis swept an arm low in front of him. After a moment it hit something rigid. A structural upright. He felt down its length and found the top of the still-sturdy handrail.

Thirty seconds later they were two floors down.

Travis stepped off of the landing and navigated by memory to where he'd left the twelve-gauge, a few yards away. It was still dry, leaning under the intact metal panel. He carried it back to the stairs.

"Hand me the backpack," he said.

He heard it shift in the darkness and then Bethany pushed it into his hands. It contained nothing but shotgun shells now. Bethany was still holding the SIG, and Paige had the cylinder.

"What are you doing?" Paige said.

"I'm going back up," Travis said. "You're going to keep heading down."

"The hell we are. You're coming with us, or we're coming with you."

"Finn and his people have the other cylinder," Travis said, "and it's their only way out of the building. The ground floor probably slammed shut like a bear trap half a second after you smacked Garner. Even the upper stairwells could have building security in them by now. Finn has to assume they do, either way. So his only exit is through the iris, on the top floor. Think of that, along with the fact that he still wants to capture or kill us. What's his best strategy?"

Paige was quiet a few seconds. Then she said, "He'll give us a few minutes to flee, and then come through the iris. That way we're not right there, shooting at his guys on their way through the bottleneck."

"Exactly," Travis said. "Once they're past that point, the advantage is all theirs. You saw the goggles around their necks. They can see in the dark and we can't. If they come through the iris in the next couple minutes, while we're groping our way down the stairs, they'll overtake us long before we reach the ground. And they know we can't use our own cylinder to go back through the iris on some lower floor—not with the building locked down. We'd be taken into custody, and we'd be under President Currey's discretion within hours. We're dead either way. The only real chance we've got is to stay here in the ruins until we're well away from this building. But that only works if someone stays up here and covers the retreat. And I'm sorry to be a dick, but it's gonna be me, and that's it."

He slung the pack on his shoulder. The weight of the shells inside felt reassuring.

"On the bright side," he said, "this is a chance to end this right here."

"Then we should all stay," Bethany said.

"No," Travis said. "We can't risk the cylinder. What Currey said on the phone is right. No one's going to believe any of this if they don't look through the iris for themselves. Garner needs it. It's more important than any of our lives."

Neither of them replied right away. In the whisper of the rain, Travis could sense them accepting the idea. Hating it, but accepting it.

"Where do we meet you?" Paige said.

"Just get down onto Central Park West and head south. Get as much distance as you can. It'll be hard in the dark, but do your best. You'll hear the shooting. Hopefully sometime later you'll hear me calling out behind you."

The seconds drew out again. Then he felt one of Paige's hands on his face. Her fingers tracing its contours. The closest she could get to a last look at him.

"Be there," she said, and then her hand fell away, and Travis heard both sets of footsteps moving off down the next flight. He listened for a few seconds, then started back up.

He reached the head of the top flight and dropped to a knee. It was as good a spot as any, and it had at least some strategic value: he could descend a few treads if he needed to dodge return-fire.

The more he thought about his odds, the more he liked them. At any distance over a dozen yards, the shotgun's spread would be at least as wide as the iris. Anyone coming through it was going to get cut to pieces.

Finn and his men had numbered seven originally. Two were dead now. Maybe more.

Travis dropped the backpack off his shoulder. He set it right in front of himself and unzipped it. Pulled it wide open so there'd be no fumbling later.

The Remington was already good for five shots—four in the magazine and one in the chamber. He felt for the loading port and mentally rehearsed sliding shells into it by feel alone. It wouldn't be difficult. He probably did it mostly by feel even in daylight.

He surveyed the darkness all around him in long, rapid sweeps. He would see the iris the moment it opened, even at the extent of his peripheral vision. He could no more miss it than he could miss a searchlight being switched on.

He pulled the shotgun's stock hard against his shoulder.

He was ready.

*   *   *

Finn stood at the open entry to the suite, listening to the larger corridor beyond. The stairwell was twenty feet away. No doubt Garner's security detail had opted for that route when they'd left, rather than wait for an elevator.

Finn listened now for other footsteps echoing on the stairs—approaching, not retreating.

He heard nothing.

But he couldn't expect to, he realized. The Secret Service might've made all the racket in the world on the way down, but other security personnel coming up to hold the stairwells would probably be quiet as cats.

He returned to the suite's living room. He had five men left. One with a broken nose and probably a facial fracture. The man was still on his feet, but he looked like he could barely see through the swelling under his eyes.

Outside, police had begun converging on the building. Their sirens sounded faint from thirty stories up. Finn noticed the winking lights of an incoming helicopter, far away across the city.

He stooped and picked up the cylinder from where it'd rolled to a stop, at the corner where the windows met the wall.

He considered the logistics of the situation.

On the other side, Miss Campbell and her friends would be making their way down the stairs by now, at whatever speed they could manage.

Unless they'd decided to stay and fight it out.

Finn turned in a slow circle. He let his eyes roam. He imagined the suite in its ruined state, pitch-black and skeletal and cold and wet. And devoid of cover. If the others really were waiting for them over there, where would they position themselves?

He continued his slow turn. And then he stopped. He was looking down the entry hall toward the outer corridor—and the unseen stairwell beyond.

He thought about it. It made sense. It was all that made sense, really.

He turned again and studied the suite, no longer envisioning its alternate form. He looked across the living room, through the doorways on the far wall, toward the distant end of the residence.

The point furthest from the stairwell.

He headed for it, waving his men to him as he went. They fell in behind him, weapons ready. Fifteen seconds later they reached the place—a sitting room with wicker furniture and bright yellow paint. It had thick canvas drapes—pulled back at the moment.

Finn pulled his FLIR headset up and secured it over his eyes. His men did the same. He raised the cylinder. He put his finger to the ON button.

And then he withdrew it. Something obvious had occurred to him.

"Shut the drapes," he said. "And kill the lights."

Travis waited. The rain had soaked through his shirt. The night was probably sixty degrees, but the dampness made it feel a lot colder.

He continued to sweep his eyes across the darkness. It was hard to say how long he'd been kneeling here. Three or four minutes, at least. Paige and Bethany should be most of the way down the building by now.

Travis cocked his head. He'd heard something.

The sound was distant, keening, rising and falling. Just discernible in the rain. It reminded him of the wolves in the ruins of D.C., but the pitch was higher. Coyotes, maybe. Or simply the wind playing through the girders.

Paige kept count of the floors as she and Bethany descended. Garner's suite had been on the thirtieth. They'd come down twenty-three flights from there.

The going was harder than she'd imagined. The metal treads were slick in the rain, and on some flights the handrail was missing. She tried to remember what the stairwell had looked like in daylight on their way up. Tried to recall any places where the landing was buckled or compromised in any way. She didn't think she'd seen anything like that—it should have stuck with her if she had—but she couldn't shake the sense that there was *something*. Something she'd noticed on the ascent. Something that hadn't mattered then, but might matter now, in the dark.

Travis had discounted the keening sound—what little of it he could hear—even though something about it troubled him.

Now he heard something else. Very faint, at first. A kind of drumming. It might have been only the rain intensifying—but he felt no change in it on his skin.

Then the sound swelled by a tiny degree, and he recognized it.

And he understood that he was in trouble.

* * *

Paige was stepping onto the fifth floor when it happened. The moment her foot came down, she remembered exactly what she'd been trying to think of, and why it *did* matter—not because of the darkness, but because of the rain.

It was a clump of maple leaves, still attached by their stems to a narrow twig. Lying there curled and damp in the afternoon light, they'd been harmless. Something to step over and forget within a few seconds.

Plastered flat now against the smooth bars of the gridwork, the clump might as well have been an oil slick.

Paige's leading foot hit it, coming down hard off the bottom step, all of her weight on it in the instant before it went out from under her.

Her arms shot down to break her fall against the steel treads—it was that or break her skull—and she was on her ass before she realized what she'd done.

"Paige?" Bethany said.

"Fuck!" she hissed—she just managed to keep it from being a scream.

She threw herself forward, away from the stairs and out across the blind void of the fifth floor, following the sound of rolling metal on metal.

The cylinder.

Rolling away from her, fast as hell.

Toward the edge.

The drumming was the sound of helicopter rotors. And the high, rising-falling tones were police sirens.

Still down on one knee, Travis spun hard toward

the sound-source, swinging the Remington around with him. Too late. A hand gripped the weapon's barrel in the darkness and shoved it upward, and then something else—probably a silencer—slammed into his temple. He dropped. Landed facedown on the grid flooring. Just holding on to consciousness.

Paige scrambled forward on all fours—there wasn't time to get up on her feet. All visual reference was gone. There was only the steel grid beneath her, and the rolling sound, somewhere in the blackness ahead of her.

She was plunging blindly toward it.

And catching up.

That was all that mattered.

Very close now—it couldn't be more than a foot or two ahead.

And then the sound simply vanished.

Like someone had neatly lifted the needle from a record.

Paige understood. Panic flared across her nervous system. Her hands grabbed for purchase on the grid—anywhere they could—to arrest her forward motion.

The hand that was further ahead came down onto nothing—it plunged into vacant space beyond the building's edge, five stories above the ground.

Her breath rushed out and for a second she was aware of nothing but her body's momentum, unstoppable, taking her over the drop-off.

Then her trailing hand closed around a bar of the gridwork, and she gripped it tightly, and her shoulder damn near came out of her socket as she wrenched to a stop. Her legs kicked out from behind her, sliding around and forward on the wet steel.

And then she was still. Her hand gripping the bar. Her body lying sideways along the edge. She could feel the girder's outer margin pressed firmly against the center of her chest.

A second later the cylinder exploded, fifty feet below.

A burst of blue-white light. Like a collapsing star. Blinding, painful to her dark-adapted eyes. It lit up the pines and hardwoods that crowded the base of the building, and the broken and canted slabs of Central Park West lying across exposed roots. She saw the cylinder's casing shatter. Saw its internal structure burst, fragile wafers of alien technology scattering over the wet ground. Strange, spherical pockets of light flickered and popped from a few components. In the larger spheres Paige saw a fish-eye view of the present-day street. Warped, distorted police cruisers with their flashers on. The intact front of the building, blazing with internal light from dozens of windows. The images lingered for less than a second and then vanished. A moment later there was nothing to see but the fragments of the cylinder's casing, their concave inner surfaces glowing deep blue in the night, haloed by the rainfall. And then they went dark too.

Travis saw it. Saw the eruption of light thirty stories below, with his face pressed to the grid, and understood. It was the last thing he saw before the toe of someone's boot connected with his head and shut everything off.

CHAPTER FORTY

He faded in and out. More out than in. His head hurt like hell.

He was lying on thin, bristled carpeting. There was something rumbling beneath it. His thinking cleared a bit, and he understood that the rumbling came from a spinning axle.

He opened his eyes. He was lying bound on the floor of an SUV. He was in the back. The rear seat had been removed to make a flat storage bay. The vehicle was still in the city. The high steel and stone and brick faces of buildings slid by overhead.

He heard Finn and at least two other men talking up front. He heard a wash of static and then he heard Finn tell someone in another vehicle—or a number of vehicles—to take 495. A minute later the roof of a tunnel drew across the view, and the city was gone. The hum of the tires echoed in the enclosed space.

Travis took in fragments of the conversation between Finn and the others. Pieced together what'd happened. They'd hauled his unconscious body down through the ruin of Garner's building and carried it two blocks to where it was safe for them to come back through the iris—inside a private garage. They didn't have Paige and Bethany. The two of them had been long gone by the time Finn's men had reached the bottom of Garner's building.

The procession of SUVs traveled for a long time on the freeway. Travis didn't bother keeping track.

Finn made a phone call. It wasn't on speaker, but over the drone of the vehicle's engine, Travis heard it ring four times before voice mail answered.

"Audra, it's me," Finn said. "Everything's tied off here, at least as well as it can be. I should be on-site about eight hours from now. I'll call you again from the air."

He hung up.

Travis considered what he'd heard. Audra. Alive. It wasn't all that surprising. He might have guessed it if he'd thought about it, given what he'd realized at Garner's place.

A few minutes later the motorcade pulled off the freeway. It took a series of turns and short jogs, and finally stopped. One of the front doors of the vehicle Travis was in opened and shut. The driver kept the engine running. Footsteps came around the back of the vehicle and then the rear window popped open. Travis heard the whine of jet engines powering up nearby.

Finn leaned in and stared down on him. He had the surviving cylinder tucked under his arm. In the dome light, the man's eyes looked deeply troubled.

"What's going to happen to you about an hour from now," Finn said, "I despise more than anything there is. I wish to hell it could be avoided. But it can't be, this time. There's too much at stake. I need to know what you know, and who else you've

spoken to. So please just cooperate with the inter-
rogators. They'll know if you're being truthful.
And it'll be over sooner."

His eyes stayed on Travis a moment longer.

"I'm sorry," Finn said. He looked like he meant
it. Then he closed the window again, pounded
twice on the roof, and walked away.

Travis saw the glow of headlights swing through
the side windows as two other vehicles backed out
of nearby spaces and took the lead. His own pulled
out and followed, and a few minutes later they
were on the freeway again.

CHAPTER FORTY-ONE

Fifty seconds before the first shots hit the motorcade, Travis was thinking about Paige and Bethany. They were all he'd thought of for the past hour. He imagined them trying to find shelter in the unbroken darkness of the ruins. Imagined their uncertainty and confusion when they hadn't heard any shooting from the top of the building. Imagined their fear now, all this time later, the reality of their situation sinking in as deeply as the cold and the dampness of the October night.

The vehicle slowed and came to a stop. The procession had left the freeway a while earlier. It was traveling through dark countryside now, halting occasionally at what Travis guessed were stop signs at remote intersections. There was no sky glow to indicate a populated area nearby.

The vehicle accelerated again.

Travis thought of Paige touching his face, feeling it. Worried for him. He wondered what she thought of him right now.

Half a minute later—no doubt precisely a half mile on the regimented grid of roads out here—the vehicle slowed again. Travis imagined they were getting close to their destination.

The moment the SUV came to a complete stop, Travis heard something, somewhere ahead in the dark.

It sounded like a playing card in bicycle spokes.

Garner watched it unfold. It took fifteen seconds from start to finish, by which time he was convinced that every man on his Secret Service detail would've done just fine in the SEALs.

The six of them advanced on the vehicles, silenced M4 carbines trained on the shattered windows up front. The lead SUV, suddenly absent its driver's foot on the brake, had coasted across the intersection and veered off the corner into a shallow ditch.

The team took another fifteen seconds to confirm that every hostile was dead—with the help of an extra bullet or two, in some cases.

One of the men, Dyer, called out to Garner. "Clear, sir."

Garner came forward from the tree cover edging the road. He had his own silenced M4 in hand—a precaution in case things had gone badly, though his men had been adamant that he stay out of the initial attack. Given all he'd asked of them, he'd felt the point was worth conceding.

Two of the men had the big rear door of the last SUV open. They waved Garner over. He arrived to find Travis Chase lying bound on the floor. At the same time he heard the others calling out to report no captives in the remaining vehicles.

One of the agents leaned in with a knife to cut the heavy zip-ties binding Chase's wrists and ankles.

Garner stood back and stared north along the dark two-lane. He could see the lights of the front gate at Rockport, a mile away. The sentries there couldn't have heard the suppressed gunshots, but it still wouldn't be smart to stay here any longer than necessary. The two cars Garner and his men had brought were parked on the shoulder, a hundred yards down the cross street.

Chase sat up in the back of the SUV.

"Paige and Bethany are dead?" Garner said.

Chase shook his head. "Not if we can help it."

Travis gave Garner the basics as they ran to the cars. Garner cursed softly when he heard Paige and Bethany's situation.

They reached the vehicles, two black Crown Victorias. Garner pointed Travis to a rear door of the lead car, then rounded the back and climbed in on the opposite side, next to him.

"How'd you convince your guys to go along with this?" Travis said.

"I told them the truth."

"And they believed it?"

Garner nodded. "Two of them served with Tangent hubs, earlier in their careers. Besides, it was easier for them to swallow than the idea of half a dozen armed men walking into my place without their knowing it."

Ten seconds later they were cruising away from the attack site at exactly the speed limit.

"Where's Finn now?" Garner said.

"On a plane. Going somewhere that takes eight hours to get to."

"Lots of places are eight hours' flight time from New York," Garner said. "Central Europe, north Africa, Brazil—"

"He's not going to any of those," Travis said. "He's going to where the flights out of Yuma were going."

"The Erica flights."

"You're saying it right," Travis said, "but you're spelling it wrong in your head. Like the rest of us were."

Travis nodded at the cell phone clipped to Garner's waist. "Bring up any mapping website. Look at northern Chile."

Garner drew the phone, switched it on, and pulled up a Mercator map of the world. He zoomed in until the northern portion of Chile filled the little screen. The most prominent city in view was a place on the coast called Arica. It had the Pacific Ocean to its west, and the Atacama Desert to its east.

"Arica flights," Garner said.

Travis nodded. "We never saw it written down in Yuma. We only heard it in the recording."

"So the panic move when everything went wrong," Garner said, "was to gather everyone in Yuma, and then airlift a select few to Arica, Chile?"

"Part of that's correct," Travis said. "The gathering and the airlift happened. Hard to say how many they transported to Arica. A hundred flights, stretched out over something like a week, could've moved tens of thousands. Maybe they flew more than that. Or less. Those details we can only guess about."

"So what am I getting wrong?"

"The same thing we all got wrong, from the very start."

Garner waited.

"We asked ourselves, from the moment we saw the ruins in D.C., what kind of accident could've caused the collapse of the world. And when we saw Yuma, we wondered what sort of crisis could've compelled people—millions of them—to leave their homes and gather in a place that couldn't possibly support them all."

"I'm still asking myself those questions," Garner said.

"And you'd be asking them for a long time," Travis said, "because there aren't any answers to them. They're the wrong questions."

"What are the right ones?"

For a moment Travis said nothing. He stared out at the dark woods going by. A few miles ahead he saw the spread-out sodium glow of a subdivision.

"Think of what we know about Isaac Finn," Travis said. "We know that at one time he was practically a saint. From the moment he was an adult he was putting himself in danger and probably every kind of misery, trying to reduce suffering in the world. We know he thinks way the hell outside the box. He left the Peace Corps and formed his own group, and brought into the fight every resource he could line up. Even things like psych profiling of populations, in an attempt to weed out the worst people and draw together the best. Those with attributes like kindness, concern for others, aversion to violence. We know it turned out to be a lost cause, and by the time Rwanda was in full swing, he'd had enough. He walked away from the whole game. Or seemed to."

"None of which contradicts the theory we all agreed on earlier," Garner said. "That Finn and his wife proposed using ELF-based systems to pacify conflict zones—at least long enough for peacekeepers to stabilize them. And that Finn is still working to realize that goal. And I agree, it's pretty damn far outside the box."

"It is," Travis said, "but I think his real goal is a lot farther out than that, and has been for a very long time. And he's not doing it alone. They're still working on it together."

"They?"

Travis nodded. "Audra faked her death. I heard Finn leave her a voice mail before he caught his flight."

For the first time Garner looked genuinely surprised. And more open to considering whatever Travis was leading up to.

"You said yourself, sir, the theory of a satellite malfunction doesn't work. We'd shut them off or shoot them down. There's no chance at all that they'd be out of control and harming people for a solid month."

"Right," Garner said. "So have you figured out what goes wrong?"

"Nothing goes wrong," Travis said. "We've been off track from the beginning, looking for a mistake that doesn't exist."

"I'm not following you," Garner said.

Travis looked at him. "When Finn switched on the cylinder inside his office yesterday, I was standing on the other side of the opening it projected. Just out of his view, but close enough to hear him speak. He stood at the iris, and he looked at the ruins of Washington, D.C., and he said, 'Jesus, it works.'"

"Meaning the cylinder," Garner said.

"That was what I thought. But I was wrong. I should have known by the way he said it. It wasn't just surprise in his voice. It was more like reverence. Pride, even. It was the sort of tone you'd hear from Orville Wright if you took him out to La-Guardia on a busy afternoon."

Travis broke his stare with Garner and looked at the soft lights of the suburb coming up.

"The collapse of the world isn't a failure of Finn's plan," Travis said. "It *is* his plan. He means for it to happen."

CHAPTER FORTY-TWO

Garner said nothing for the next several seconds.

"I won't pretend I understand his motivation," Travis said. "Or the motivation of anyone who goes into a conflict zone and tries to make things better for people. Someone like me doesn't have the first clue, and never will. But I have to think there's a burn-out rate like no other. I have to think that for everyone in that line of work, there's a moment that comes sooner or later when you really understand the size of the problem, and the limits of your own capacity to do anything about it. I'm guessing, but I bet it feels more like a cement truck than a last straw. In Finn's case, if I'm right about the rest of this, then it was even bigger for him. I think he lost hope in a lot more than just Rwanda. I think he was looking at the whole human picture by the time he walked away from that place. Like he wished he could just end the world and start over. And maybe he's not the only person who's ever felt that way, at a low moment, but in Finn's case there was something that set him apart: he was a pillow away from the one person on Earth who could actually make that happen."

Something changed in Garner's expression. Travis saw him working it out.

"Oh, Christ . . ." Garner said.

"Finn isn't stupid," Travis said. "Neither is Audra. They must have known, even before they submitted that paper to the *Independent*, that using ELF satellites to sedate conflict zones would be politically toxic. But I doubt that was ever their goal, in the first place. I think the paper was only meant to put the subject out there, get people talking about it, especially the kind of power players who'd be interested in the implied technology. The point was just to get the ball rolling so that someone would actually *build* ELF satellites, because that was the critical piece of the real plan. So when the paper got rejected, and Audra's father stepped on it, they must've decided to get the ball rolling themselves. There would've been lots of reasons for Audra to leave Harvard and take the job with Longbow Aerospace. Re-immerse herself in the design field, make industry contacts to go along with Finn's political ones, that kind of thing. And at some point she got them to agree to build the satellites she wanted, disguised as comm satellites that didn't work worth a damn. I guess she faked her death so her role in the project would never come under scrutiny. There'd be a lot she'd have to do over the years, and she wouldn't want to answer questions about any of it."

Garner was still thinking it all through. Making the connections Travis had made earlier in the suite.

But not all of them. He shook his head. Looked at Travis and waited for him to go on.

"You said that the initial uses of ELF in the fifties, just by accident, triggered suicides, and also bouts of euphoria."

Garner nodded.

"And in the years after that, when governments tried to weaponize the technology, they dialed in on exactly how to create certain responses, and how to vary the intensity."

"Yes."

"So a global network of satellites with that capability could paint the whole world in zones ranging from suicidal to dancing in the streets. Anything the controllers wanted."

"I suppose."

"All right. Then it works. You could use the technology to herd people. Like livestock. Entire populations, all at the same time."

Garner's eyebrows knitted together, like he agreed with the point but didn't see its significance.

"Imagine it from any random person's view," Travis said. "What would it be like on the receiving end of this technology? One day everything's fine. The next day, you wake up and you don't even want to move. You're miserable lying there, but the thought of getting up makes you miserable too. You don't even know why, but there it is. Every part of it overwhelms you, and you realize there's nothing on your horizon that makes you happy. Nothing pulling you forward. It's not like any sadness you've ever felt before. It has no cause. It's just there. But knowing that doesn't make it go away. You lie there thinking about that, and you start to get scared. You realize you're having a serious problem, and you think maybe you better go talk to someone about it. Maybe pretty soon, too, because you don't know what you'll do to yourself if this keeps up for any length of time. Now imagine you find out, over the coming hours, that it's not just you. That it's happening everywhere, to everyone, all at once. Picture it. Make it as real as you can. Think of the public reaction. People would know something was going on, but they would have no idea what. It'd be the strangest damn thing anyone ever saw. It would make the news, obviously, but how would it be covered? What would they say? What the hell would *anyone* say, except to wonder what was happening to them, and how anyone was going to fix it?"

Garner looked chilled at the idea. His eyes were far away now, seeing his own version of a day like that, the effect bringing cities to a dead stop.

"Imagine it gets worse the next day," Travis said. "And the day after that. Until you're ready to just end it. You no longer even care what's causing it. *No one* cares. All that matters is how bad it feels. The papers are calling it *Bleak December*. That's all they've got. A name. Still no real information. Another day, and it's worse yet, and right then, when you're thinking in specific detail of how you're going to end your life, a friend calls and asks if you're watching the news. You turn it on, and there it is. The one place where this effect simply isn't happening. Yuma, Arizona. No one knows why, of course. And no one cares, either. What matters is that it's true. You can see it even in the background of the coverage. You can see people already arriv-

ing there from other places, and it's obvious from
their body language that they're not sad anymore.
They're better than not sad. They're euphoric."

In the dim interior of the car, it was impossible
to discern Garner's skin tone, but Travis imagined
it'd gone pale.

"Think of Finn's original plan for conflict
zones," Travis said. "Profile everyone. Weed out
the bad. Keep the good. People with just the right
attributes for a peaceful society. I think even when
he'd decided the whole world was the problem, he
still thought that idea was the solution. Just on a
bigger scale. A global scale."

Garner looked at his phone again, the map of
northern Chile still on the screen. He backed it
out and dragged it until both Chile and the United
States were visible in the frame. He drew imaginary lines with his fingertip, tracing routes from
all over America toward Yuma. And then a single
line: Yuma to Arica.

"You're saying he wants to kill the world except
for a few tens of thousands of people," Garner said,
"and then use them as some kind of seed population to start over, in Arica?"

Travis nodded. "We can stay away from what
we'd have to guess about; what we already know is
enough. We know ELF can be used to move people
around en masse. Push and pull them at will.
You could empty a city like Arica of its original
residents. Draw them off to their own version of
Yuma, up or down the coast. You could kill them
once they were there. Turn up the signal until the
depression is unbearable. Kill the rest of the world
too, outside the United States. And within the

U.S., we've seen for ourselves what happens. Everyone comes to Yuma, with their cars packed full of whatever they think they might need. They've already heard something about flights going out of there, and they'd be happy enough to catch one of them, but what they want more than anything is just to reach Yuma itself. Because then the pain will go away."

Silence came to the car. They were passing through the suburb now, the two-lane bisecting separate reaches of it. Travis saw an overpass far ahead, where 495 crossed the road.

"And how would Finn select the ones he wanted to keep alive?" Garner said. "Would he do that right on-site in Yuma, as people begin to show up?"

Travis shook his head. "He could've done that part years in advance. He'd probably *have to*. He'd need at least some people with critical knowledge. Scientists, tradespeople, doctors. The rest could come from the profiling, which could be conducted over a span of years on people who probably aren't even aware of it. Finn's best attempt at choosing good neighbors. That process is probably already finished."

Garner was still thinking it all through. Travis could see that he understood it. It was acceptance he was struggling with.

"Once these people are actually down there," Garner said. "Once they're in Arica, however many there are, ten thousand, fifty thousand . . . to be self-sustaining, they'd need so many things. I'm sure the city's existing water supply could be kept running, however it already works. Same for irrigated farming. But what about power? What about manufactured things we take for granted? Everyday items that wear out over time. Even clothing."

"You could use solar power," Travis said. "Arica has to be about the best place on Earth for it. And all the panels in the world would be left for the taking. *Everything* in the world would be left for the taking, at least until things started to decay. But in places like Vegas and Los Angeles, useful objects and materials would last a long time. You could send salvage flights up there for decades, if you had to. But I don't think you *would* have to."

"Why not?"

"Because that's what the gathering site at Yuma is for. Think about it. All those cars, packed with the basic necessities people would naturally bring along. Clothing, dishware, in some cases computers or other electronics. All of it neatly stored in a place where it'll last forever. For years after the settlement of Arica, flights could come up to Yuma and methodically gather that stuff. Take it back down there and store it in the Atacama. For a small enough population, it'd be a thousand years' worth of everything they'd ever need."

Travis watched Garner process it. Watched him try to, anyway. The man closed his eyes and rubbed them. Exhaled heavily.

"What else explains Yuma?" Travis said. "What else explains *any* of this stuff?"

Garner opened his eyes again. Stared at the cross streets going by, each lined with dozens of homes.

"How could anyone actually do it?" Garner said. "All those lives. How could someone sign up for a thing like that?"

"Is it really so hard to believe?" Travis said. "The

concept is hardwired right into our culture. We tell little kids in Sunday school a story just like it, and in that story it's not exactly the bad guy who makes it happen."

"Christ's sake," Garner said. "That's not meant to be taken literally."

"No, but you might ask yourself how the story got to be popular in the first place. Don't you think it just appeals to people, on some level? You look around at the world and all its bullshit. This group hates this group, because of something that happened this many centuries ago, and these other people are suffering for it. I'm not saying I agree, but I can understand the attraction of the idea. The notion of just scraping everything clean and starting all over. And I haven't seen a tenth of the ugliness Isaac Finn has seen."

"But Currey," Garner said. "All the rest of them. I just don't understand it. Cultured, educated people, trusted to govern. All of them standing up to be counted as part of something that's . . . objectively evil."

"We don't need to look to scripture for an example of that," Travis said. "We don't even need to look past living history."

Garner turned and met his eyes. Travis saw a chill pass through him. Along with acceptance, at last.

The driver tapped the brakes and slowed. "Coming up on the L.I.E., sir. Back to the city?"

"I don't think so," Garner said. "Pull off for a minute."

The driver parked on the shoulder, a hundred yards shy of the first on-ramp. The trailing car followed suit.

Garner took out his cell phone again, but didn't dial a number. He glanced at Travis. "You're sure Finn is going to Arica right now?"

"Can you imagine any place he'd rather go, with the cylinder? Now that he thinks the loose ends are tied off, he's free to go see what's there, on the other side—the end result of his dream."

Garner considered it for a few seconds. Then he opened the phone and dialed. While it rang, he switched it to speakerphone.

"Who are you calling?" Travis said.

"A lieutenant general I know in the Air Force. Heads up the Reserve Command."

"You trust him?"

"He used to rat me out for cutting class, but we're better since then."

The line clicked open and a man said, "This is Garner."

"So's this," Garner said.

The man on the phone said, "Rich, how are you?"

"I'm good, Scott. But I need a favor."

"Name it."

"I'm on Long Island, just east of the Army depot at Rockport. Williston Air Force Base is out here somewhere, isn't it?"

"About twenty miles further east."

Garner looked at the driver and nodded. The guy put the car in gear and pulled out. He accelerated to pass the westbound on-ramp and put on his blinker to take the next one.

"I need a lift," Garner said. "For myself and seven friends. What's the fastest thing they have stationed at Williston?"

"The fastest transport?"

"The fastest anything."

"I know they've got a wing of Strike Eagles. Those'll go Mach two without breaking a sweat. They could ferry one passenger per plane, if you swap out the weapon systems officer."

"We don't anticipate any dogfights," Garner said. "We just need to win a race. And I need you to keep this in the back channels, Scott. All the way. No one learns about this who isn't flying the planes, clearing them, or waving them off the aprons."

"What the hell's going on, Rich?"

"Nothing good. Keep your communications off the primary channels. Use something secure. But make damn sure you don't use the Longbow satellites. We have reason not to trust them."

"Those would be no good anyway, tonight," Scott said. "I'll find a different option."

Garner cocked his head. "Why are the Longbows no good tonight?"

"Don't know. It's the strangest thing. The whole constellation, forty-eight satellites in all, went into some kind of standby mode about three hours ago. No one can get access."

Garner turned to Travis, and in the glow of the freeway's overhead lights, the man's expression went cold.

"Holy shit," Garner said.

CHAPTER FORTY-THREE

They were in the air thirty minutes later. Travis's F–15E was the third off the runway. Its wheels left the ground and a second later Travis felt like he was lying on his back, and that he weighed about five hundred pounds. There were four green-screen displays in front of him, left to right in a row. They were full of visual data and numbers, most of which he couldn't make sense of. One he could: altitude. That number was climbing rapidly.

The fighter leveled off at thirty thousand feet. Travis looked to his left and right, and saw the southern coastline of Long Island passing far below. A continuous vein of light reached west to the bright sprawl of New York City, then snaked away down the seaboard into the hazy summer darkness.

Travis saw the light-points of the first two jets' engines ahead. A moment later his plane caught up and settled into a line beside them. Over the next three minutes the remaining five aircraft joined the formation, and then Travis felt the lying-on-his-back sensation again, not because of a climb but simply due to acceleration. All eight fighters were ramping up to nearly their maximum cruise speed, which was more than three times as fast as whatever kind of private jet Finn was traveling in. Travis had already done the math. Even with Finn's ninety-minute head start, the eight of them were going to beat him to Arica by almost four hours. It was enough to make Travis regret the fifteen years he hadn't been a taxpayer.

The force pushing him into his seatback receded as the jet's speed topped out. He stared at the coastline again, already falling far behind. He looked at Manhattan and thought of Paige and Bethany, huddling in the darkened ruins of the place. It was hard to imagine that they could be holding on to even a strand of hope.

Travis watched the black nothingness of the Atlantic for a long time. He felt tiredness steal over him. He closed his eyes for what seemed to be a minute or two, and woke to the sound of the jet's engines whining, their power level rising and falling from one second to the next. He looked up, and through the instrument glare on the curved canopy, he saw the shape of a massive four-engine aircraft above and just ahead of the F–15E. He saw a refueling boom coming down, little airfoils near its tip keeping it roughly stable.

Travis leaned a few inches to the side, looked past the front seat and saw the pilot's hand making feather adjustments on the stick, steady but tense.

"How many times do you have to do something like this before you're comfortable at it?" Travis said.

"I'll let you know if I ever get there," the pilot said.

It didn't sound like sarcasm. Travis decided not to distract the guy with any more questions.

They reached Arica half an hour before sunrise. From above, the city was a broad crescent of light hugging an inward curve of the sea. Travis could get no sense of the desert except its emptiness—the landscape was black and formless under the deep red sky.

The fighters touched down, offloaded their passengers and were gone again within a few minutes.

A number of airport security officials, as well as local and Chilean federal police, were waiting. Garner spoke to them alone for ten minutes, while Travis sat aside with the agents. He watched Garner make his case. No doubt it was a fairly big deal to land in someone's country and ask permission to personally detain the passenger of an incoming private jet—and to request that it all be kept secret. Travis wondered how many people of lesser clout than a former American president could've pulled it off.

They sat in the lounge overlooking the tarmac. They waited. Garner called his brother and got an update from satellite and ground-based tracking stations monitoring Finn's aircraft. It was right on schedule.

From the airport lounge Travis could see the city in one direction and the desert in the other. Arica was a beautiful place. In the predawn its structures stood silhouetted against the pink ocean. Most of its streetlamps were still on, their light softened by the breaking day. Toward the south end of the city's shoreline, a giant stone formation punched up out of the ground, shaped like an overturned ship's hull. It was at least four hundred feet high.

Then there was the desert. Which was simply empty. It stretched away south and slightly east of town, hemmed in by shallow rises of the land on both sides—these too were empty. There was just nothing out there past the city's edge. Not so much as a lonely weed.

The sun came up and the sky went pale blue. There wasn't a trace of cloud in it, in any direction. Travis wondered if there ever was.

Finn's plane was on approach. Two minutes out. Travis was standing in the dim interior of a mechanical room, just inside a door that accessed the tarmac.

He was holding an HK MP7 that'd been provided by airport security. So were the Secret Service agents. Garner had one too, but at the agents' insistence he wasn't going to participate in the action. He seemed annoyed about it, but only a little. Travis guessed that he'd only agreed because he didn't *expect* much action. As far as anyone could tell, Finn was traveling alone. Even if he *did* have security with him, a light business jet couldn't hold enough people to counter the strength that was waiting here. In addition to Travis and the agents, the local and federal police had dozens of armed officers concealed among the airport's structures. Garner had thoroughly convinced them that Isaac Finn was not someone they wanted on their soil.

Someone in the tower spoke over an intercom. "Ninety seconds."

Travis glanced at Garner in the vague light. "The police are clear that we're taking point on this, right?"

Garner nodded. "The way we're doing this, they'd prefer their people not become involved at all, beyond providing a show of force. Makes it easier to pretend it never happened."

"All I care about is making sure no one shoots at the plane while the cylinder's inside," Travis said. "It'd be the same as opening fire while Paige and Bethany were in there."

Garner took his point. "Should be no need for any of that. Just let him open the door and exit the plane, and then move on him. He's not prepared for it. What can he do?"

Travis didn't answer. He wasn't ready to relax even that much. He looked through the two-inch crack in the door. He could see most of the runway and the swath of sky through which Finn's plane would descend.

Then he saw the plane. First a glint and then a distinct shape. A speck of a fuselage flanked by jet engines.

Nearer, he could see the idling maintenance trucks that would pull out and block the runway at its midpoint, once Finn had disembarked from the aircraft.

The plane's details resolved by the second. Travis saw the landing gear swing down and lock when it was thirty seconds out.

There was only the faintest bark as its wheels touched the runway. It settled onto its nose gear.

The engines' thrust reversers deployed, and a moment later the aircraft was rolling slowly to a stop. It halted forty yards from where Travis was standing behind the door.

And then the maintenance vehicles moved. One went first. The rest hesitated a few seconds and then followed.

"Goddammit," Travis said. "It's too soon."

He heard Garner breathe out slowly behind him, sharing the sentiment.

Then the jet did exactly what Travis expected it to do: it began to turn in place. He guessed the reason was nothing more than a courtesy to its passenger: the plane's door was on the side opposite the terminal building. The turnaround would correct that.

The plane was most of the way through its half-rotation when it suddenly stopped. Travis had just enough of a viewing angle on the pilots to see that they'd spotted the maintenance trucks. They seemed thrown. They traded looks. Their mouths moved.

"Fuck," Travis said.

He could picture Finn at the back of the little plane, looking up sharply at what the pilots were saying. Putting it together, just like that.

For the longest time nothing happened. The pilots were still talking, looking from each other to the vehicles. If Finn was asking them to take off again, it was in vain. No way could the jet get up to speed in the distance available. Even the taxilane was blocked now.

Travis guessed that a minute had passed since the plane had stopped turning. Maybe it'd been longer.

Then both pilots looked behind them into the cabin and flinched at something. They tore their headsets off and came up out of their seats. In almost the same instant, Travis saw smoke begin to curl into the cockpit along the ceiling.

"What the hell?" Garner said. "Is he committing suicide?"

And then Travis understood. "Oh shit."

Half a second later the plane's door opened. It started to ease down on its friction-hinges, and then the pilots pushed it violently from the inside, and climbed out past it.

Travis was already running. He'd shoved open the door of the mechanical room. He was sprinting as hard as he could over the tarmac, MP7 in hand. The pilots saw him coming and froze for a second, their eyes on the gun. Then they broke to the left, getting the hell away from both Travis and the plane.

The smoke was rolling out from under the top of the doorway, thick and black. The door had fallen fully open by now, its stair steps resting level. Travis could see the light of flames playing over the aircraft's interior.

He covered the last few yards and vaulted up and over the stairs. Tucked in his arms, ducked and landed on his feet inside the plane, his shoulder slamming against the opposite sidewall.

Everything aft of the cockpit was burning. Travis saw broken liquor bottles everywhere. The fire had spread from their spilled contents up the sides of the leather seats, igniting the foam within. The smoke was thickening by the second.

Finn wasn't inside. Travis hadn't expected him to

be. All that was there was what Travis *had* expected.

The iris. Hovering by itself, detached, just shy of the cabin's back wall ten or twelve feet away. Through the smoke, Travis could see nothing beyond the iris but harsh sunlight, exactly the way it shone in the present Arica. Finn had already gone through.

How long had the iris been open?

If Finn had detached it right after the plane stopped its turn, the thing could contract shut any second now.

What would happen if a person were halfway through the opening when it closed? Something told Travis the iris didn't have the kind of safety features found in elevator doors.

He lunged forward. Into the smoke. Past the flames. Threw his arms ahead of him, the MP7 still in his right hand, and dived.

He passed through the open circle into bright light. He felt the iris's edges draw sharply inward and slam against one of his shins, and then he was through, both feet clearing the margin. He saw the ground coming up beneath him—not the runway blacktop that'd been there in the present, but a gridwork of paver stones. He kept hold of the gun with one hand, and threw the other downward to break his fall. He hit hard, took half the impact with his hand, then tucked and rolled to let his shoulder take the rest. The move wasn't graceful, but it worked. He ended up on his back, the MP7 slamming hard onto the pavers but not discharging. Still gripping it, he pitched himself sideways and got up into a crouch, eyes everywhere for any sign of Finn.

But he couldn't see anything. The air was thick with black smoke from the just-closed iris. He could make out low, boxy shapes here and there, ten to twenty feet away in several directions. Waist high, they caught the wind and made it swirl, trapping and churning the smoke.

Travis took a step and heard his foot kick something tiny and metallic. It skipped away over the pavers before he could get a look at it, but he knew by the sound what it was: a bullet cartridge. He glanced down and saw two more beneath him. He stooped and picked one up. Thirty-eight caliber. He pictured Finn, sometime in the last ninety seconds, fumbling rounds into a revolver on this very spot.

He scanned his surroundings again. Still no sign of Finn, but the smoke was already thinner. The box shapes were resolving. He could see now that they were made of concrete, and were open on top. They were half filled with dirt—planter boxes of some kind, but there was nothing growing in them.

He couldn't stay here in the open any longer. He chose a planter at random and sprinted for it, MP7 leveled in case Finn was already hiding there. He passed the first corner: nothing but open space beyond it. He ducked low and made his way down the box's length, and took the next corner without pause. That side was empty too.

He advanced on the last obscured face. The smoke was thinning by the second. This kind of cat-and-mouse stuff was all luck when it was one-on-one. A team of four people or more could use tactics, cover each other's backs, but between single opponents it was almost purely random. Finn would be around this next corner or he wouldn't. If there, he'd be facing away or he wouldn't.

Travis took the corner.

Finn was there, crouched five feet away, his pistol aimed straight back at Travis.

For three seconds neither made a move.

The cylinder lay at Finn's feet, safely out of the crossfire; Travis saw it without breaking eye contact.

Travis considered the situation. He could pull the trigger on the guy right now and probably resolve the whole thing. The risk was that, even with half the guy's head missing, motor reflex could still fire the .38—and probably hit the target, at this range. Travis thought he'd probably take the risk, if it were just his own life on the line. But it wasn't.

"The two women who were with me in New York," Travis said. "They're still there. They're stuck in the ruins." He indicated the cylinder with his eyes. "I need that to get them back. I'm not leaving here without it."

Finn's gun hand remained steady. "That's not going to happen. If you take this, Garner can still stop me."

"Garner's stopping you as we speak. He knows about Longbow. He knows you're activating the satellites. He's on the phone right now setting up raids at all their corporate properties. I imagine one of them will net Audra."

Each piece of information seemed to rattle the man more deeply, though Travis thought his reaction was missing something. It looked like unwilling acceptance where surprise might have been.

"You had to know it was over," Travis said.

"From the moment Paige slapped Garner last night, you were never going to pull it off."

Finn shook his head. He took the cylinder in his free hand and moved back two feet, rising to full height as he did. The .38 stayed level.

Travis stood upright, too. He felt sunlight begin burning his neck through the dissipating smoke. Visibility was better: it was like standing in a thin fog, though the light glared through it everywhere. Travis still couldn't see beyond the nearest forty feet of paver stones and planter boxes. This place seemed to be a plaza of some kind, where the airport had been in the present.

Finn's eyes narrowed. They didn't quite leave Travis, but they moved a little, like the man was reading a list of options in his own head. Looking for some way to salvage his plans. He took another step back. Nine or ten feet away now. Travis saw the risk of getting hit by a reflexive shot begin to drop. He kept the MP7 sighted for a head shot.

"I'm sorry about your friends," Finn said. "I mean that. But I can't just let you take this thing."

He retreated a step further. Maybe he thought he could make a run for it. Put some distance behind him and cross back into the present, somewhere else in Arica. Then try to call Audra and warn her.

The MP7 required four ounces of trigger pressure to fire. Travis applied two.

Finn backed up again.

And then the wind shifted.

Whichever way it'd been blowing before, the boxes in the plaza had spun it in circles. Now it came on dead straight from behind Travis, its speed seeming to double, and in the span of five seconds the smoke drew away like a veil.

Finn took a sharp breath.

Travis felt his own eyes widen involuntarily.

They might as well have been standing in Midtown Manhattan. The Arica they'd seen in the present was long gone, and in its place reared a skyline of concrete and glass and steel, some of its towers standing to a height of seventy stories or more. Broad avenues crisscrossed at their bases, complete with traffic lights and crisp white lines. Along the length of the nearest street, Travis could see the downtown district snaking up the coast for over a mile, and the height and density of the structures held consistent for most of that distance.

None of it lay in ruins. The skyscrapers' glass faces looked like they'd been washed yesterday. The sidewalks were immaculate. Vehicles stood parked at curbsides, 2011 models or earlier as far as Travis could tell. Wooden benches framed the plaza, their green paint gleaming in the desert sun.

Yet nothing moved. Beyond the filled parking spaces, the streets were deserted. Through ground-level windows, every visible lobby sat vacant. The traffic lights were dark. The tires of every vehicle were flat and beginning to crumble. Arica was imposing and beautiful and pristine, but it was also abandoned. For how long, Travis couldn't guess.

"It worked," Finn said. He looked around at the place while keeping the gun on Travis. "The survivors flourished here. They made it."

"For a while. What does it matter? They're dead now."

"We don't know they're dead. We don't know what happened here."

"Couldn't have been good."

Finn looked at him. Some kind of new hope flickered in his eyes. "It's enough that it worked at all. And if I search this place for even a few hours, I can probably find out what happened to it. Find out how to avoid the problem."

"We could've found this place bustling and it still wouldn't be worth killing the world for it," Travis said.

"The world's going to kill *itself* sooner or later. Why shouldn't at least some of us live?"

"Neither of us is going to convince the other. If you want to stay here, feel free. But I'm taking the cylinder with me. I'm going to New York to get my friends."

"You're not," Finn said. "I really am sorry, but you're not. You don't have time, anyway. Look."

He held the cylinder toward Travis, showing him the side opposite the row of buttons. In the harsh light it took Travis a few seconds to see what the man was talking about.

Along part of the casing's length ran a line of blue lights, pencil-eraser-sized and spaced at centimeter intervals. They shone softly and diffused from just beneath the black surface, and extended to a little over a third of the cylinder's long dimension.

"They appeared last night," Finn said. "Right after your friends broke the other cylinder. At that time the lights covered the whole length, but they've been disappearing steadily since, like a countdown. Whoever built these things must not have wanted anyone using one without the other. My guess is, when the last one of these lights goes out, this thing becomes a paperweight."

Travis's mind was already doing the math. The

other cylinder had broken maybe nine hours ago. If that amount of time had burned not-quite-two-thirds of the countdown, he had something like five hours left.

Five hours to reach New York and find Paige and Bethany.

He thought of flight time, and search time, and shit-happens time. Five hours. Was it even close to enough?

"You're wasting your time thinking about it," Finn said. "I'm not giving this to you. Not now that I've seen this place." The man took another step back. "I'm sorry," he repeated.

"So am I," Travis said, and pulled the trigger the rest of the way.

Nothing happened.

CHAPTER FORTY-FOUR

The MP7 didn't even click. It wasn't empty—Travis had loaded it himself and chambered the first round. When he applied the last two ounces to the trigger, the mechanism simply froze.

He squeezed harder. Nothing.

His eyes dropped from Finn and focused on the MP7's action. There was a stress ripple in the metal, where the weapon had hit the paver blocks earlier.

He looked back up at Finn.

The man knew. Even without a click, Travis's body language had said everything.

Finn advanced two steps, his eyes narrowing. The .38 trembled a little in his hand, but he held it tightly.

"Put it down," Finn said. "Then turn around and get on your knees."

Travis exhaled, the breath almost a laugh. "Why the hell would I do any of that? If you're gonna shoot me, just do it."

Finn made no move to come closer, but he took a breath and the gun went still in his hand.

"I hope you don't feel it," Finn said, and Travis saw his forearm tense for the pull.

Then Finn's head came apart, the sides of his skull blowing out like a shaped charge had gone off inside it. A split-second later the flat crack of a high-powered rifle broke across the plaza, and Travis flinched against his will and turned toward the sound.

Thirty yards away, a figure dressed in white rose from concealment behind another planter box.

In his peripheral vision, Travis saw Finn crumple to the ground. The .38 hit with a soft clink and didn't fire. The cylinder rolled out of his other hand and settled gently onto his abdomen, as if his body's last impulse had been to protect the thing.

Travis dropped the MP7 and raised his arms at his sides, and kept his eyes on the shooter.

The newcomer held the rifle at ready without aiming it, and for a moment simply stared, assessing the situation. Travis could make out no detail of the face: the body was covered in white from top to bottom, including a loose hood with some kind of mesh screen at the front. The outfit seemed designed to reflect away sunlight while letting in the breeze. Probably a necessity in this place.

The figure stared a moment longer, then slung the rifle on a strap and stepped out from behind the concrete box. It strode across the plaza toward Travis, its movements measured, unhurried.

Travis could only stare. He felt too numb to even be afraid.

The figure came on, twenty yards away now. Ten. It stopped just out of handshake range and stared at him. Through the glare of light off the mesh fabric, Travis could just get a hint of the face. But he'd stared at it for only a second when something else drew his gaze: a bright red disc on the back of the newcomer's hand, just visible past the edge of the sleeve. The disc was the size of a quarter, and stuck to the skin somehow. Travis looked closer and saw what he already knew would be there: near-microscopic tendrils, binding the disc to the hand.

He looked at the face again, and recognized it through the mesh half a second before the figure lifted the hood.

The eyes were the same as he'd always known them—huge, brown, intense—but everything else had aged a bit, to somewhere between fifty and sixty years.

"Travis," the newcomer said.

Travis swallowed and found his voice. "Paige."

CHAPTER FORTY-FIVE

For the next five seconds they said nothing. Travis heard the sound of waves breaking, the soft crashes echoing through the high-rise canyons.

Then a voice crackled over a radio, somewhere on Paige's body, the words inaudible. She reached to her waist and drew the device from a fold of her cloak.

She keyed the TALK button. "I missed that. Say again."

A man spoke, his tone all but lost to static. "I asked what you're shooting at."

"I'll explain when I see you," Paige said. "I'm safe."

"Did you find out what the smoke came from?"

"Not exactly. Let me get back to you."

"Be careful."

The man clicked off, and Paige stowed the radio. By then, Travis realized he'd recognized the voice, even without discerning its tone. Its rhythm and cadence had been more than familiar. Much more. He felt his balance falter.

Paige stepped closer to him. She raised a hand

and touched his face, gently. Her thumb traced his cheekbone, feeling the texture of his skin.

He saw the obvious confusion in her eyes, mixed with some fragile understanding, and thought he knew what it was. Paige—the other Paige—had described it to him last night in Garner's living room. Getting it without getting it. The Breach had taught her to do that.

Still, there had to be a thousand questions. He thought he saw those in her eyes too, along with a reflection of the thousand he wanted to ask.

How the hell had she gotten here? Not on board one of the flights from Yuma. No way would she have taken part in any of that, ELF effects or not. She couldn't have left all those people behind to die.

She must've come here later on, long after Bleak December had gone. If anyone in the world could've survived Umbra without going to Yuma, it would've been Tangent personnel at Border Town, with all their exotic resources. And no doubt Bethany had been right: Paige had found him before the world had ended. Had found him and kept him alive.

Those thoughts echoed in his head for maybe three seconds, and then they were gone—drowned out by the only thing he could afford to think about now.

The cylinder.

The line of blue lights.

And time—draining away like blood from a nicked artery.

Every minute he stayed here might be the one that doomed Paige and Bethany in New York.

The thumb—shaking now—retraced its path across his cheek. He raised his hand and closed it softly around hers.

"I have to leave," he said. "I have to leave right now. I'm sorry I can't explain any of this."

She shook her head, dismissing the apology, and took her hand away from his face. "Go."

He held her gaze another second, in spite of his urgency, then turned and crossed to Finn's body in two running steps. He lifted the cylinder and aimed it to put the iris just shy of the fallen shell casings where he'd come through before—where the smoke from the burning plane would hide his arrival in the present.

He put his finger to the ON button.

"Wait."

He turned. Paige was just behind him. She put a hand on his shoulder.

"I can't wait," he said. "I might not have enough time as it is—"

"There's something you need to hear. It's more important than whatever you're on your way to do."

"If I'm thirty seconds late, people are going to die. One of them is you."

If that news affected her, she didn't show it.

"That's a necessary risk," she said. "Listen to me. It'll take more than thirty seconds, but I'll go as fast as I can."

Her eyes were as serious as he'd ever seen them. Scared, too.

He withdrew his finger from the button, and faced her.

"I know about the message I sent back through

the Breach," Paige said. "And I know you created and sent the Whisper."

Travis felt his grip on the cylinder weaken. He pushed it against his side.

"You told me everything," Paige said. "The *other* you told me. The one I just talked to on the radio. You explained it the same day we sealed the Breach."

Travis stared. He'd never imagined a scenario like this, in which he could learn exactly how Paige would react to the news he'd been keeping from her.

She seemed to read the question in his eyes.

"I took it better than you expected," she said.

In a way, that response was almost as surreal as finding Paige here at all. Travis shook his head. "How is that possible? I created the Whisper, Paige. All the deaths in Zurich were my fault. All the deaths in Border Town. Your friends."

"I took it well because I understood things you didn't. Things about the Breach, and what it would take to send something back in time through it. Tangent knew, long before we had the means to actually *do it*, what would be involved in the process. Dr. Fagan had it all worked out, like the Manhattan Project scientists had the bomb yields calculated before they ever set one off. The machine that would transfer something into the Breach—an *injector*, Fagan called it—would be unstable almost to the point of uselessness. And there's no way to engineer around that. A person trying to operate it would have to position it right in front of the Breach, then stay there with it and shepherd the process to the very end. There's no practical way to automate it, or even to do it remotely. You'd have to be there. Right there."

"None of this matters," Travis said. "Some other version of you, in the original timeline before anything changed, decided I had to be killed. She sent the note back. And some other *me* sent back the Whisper to block that note and save his own ass. He could've given the Whisper strict limits—like don't kill anybody—but he didn't. He didn't give a shit about anyone but himself—myself."

"The Whisper was a computer beefed up with Breach technology. It would be very unpredictable. It's likely the other Travis had no idea how ruthlessly it would do its job."

"That's a guess at best, and it absolves him—me—of nothing. I sent that thing back out of selfishness, simple as that."

"You're wrong. Selfishness couldn't possibly account for it."

"How can you know that?"

"Because anyone sending something back, standing with that machine in front of the Breach, would have to *still be there* when the injection actually happened. And it's a violent reaction. Hyperviolent. The temperature in the receiving chamber spikes to over four thousand degrees, and stays there for about a minute and a half. You see what I'm saying? To send something back in time through the Breach, you have to die."

Travis stared at her. Whatever he'd meant to say next, it was already gone from his mind. He considered her words, and their implications.

Paige went on. "The version of me that sent that message back must've really believed it was necessary. She gave her life to do it. But when you coun-tered her move, you gave *your* life too. That couldn't have been selfishness. So whatever I thought was worth killing you for, whatever it was you were doing, there must have been more to it than I knew. Like it looked evil from my point of view, but you knew better. Maybe you just couldn't share it with me. Maybe it was that bad. But necessary."

Travis looked down, his eyes going to the cylin-der at his side. The soft blue lights, like stair treads up to a gallows platform.

"I'm telling you this because it matters," Paige said. "You have to go back to Tangent. You're sup-posed to be there. That other version of you, acting on better information than *any of us* have, died to put you there."

"Then why didn't he have the Whisper tell me everything? Just lay it all out in steps?"

"I've had seven decades to think about that. My guess is, if the Whisper had told you what you're expected to do someday . . . you wouldn't do it. Your future self could've guessed that even more easily."

The information seemed to churn around Travis, like the smoke had done minutes earlier.

"Can we just seal the Breach?" he said. "It worked for you guys."

Paige inhaled sharply. "No. Jesus, I would've forgot. Do *not* seal the Breach."

"But it worked. It's still sealed now, after seventy-three years."

She was shaking her head, eyes wide. "The seal held, but it's been a disaster. The best we can tell, entities that build up in the tunnel get destroyed by the pressure, over time. In some cases, the destruction releases energy, and that energy still makes it out into the world. *A lot* of energy, for some of them. Radiation. Strange kinds we can't even identify. We get the effects even this far away."

Travis looked around at the empty city, and began to understand.

"Yes," Paige said. "This place is all but dead because the Breach is sealed. Most of the world would've been, by now, if it hadn't ended already. Don't seal the Breach."

At the bottom of his vision, Travis saw movement. He looked down. One of the blue lights had just vanished.

"Christ," he said.

"Go back to Tangent," Paige said. "I don't know what's coming, but you need to be there when it hits. It probably matters more than either of us realizes. *Go.*"

He nodded, leveled the cylinder, turned it on, and hit the delayed shutoff. Black smoke churned from the iris.

In the seconds he had to wait for the light cone to vanish, Travis faced Paige again. He stared at her eyes.

She was beautiful.

She always would be.

He'd known that the day he met her.

He wondered now if he would ever see her this age again. In their own timeline, however it might play out, what chance did they have of growing old together?

He saw the reflections in her eyes sharpen. She blinked at a sheen of tears.

Then the light cone vanished, and he turned away from her and didn't look back. He sprinted for the opening and vaulted through into the smoke plume.

Sirens. Shouting voices. Blue and red flashers strobing through the smoke. He held his breath and ran, and came out into clear light beside the gutted husk of the jet. Fire crews were laying streams of water and foam into it. Travis hardly noticed them. He scanned the onlookers gathered at the periphery of the scene, most of them near the terminal. He saw Garner, and sprinted toward him as fast as he could move.

CHAPTER FORTY-SIX

Paige stacked the pine boughs close to the fire. Hopefully they'd dry within a few hours. The fire was hard to keep going. Everything was waterlogged.

The night had been hell. From Garner's building they'd gone south as quickly as possible, which wasn't very fast through dense trees and over broken concrete, all in perfect darkness. For the first fifteen minutes Paige had told herself that everything could still turn out okay. They would hear a series of shots from the Remington far behind and above them, and then they would hear Travis calling, and with any luck at all he'd have the other cylinder when they met up.

It was a lot to ask for, and they didn't get any of it.

By the second hour, still making their way south, both she and Bethany had stopped saying anything hopeful or encouraging. Then they stopped talking altogether. Neither knew what the hell to say.

Occasionally they passed by places in the darkness where the rainfall seemed to be splashing down into deep water. They had no idea what the places might be, but the thought of accidentally stepping into one was terrifying. They were wet enough from the rain, though at least the trees kept them from being completely soaked. To fall into standing water and be drenched to the skin, with no means of drying off or getting warm, would be serious trouble.

Finally they just stopped. They had no idea how far south they'd gone, or even if they'd held to their intended path. They felt out the lower branches of a thick pine, made their way up ten or twelve feet, and found a raft of boughs spaced tightly enough to serve as a platform.

They lay in the darkness a long time, trying to fall asleep. They heard animals moving through the forest below, sometimes passing directly beneath where they lay. Maybe just deer. There was no way to tell.

Paige slept. She woke sometime later, the city still pitch-black, the rain still coming down. She heard Bethany crying, trying not to make any noise, but failing. Her breath was hitching and her body was shaking hard enough to move the branches. It was as terrified and lonely a sound as Paige had ever heard. She pulled Bethany against herself and held on tightly. It seemed to help.

When they woke again it was morning. The rain had stopped but the overcast and the chill were still there, pressing down on the ruins.

They climbed to the ground. Paige saw at once where they were. The southwest corner of the park. She also saw what the pockets of deep water were. Subway stairs. The access to Columbus Circle Sta-

tion was flooded to within a few feet below street
level. Not from the rain, Paige was sure. It was
only the natural water table of the island, in the
absence of pumps to keep the tunnels clear.

With daylight they found dry wood: a dead sap-
ling in the partial shelter of an intact stone entry-
way. They broke it into kindling and piled it on the
dry concrete below the entry. Paige used a sharp-
edged rock to carefully deform and take apart one
of the SIG's .45 ACP bullet cartridges. She spread
the powder in a fine layer beneath one edge of the
kindling, and set the cartridge's primer at its center.
Then she slammed the rock down onto the primer.
The powder flashed, and a few of the twigs' ends
smoked and glowed for a second, but nothing else
happened.

The third cartridge—out of four that'd remained
in the weapon—did the job. After that it was only
a matter of finding dry enough wood to keep the
fire burning. They tended it all morning and into
the afternoon. They still hardly spoke.

Travis watched New York rise out of the afternoon
haze far ahead. The aircraft—an F–15D this time
instead of an F–15E, the distinction making no
difference to its top speed—began to descend, and
for the moment its speed actually ticked up a bit,
from 1,650 miles per hour to 1,665.

The fighter had originated from Homestead Air
Reserve Base near Miami. It'd left there for Arica
within five minutes of Travis's return through
the iris, into the smoke of the burning private jet.
Miami was only marginally closer to Arica than
New York was. About three thousand miles in-

stead of four thousand. But it was the closest place available that had two-seater F–15s.

Travis and Garner had done what they could to speed up the process: they'd secured the use of a Piper Cheyenne, the fastest thing based at Arica, to fly Travis north and shorten the F–15's trip. In theory, the Piper could've flown about six hundred miles while the fighter flew twenty-four hundred, saving the F–15 a round-trip distance of twelve hundred miles and putting Travis in Manhattan about forty minutes sooner than originally planned. In practice, that wasn't possible. Six hundred miles north of Arica there was nothing but the biggest jungle on the planet, and no airport in sight. The only viable option had been Alejandro Velasco Astete International, in Cusco, Peru—three hundred fifty miles from Arica. Travis had landed there and waited for the F–15—the move had bought him maybe twenty extra minutes to reach Paige and Bethany. Every second of them would count.

There'd been plenty of time to do the math, between the flying and the waiting. Travis had watched the line of blue lights continue to disappear, measuring the interval with his watch timer. Each light winked out twenty-eight minutes and eleven seconds after the one before it. Once he had that locked down, he was able to determine the exact time when the cylinder would stop working—assuming Finn's guess had been right, which it damn near certainly had. Speaking over the aircraft's radio with both Garner and his brother, Travis rehearsed every step of the process they'd lined up. The hastily planned scramble that would begin the moment the F–15's wheels touched down at LaGuardia.

On paper, it worked. *Could* work, anyway. If everything went just right. Especially at the end.

New York rose into detail ahead.

Exactly six minutes left on the cylinder.

Too goddamned close. Travis felt his hands sweating on the thing.

Manhattan gradually slid to the left of center as the plane made for the airport. The deceleration pulled Travis forward against his seat harness—he was pretty sure this wasn't the normal rate at which the plane slowed for a landing. LaGuardia's crossed runways resolved. Travis drew an imaginary line from there to the bottom of Central Park, and tried to guess the distance. Five or six miles, he thought. By road it would be twice that, and there was no telling how long the drive would take. He didn't know New York well enough to even guess, but he knew it would take a hell of a lot more than six minutes.

Which was why he wasn't driving.

By the time the F–15 lined up on its approach and settled into the glide path, half a mile out, Travis could already see the helicopter waiting. Not even parked on an apron—just sitting there beside the runway, right where the F–15 was going to come to rest. It was a big, hulking son of a bitch. A Sea Stallion, Garner's brother had called it. Eighty feet long, twenty-five feet high and wide. A massive six-blade rotor assembly on top. It could fly at about two hundred miles per hour once it was up to speed. It would cover the distance from LaGuardia to Central Park in a little over two minutes.

The F–15 descended through the last dozen yards of its altitude and hit the runway.

"Gonna roll fast and brake hard at the end," the pilot said. "Buy you some seconds."

"I'll need them," Travis said.

The cylinder had four minutes and fifteen seconds left.

"Hang on."

There wasn't much to hang on to. Travis saw two metal struts along the sides of the seatback in front of him. They looked sturdy enough. He braced his hands against them, and a second later he heard the airflow over the jet's body change radically, and his chest was pressed harder than before against the harness straps.

He saw the Sea Stallion just ahead. It had a tail ramp like a cargo jet, lowered and facing the runway. There was a crewman standing at the foot of the ramp. Overhead, the giant rotor was already spinning. Travis could see the mammoth aircraft rising on its wheel shocks, like it was just a few hundred pounds shy of lifting off.

The F–15 stopped twenty yards away from it. The plane's engines powered down immediately, their pitch dropping through several octaves per second—again Travis had the sense that normal procedures were out the window here. The pilot punched the canopy release and shoved it up and open. Travis stood up in his seat and bent at the waist to clear the angled canopy. He tucked the cylinder under his left arm and held it there as tightly as he could. Then he leaned forward, right out of the cockpit on the left side, grabbed the edge with his free hand and let his body swing down and out.

It was over ten feet from cockpit to ground. His shoes were three feet above the tarmac when he let go; he landed hard, straightened up and sprinted for the chopper. He glanced at his watch as he ran. Three minutes and fifty seconds.

They sat at the fire, eating apples from a tree Bethany had found at the southern edge of the park. Something had eaten everything below about eight feet, but the rest had been untouched.

Paige watched the long needles of a white pine bough curl in the flames.

"It's mid-October," she said. "Any night from now on could freeze. We need to go south if we want to survive."

"Do we *want* to survive?" Bethany said.

Paige looked at her.

"I'm sorry," Bethany said. "I'm not trying to be a quaalude, but . . . what's the point? Unless I seriously, seriously misunderstood high-school biology, we're the end of the line, right? You want to live to be a hundred here?"

Paige lowered her gaze to the flames again and tried to think of an answer to the question. It was essentially the same one she'd been asking herself since the middle of the night.

The Sea Stallion crossed the East River at a height of two hundred feet, just north of a long, narrow island that paralleled the Manhattan shoreline. A second later the aircraft was screaming over the rooftops of the Upper East Side, banking in long, gentle arcs to avoid the taller structures.

Two minutes, thirty seconds.

Travis was standing upright, holding onto the doorway in the forward bulkhead just before the flight deck. Other than himself, the only people aboard were the pilot and co-pilot. Behind Travis was the cavernous troop bay. Its long side walls were lined with bench seats made of steel tubing and canvas. The walls themselves were just the structural ribs of the fuselage and the metal outer skin. Hydraulic lines and wiring conduits ran everywhere. Harsh overhead fluorescent panels lit the space.

The co-pilot turned in his seat and shouted over the thrum of the rotors and the turbines driving them. "Our orders are pretty damn specific. In addition to the phrase *haul ass* being emphasized about a dozen times, here's how I understand it. We land in the biggest clearing toward the south end. We leave the ramp closed. We face forward and we don't pay any attention to you for the next two minutes."

"That'll work," Travis said.

"What the fuck do we do after that?"

"Whatever you want," Travis said. "I'll be gone by then."

The guy stared at him a few seconds longer, waiting for the rest of the joke. When it didn't come, he just shook his head and faced forward again. He mouthed something Travis didn't catch.

They passed over Fifth Avenue at a diagonal, still doing just under two hundred miles per hour. The pilot started cutting the altitude, even as he kept the forward speed maxed. Travis saw the clearing ahead, coming up very fast. They covered most of the remaining distance to it in just a few seconds.

"All right, hang on tight," the pilot shouted.

Travis gripped the doorway with his right hand. He held the cylinder tight against himself with his left. He saw the pilot pull back hard on the stick, but for the next half second nothing happened. Then the park and the skyline, visible ahead through the windscreen, dropped away sickeningly as the chopper leaned back into a steep tilt. Nothing through the windows but blue sky. In the same moment its massive tail swung around like a boom, and when Travis saw the park again it was turning like a schoolyard seen from a merry-go-round. He saw people below, running like hell to get clear as the chopper descended fast.

Just before touchdown Travis looked at his watch. One minute, forty seconds.

Paige was still thinking about Bethany's question when the sound started up. A heavy bass vibration through the trees, like a bank of concert amplifiers playing no music, but simply cranked to full volume and humming. There was a rhythm to the sound, as well. A cycling throb. Like helicopter rotors.

Bethany flinched and turned where she sat, looking for the sound source along with her. It was almost impossible to get a fix on. It was deep and diffused and everywhere.

Then they heard a man shouting, from very far away.

Travis.

Shouting for them to answer.

And shouting for them to run.

* * *

Travis ran to get clear of the iris, not because he knew which direction to go, but just to get away from the turbine sound—he needed to listen for Paige and Bethany. He looked back once, and through the opening he saw the fluorescent-lit interior of the Sea Stallion. On this side, the iris was surrounded by the massive pines and hardwoods that'd long since filled in the clearing.

He stopped fifty yards south.

He shouted for Paige and Bethany again.

He listened.

Nothing.

Nothing he could hear over the chopper, anyway. It'd never occurred to him to have the pilots shut the damn thing down. He just hadn't thought of it, against the clamor of everything else he'd been focused on. No time for it now. He looked at his watch.

Fifty seconds left.

He shouted again.

A second later he heard them. Far ahead and to the right. He broke into a sprint, holding the cylinder tight and dodging side to side through the trees. Their voices sounded very far away. Maybe far enough that there was no real chance, even with them closing the distance toward him. He ignored the thought. It didn't serve any purpose. He simply ran.

An even less welcome thought followed: his math on the timing could be off. Maybe by as much as ten seconds. He'd tried to nail it down as accurately as possible, and where he'd been forced to round off, he'd done so conservatively. It was possible that he had a few more seconds than he thought—but he could just as easily have fewer.

He glanced down at the cylinder as he ran. Its final blue light stared back at him impassively.

He kept shouting.

He could hear their replies now even over his own running footsteps.

Closer.

But only a little.

Thirty seconds.

He sprinted faster. Felt his leg muscles burn with acid, and welcomed the pain.

He listened for Paige and Bethany, and realized he could hear more than their voices. He could hear their bodies crashing through the trees. They were closer than he'd imagined. Much closer. There was still time.

Then he broke through the interlaced boughs of a pair of pines and saw the real source of the crashing sound.

Not Paige and Bethany.

A clutch of white-tailed deer. Thirty or forty of them, streaming through the trees, two or three abreast. Spooked by what they'd never heard before: human voices. The animals crossed his path just ahead at a diagonal, damn near running him down. Two hundred pounds apiece and moving at thirty miles an hour. Blocking his way like a train thundering across a road.

"Fuck!" he screamed. He saw the nearest of the animals draw hard aside from him, the formation bulging away but not slowing or scattering.

The instant they'd passed he began to sprint again, but even as he did, he heard Paige calling, and the sound was still agonizingly faint and distant.

He looked at his watch.

Ten seconds.

He stopped running.

He stared down at the blue light again.

He'd decided hours earlier, before he'd even left Arica, what he would do if it came to this. If time were almost up, and there were no chance of saving Paige and Bethany. If all he could do was get himself back through the iris.

It'd been no choice at all. Not then and not now.

Travis opened his hand and let the cylinder fall to the soft earth at his feet. It rolled a few inches and stopped, with the blue light facing him.

He sat down and rested his arms across his knees.

Five seconds.

Paige ran as hard as she could. Bethany kept up beside her. They ducked branches, shoved others aside, vaulted deadfalls.

It hardly entered Paige's mind to wonder what the hurry was. There was no room in her thoughts for anything but exhilaration. A wild, animal joy. She couldn't recall ever experiencing this sudden and steep a reversal of emotions. She ran. She didn't care why.

Zero seconds.

For the moment, the blue light stayed on.

Not surprising. Conservative estimates. It would die in the next few seconds.

Travis heard footsteps and small branches breaking. Paige and Bethany were still far away. Well over a minute out. He heard Paige call for him again. He didn't answer. Suddenly shouting felt like a lie. They'd find him soon enough. He'd explain.

At five seconds past zero the idea came to him.

It hit like a physical thing. He couldn't believe he hadn't thought of it hours earlier, along with all the other preparations.

He threw himself forward and scooped up the cylinder. He aimed it roughly level with the ground and jammed his finger against the ON button. The iris appeared and he saw the sun-drenched leaves of thin forest undergrowth in the present day, and heard the whine of the Sea Stallion again, hundreds of feet away. In the same instant he pressed the delayed shutoff button. He watched the light cone brighten.

His gaze fell and locked onto the last blue light of the timing line. He was certain of one thing: if the cylinder died before it detached from the iris, the iris would die with it.

He stared at the light cone, shining intensely as it charged the projected opening.

The seconds drew out like exposed nerves.

Then the light cone vanished, and the timing light vanished, and if there was even a hundredth of a second between the two events, Travis couldn't tell.

He looked for the iris.

It was still there.

Still open.

Central Park waiting on the other side.

While he was looking at it he heard a hiss and felt the cylinder vibrate in his hands. He looked down and saw wispy tendrils of smoke issuing from inside the casing, coming out around the three buttons. The thing was dead.

Travis got to his feet and shouted for Paige and Bethany, loud enough that pain flared in his throat.

* * *

Paige hadn't heard Travis in the past half minute. Now she heard him again, and at this range she caught in the sound what she'd missed earlier: panic.

He was screaming for them to move as fast as they could.

Paige had felt like she *was* moving her fastest, but hearing the tone of his voice, she found she could move a little faster. So could Bethany.

Travis kept shouting, providing a source for them to fix on.

He wasn't even looking at his watch now. It didn't matter. They'd make it or they wouldn't. It was hell not being able to run toward them and help close the distance. He could only stand there, shouting, unable to hear their approach.

Paige saw him. Fifty yards ahead. Saw him react to the sight of them. Saw the iris hovering open just beside him as he waved them on.

She also saw the cylinder, lying discarded on the ground. She saw just the faintest trace of something coming off of it. Like smoke.

She got it without getting it.

Got it enough to understand it was time to move her ass a little faster still, and to urge Bethany ahead of her.

"Dive through it!" Paige shouted. "Don't slow down!"

She saw Bethany nod.

They covered the last distance, and Bethany went through the opening like a kid through an upheld hula hoop. Paige followed. She passed across the threshold into a world of filtered sunlight and the rumble of traffic and some kind of heavy turbine engine whine. She hit the ground at the base of a shrub, and looked up. She was just at the edge of tree cover, looking out at a broad, sunny expanse of the park that could only be Sheep Meadow. Hundreds of people ringed the space, and—pretty damned improbably—there was an Air Force-marked Sea Stallion parked out in the middle. Paige had just absorbed that fact when she felt Travis hit the ground next to her legs. She turned to look at him, but saw that he wasn't looking back at her. He was looking up toward the iris behind them.

But by the time Paige followed his gaze, no more than a second after Travis landed, there was nothing to see but shrub leaves and blue sky beyond. The iris had already disappeared.

CHAPTER FORTY-SEVEN

Travis got his final update on the entire situation four days later. He got it by phone from Garner himself. Travis was seated near the back of a United Airlines 757 on approach to Kahului Airport on Maui.

Longbow Aerospace had been raided. The process had been well underway even by the time Travis landed with the dying cylinder in Central Park. The raids were authorized by the few mid-level Justice Department people that Garner explicitly trusted, and within hours the evidence had been exposed: control hardware and software for the strange and surprising instruments that were really in orbit aboard the Longbow satellites. By then the information was in too many uncorrupted hands for anyone to head it off. Not even President Currey could contain it.

The real story was never going to go public as anything more than a rumor. Travis had expected that. But the stand-in story was close enough: Longbow had knowingly put a weapons platform in orbit that violated several treaties and international laws. They'd done it without the government's permission or even its knowledge—though many individuals within the government were tied to the incident. People were talking. Turning on each other. Names were being named. Including that of Audra Finn. She'd been taken into custody during the initial raids, and had already become the face of the story in the media. The faked death was just too irresistible a detail. Authorities were eager to speak to Audra's husband, as well, but no one could seem to find him.

In strict legal terms, President Currey was well insulated from Longbow and the investigation surrounding it. But hundreds of powerful people in Washington who hadn't been in Finn's inner circle learned in detail what Currey had really been a part of. These men and women, at all levels of Justice and even the CIA, had no trouble grasping the severity of what had almost happened. Any one of them could stand in their children's doorways late at night and consider Currey a man who'd intended to kill them. It wasn't a good situation for the president. He knew it too.

He resigned from office three days into the investigation—yesterday. By that time, comparisons to Watergate had already fallen away. This was something much bigger. Essentially, the entire administration was stepping down. There'd been constitutional scholars on all the cable news nets talking about the event in terms of its logistics. Who the hell was in charge now? And how would that person be selected? Congress had managed to agree, pretty overwhelmingly, on at least a temporary solution: Richard Garner could come out of retirement. Maybe he could even finish out the term he'd been elected to, and 2012 could be another election year as scheduled. No one had offered much resistance to the idea, and Garner had been sworn in two hours before calling Travis on the plane.

All that remained to be squared away were the satellites themselves. They still had plenty of station-keeping propellant on board. Enough to boost them way out into what was called a disposal orbit, where they'd be harmless. But in the end, nearly everyone with any say in the matter had voted to go another route: push the damn things right down into the atmosphere and burn them to cinders.

"You should have a pretty good view of the show from Maui," Garner said. "First re-entry is a couple hours from now between Hawaii and the Marshall Islands. About half of them should burn up over that area, and they'll all be gone within the next twenty hours."

"I've got a place in mind," Travis said.

"Reservation for Rob Pullman?"

"His last."

"If you want my advice," Garner said, "try not to have the room to yourself all night." He managed a laugh. "But who the hell am I to tell people what to do?"

They said good-bye and ended the call.

Travis rented a car at Kahului, went west to Highway 30 and took it south. He followed it clockwise around the broad sweep of the island's western half, the Pacific at his left blazing with scattered evening sunlight. He passed upscale residential districts and clusters of hotels along the shore. Half-way up the west-side coast he took a left off the highway, and took another a quarter mile later. He pulled into the Hyatt Regency Maui, got out and followed a footpath to the beach. He stopped at the margin where the stone tiles met the sand.

He saw Paige after only a few seconds. She was sitting alone on a towel, staring at the sea. She hadn't seen him yet.

Travis took out his wallet, withdrew a folded paper he'd kept in it for over two years, and stepped onto the beach.